DEMON

Also by Shane Peacock

Eye of the Crow
Death in the Air
Vanishing Girl
The Secret Fiend
The Dragon Turn
Becoming Holmes
The Dark Missions of Edgar Brim
The Dark Missions of Edgar Brim: Monster

the **Dark Missions** of
EDGAR BRIM

DEMON

SHANE PEACOCK

Penguin Teen, an imprint of Penguin Random House Canada Young Readers,
a Penguin Random House Company

Library and Archives Canada Cataloguing in Publication
data available upon request

ISBN 978-0-7352-6272-0

Library of Congress Control Number: 2018946080

Acquired by Tara Walker
Edited by Lara Hinchberger

Cover images: (skull) NaDo_Krasivo / Shutterstock Images;
(snakes) Zhivova / Shutterstock Images; (horns) © ccoimages / Dreamstime.com;
(leaves) Pepin Press—*Graphic Ornaments*

Designed by Jennifer Lum and Rachel Cooper
Printed and bound in Canada

www.penguinrandomhouse.ca

1 2 3 4 5 6   24 23 22 21 20 19

Penguin
Random House
PENGUIN TEEN CANADA

To Johanna,
who heard the stories coming up from down below.

I must abandon life and reason together, in some struggle
with the grim phantasm, FEAR.

∞

Edgar Allan Poe, *The Fall of the House of Usher*

If we could learn not to be afraid,
we could live forever.

∞

Don DeLillo, *White Noise*

1

Howl

Far away from home, from comfort and sanity, up in the arctic mountains of Spitsbergen Island, the sound vibrates in the frigid air, comes racing toward the sea and enters Edgar's soul. It is a cry of anguish and it terrifies him. He stands on the little ship amidst the human blood and severed limbs and smashed skulls that the great whale has left in its wake, unable to move. Lucy and Jonathan are on the shore just an arrow shot away, motionless too. Tiger lies beneath them on the hard ground, awfully still.

"That sounds like the devil," whispers the wounded captain, still on all fours.

"Bring her," Edgar calls to Jonathan as he motions toward Tiger, a tear rolling down his cheek.

Though his friend is a young man with arms like a strongman, he cannot do it. Instead, he drops to his knees and buries his head in his hands. Lucy bends down and, summoning a strength beyond her physical powers, lifts her fallen companion and then staggers toward the boat with her, Tiger's limbs limp and extending toward the rocks. Edgar gets to them in an instant, reaches over the railing, and takes his dearest friend from Lucy, shocked to feel how light she is. He stares down at her twice-broken nose and pale face, framed by short, raven-black hair. She is still so beautiful, even in death. *Tiger.* The indefatigable, the unconquerable, the inimitable Tiger, laid low by the monster they had pursued to this godforsaken place. The tilted boat is jammed against the high, rocky shore. Lucy clambers up and onto it as Edgar walks with Tiger in his arms across the deck, holding her close. He puts his forehead to hers and then sets her down, away from the blood. He presses his finger to the jugular vein on her neck and tries to tell himself that he feels a very slight pulse.

The cry echoes across Spitsbergen again and the captain cowers.

"Do you have binoculars?" asks Edgar in a monotone.

The captain points to them, their straps somehow still holding fast to a hook on a mast, but their lenses smashed. Edgar takes the binoculars in both hands and points them upward into the mountains. The cry comes one more time. Edgar stares through the broken glass, seeing a thousand images, but he focuses on one: a distant figure, only slightly less white than the snow. It is holding its face toward the sky as if it has just let out a howl. Below it lies the broken body of another polar bear, the one the monster had killed with his bare hands less than an hour before. Did the horrific cry come from this looming animal, or from something else?

The bear gazes down again at the corpse and sniffs. Then it crouches and looks around, as if prepared for an attack.

"We need to get moving."

As Edgar says this, the whaling ship shudders and rights itself, pushing off from the rocks on its own and bobbing out into the water.

"Satan is taking us," cries the captain. "He sent the giant whale to destroy us and now he is taking us!"

Jonathan is still on the shoreline and looks as though he wants to stay there.

"Come!" shouts Edgar, and Jon gets slowly to his feet and leaps for the boat. He barely makes it, gripping the edge above the gunwales and pulling himself up and over the railing. He flops onto the deck like a hooked fish.

"Captain," says Lucy, "we need you to gather yourself, so we can ready the ship and sail south."

"We must clean this up," says Edgar, glancing around at the carnage on deck. "And we need to build a bed for Tiger."

"What for?" mutters the captain. "She's dead."

"HOLD YOUR TONGUE!" shouts Jonathan. He rises and moves toward the old sailor, but Lucy steps between them and wraps her arms around her brother.

Edgar and Lucy take charge of the boat, encouraging the captain to sail and Jonathan to put his mind and body into building a crude bed and finding dry blankets for Tiger. He does his job like a dead man, lifting his love into the bed and setting her down gently, feeling her neck for a pulse too—but he cannot find one. He puts his ear down to her chest and then his nose to her lips to see if there is any breath there. He looks as though he is not sure of what he hears or feels.

Edgar wonders where Tiger's mind is: in a peaceful place like heaven where all her cares and pain are gone? He knows he cannot let his thoughts dwell on her, his great ally who defended him when he was small, whose bravery was unsurpassable . . . because she has departed from him forever. He cannot believe that he is even functioning, but Lucy's courage pushes him to get necessary things done. As the boat floats out of the bay, through the fjord and into the Arctic Ocean, they shove the dead bodies of the sailors overboard, looking away from the severed parts so the sight of them does not turn their stomachs. Then they swab the deck.

They are a good distance south and nearly finished their gruesome task when the sun begins to dip toward the horizon. Edgar is so spent that he stops to lean on his mop and gazes at Lucy, who is down on her hands and knees scrubbing, not pausing for an instant. Her copper-colored hair, somehow still shining, is spread over the back of her thick winter coat, her long nose points toward her work. He tries not to stare, but he cannot stop himself. She is the smallest of the four of them, but there is something inside her that he knows he doesn't have, that none of them has. She looks up for some reason, as if she has the power to know when someone is watching her, and smiles at him.

"Somehow, you and I are still moving," he says quietly.

Lucy looks around. Jonathan has collapsed on the boards next to Tiger, his hand still on hers; the captain slouches near the wheel.

"We do what we have to do," says Lucy.

She has no idea how he feels inside, what he has to conquer even to speak, and he cannot tell her. A nearly seventeen-year-old boy cannot tell a girl, especially one as interesting as her, how desperately fearful he is, how fear has plagued him all his life. She knows of his nightmares and his electrifying visions of the hag, the old woman who began haunting him in his bed when he was a child, pressing down on his chest so he could barely breathe. But

4

Lucy doesn't know how often the old crone still comes; that it attacks him frequently by day even now; that it was on this very boat, as real as it had ever been, just before he slew the monster Godwin with a brutal iron harpoon. Somehow, he has not collapsed like Jonathan, who is so physically powerful and speaks so bravely. Edgar stands before Lucy, hiding his fear like an actor, his brave face a lie, his flaming red hair billowing in the mild arctic air.

"You look . . . nice . . . just now," she says, and bows her head back to her work.

"Lucy."

"Yes?" Her face comes up quickly, her blue eyes intense.

"Remember what Mr. Shakespeare said to us. He said something worse, even worse than Godwin, would come after us if we killed another creature."

She nods.

"Has it?" he asks.

Lucy doesn't say anything right away. He thinks of the creature they murdered on the stage of the Royal Lyceum Theatre just a month ago, the revenant some would have called a vampire, and remembers severing its head with the company's guillotine prop. He hears that harpoon sucking into the huge chest of the Frankenstein creation that was masquerading as Dr. Godwin and sees it staggering toward him onto the boat and its eyes looking up at him as it sank beneath the cold arctic water.

"Will it, Lucy?"

"I don't know," she says.

They hear a faint moan behind them. Lucy and Edgar turn.

Tiger's eyes are open.

2

Home

A few days of sailing south takes them to the Orkney Islands. Tiger has sat up once or twice and is beginning to say a few words. They stay well away from the islands and no one dares to recall anything about the events that recently transpired there, when Godwin, revealed as a yellow-faced, black-lipped monster, made of human body parts by some devil long ago, heavily muscled and without a soul, took them on the beginning of the terrifying hunt that ended in its death. Thinking of it means pondering what might pursue them next and they cannot bear that. There have been no other cries in the air, nothing but silence on the flat, gray seas, which gives them a small measure of comfort.

Edgar, however, cannot resist scanning the horizon behind them with the binoculars at regular intervals. He sees shadows and shapes out there in the distance—things that could be nothing . . . or something following.

They make for the northern coast of Scotland, where the captain will drop them and head for his native Norway. As they float into the little harbor at Thurso, Edgar stands on the deck next to

Lucy and hears her say, "We both know what the next one will be." He turns to her.

"Pardon me?"

"I didn't say anything," she says, looking at him with some concern.

He turns back and stares straight ahead.

It is dark when they get into town. They walk glumly through the narrow streets past grim stone buildings until they find an inn. Tiger, who is plagued with a blinding headache and can barely walk, is being all but carried by Jonathan. It saddens Edgar to see his friend unable to summon her usual fierce independence. At the inn's door, Jonathan hands Tiger off to Lucy's care, and they separate for the night, the girls to one room and the boys to another across the hall.

"Don't worry, Edgar," says Jonathan when they are in their beds and the lights are out, "I am myself again and I am not afraid of anything when I'm right. I will not leave the group until I am sure you are all safe. I will not even start my course at military college if I sense we are in the slightest danger. Think about it, though—we have killed the two freaks that came after us! Shakespeare knows nothing. He is a lunatic, my friend. In fact, if anything pursues us, we can use the little fellow as ammunition—he would fit nicely into our cannon. But why would we believe anything he says?"

"Because he has been right, twice," Edgar wants to respond. Instead, he simply turns over and tries to sleep. Their door, which does not latch properly, keeps creaking slightly open and then closing in little slams.

———

The hag comes for Edgar in the night. He sees the door open wide and then shut behind her as he lies in bed, unable to move, paralyzed as he always is when she appears. She grins at him in the darkness, her face somehow dimly lit. A rancid smell infests the room. Edgar turns his eyes toward Jonathan. But he is fast asleep, snoring lightly. Edgar cannot believe his friend has not heard the old crone.

She is not real, he tells himself. *Face her.* He hears his father's words. *Do not be afraid.*

But she is coming closer and he still cannot move.

She slides onto his bed and gets astride him, driving her bony knees into his ribs and her elbows into his chest as she lowers her wrinkled face to his. Her teeth are yellow, her breath putrid, but he cannot turn his head. He wants to vomit, but no part of his body can move, not even his stomach muscles to force food up his throat. He cannot breathe either—his chest is collapsing onto his heart and lungs. The fear is taking control of him again. She has never seemed so real.

"I am the devil," says a voice, though the hag's thin, white lips do not move. The sound seems to be coming from the door, which appears to be staying slightly ajar now.

Then the hag vanishes and Edgar leaps from the bed, screaming. Jonathan springs up, bare-chested, standing on his straw mattress.

"WHAT?" he shouts. "WHAT IS IT?"

Edgar is in the middle of the room in his underclothing, feet wide apart, looking frantically around him.

"I . . . I . . ."

"WHAT?" asks Jon a second time.

8

Their door opens wide and Lucy enters, her coat pulled over her underthings. She turns on the electric light.

"Edgar?"

He sees her standing in the very spot where the hag had entered, but she is the opposite of the freak. She is heaven while it was hell. He gasps and says nothing. Jonathan steps down from the bed.

"What was it? I'll pursue it!" he cries.

"No! It . . . it was nothing," says Edgar.

"Nothing?" asks Jon.

Lucy puts a finger to her lips to silence him as Edgar staggers past them toward the door.

"It was just a dream," she says, "just a dream."

Edgar stands there looking into the empty hallway. "Yes," he says. "A dream."

In the morning, he lets Jonathan go out first so he can examine the floor near his bed. He can see his own light footprints on the dusty stone surface, but it seems to him that there are more disturbances there—smaller ones, more like a woman's. Then, in the hall, he thinks he sees too many large ones, but they must be his own and Jonathan's.

"Perhaps," he says to himself, "Lucy came in later to check on me." He wonders, though, if that really could have happened.

They speak quietly at breakfast and do not say a word of the nightmare, not wanting to excite Tiger, who is able to eat a little. Edgar examines the woman who serves them, wondering if she could have entered their room for some reason in the night.

———

On the train ride south toward London, all the way to Inverness Station and down past Edinburgh, they speak of other things, anticipating their return home, pretending that everything is well and repeating how wonderful it was to have saved themselves from the aberration when it seemed it had them at its mercy. Jonathan acts particularly jolly.

Lucy asks Edgar about his plans for the future, the interest he once expressed in being a writer, his fascination with frightening stories. He answers her in short sentences and tries to engage her about her own ambitions, about which she is evasive. Inside, Edgar is bursting with anxiety and it is making him intensely conscious of everything, even words as they come out of his mouth. It is as if he were watching himself and his friends and they are all in a story that he knows will come to a desperate end. *Dread.* It dominates his feelings. He dreads everything, every possibility, and can barely keep his face from crumbling. Any movement, however slight, makes him jump, even passengers strolling by their seats. *Something is in the train, near them, watching!* It seems a certainty. If his three allies notice the distress in his eyes, they say nothing about it. After a while, Jonathan gets up to stretch his legs and walks away down the aisle. Tiger has fallen asleep.

When her brother is out of earshot, Lucy reaches out and puts a gentle hand on Edgar's knee. "I know what you saw in the night," she whispers. That is all she says, but she continues to look at him with kindness. It calms him a little.

"A voice said it was the devil."

"But it wasn't. It wasn't even real."

"It IS real!"

"Edgar—"

"I . . . I don't mean it was flesh and blood—though it may have been—but you . . . I can't explain to you, to anyone, how real it is to me. I feel cowardly for saying this, Lucy, but I am terribly afraid. I am afraid of what is behind me and in front of me, of the very air we breathe. I cannot stop my heart from pounding."

He is disappointed in himself—he had thought he had changed so much, but now he seems back at the beginning: a frightened boy wounded by perpetual nightmares, a child easily bullied.

"You don't appear that way. You simply look like my friend Edgar, as sturdy as you were up there on the island when you slew the monster." She takes his hand and squeezes it.

He relaxes a little again. The whirlwind in his mind begins to slow.

"I am *still* worried that little Shakespeare was right, Lucy. Something worse will indeed come for us, and soon." He leans forward and speaks softly, "Maybe it's here."

She glances down the aisle, then out the window and then back at him. "We faced the others, did we not?"

They sleep through the night on the train, Lucy leaning against Edgar and Tiger against Jon. They get to the station and walk out onto Euston Road under a boiling July sun. London is bustling around them, arteries jammed with people and horses and carriages and a few sputtering motorcars, everything loud and smelly as always. All that noise, all the bustle, is helpful to Edgar. He is home and feels anonymous and hidden in the crowds.

11

"It's as hot as hell," they overhear a man say to another, "never seen it like this."

The four friends pause before they cross the street.

"Tiger, come with me," says Edgar, taking off his sweat-soaked black jacket and extending a hand. "You can stay at Thorne House. Annabel will be happy to have you; she is lonely these days, now that my adoptive father is gone. We can offer you a quiet home and the best of care."

"No," she says. She is walking on her own now and traces of her old spirit are coming back.

"Of course," says Jonathan and smiles, "she would like to stay with us. I shall—"

"I am going home. I will be fine."

"No," say the other three together.

"That just makes me want to be on my own even more!" Her words snap in the thick city air, just as they used to.

The others say nothing for a moment and then they all burst out laughing. It is like another tonic to Edgar, and before he knows it, he has let her go. She walks away, heading straight south to the river and Brixton, her head held stiffly, as if it still hurts. She has not complained of any pain for a while, but they all know that means nothing—Tiger never complains.

Edgar takes his leave of the other two, lingering a bit with Lucy's hand in his before separating: his friends turn north toward Kentish Town and the old Lear home, and he proceeds southwest to Mayfair to be with Annabel Thorne, the only mother he has ever known.

3

In the Flesh

Annabel greets him in the vestibule on the gleaming black-and-white marble floor with both arms outstretched to envelop him. He has the sense that she was already nearby, as if looking out the windows, in constant wait should he appear. She is still dressed in her widow's weeds, black from head to foot, though she has somehow managed to find a dress that shows her ankles to good effect. She has magically made it cool in Thorne House too.

"My dear boy!" she veritably screams and grips him in a vice-like hold that he doubts even a monster could loosen. Then she pushes him back and looks him in the eye.

"Why did you not return home when news of that awful hotel fire was in the papers? It was a full two weeks ago. Your uncle burned to death! Dr. Godwin gone missing, presumed dead! Surely all that news reached you. You were only in Scotland, so you said. It is not the backwaters . . . well, actually it is, but did no one tell you?"

"Yes, Mother, I knew something of it, but not details and—"

"What, in the first place, pray tell, was this urgent hospital business to which you had to attend? And why did it keep you away even when such horrors were happening to your superiors down here? Did you take a side trip to Australasia or the blooming Arctic Ocean? I was without word after the first day you were gone!"

He has gotten better at lying but it is always difficult to deceive Annabel Thorne.

"I—I . . ."

"Actually, you seem like your old self again."

"Thank you."

"That is not a compliment! Your *old* self! A sad, bag-eyed and morose little thing, instead of the later model, the one that loves his mother, tries to be happy and helpful, and gets on with life. Surely, the passing of your uncle and the vivisecting Dr. Godwin cannot be *so* devastating to you, can it? You did not like Vincent Brim at all. I know it! No great loss concerning Godwin either, I say. I did not care a farthing for him! It is not their deaths that have turned you this way. Have you been thinking?"

"I beg your pardon?"

"Thinking!"

"I don't understand what—"

"I have been reading a great deal while you were away, and there are new people about who study the brain, the feelings and the nervous disposition in an entirely different way these days. There is a young man in Austria by the name of Freud who is at the forefront of all of this, and he has written a wonderful study or two about it. Nervous disorders! Phobias! Neurasthenia! We are becoming a world full of contemplators and worriers and anxious sorts, depressing people always thinking and thinking and thinking . . . about ourselves! It causes all sorts of unneeded stress to your nervous system. You must DO, Edgar, DO! Stop all this inwardness." She pauses for a moment. "Then, of course, you might simply be in love. Are you, Edgar? Is it a Scottish lass? Do tell!"

"Mother, I am merely fatigued, and yes, a little saddened by the terrible human cost of that fire. I will go to my room and have a good night's sleep and return a new man."

But in the night, his enemy comes again.

He is struggling to sleep when he hears her moving up the stairs, a light tread but her hobbled gait recognizable, the pace of a witch from a dark fairy tale, like the ones that his father used to read aloud, the ones that seeped into his infant brain. One is not supposed to truly *hear* the things that are happening in a story, but Edgar Brim could. It was as if someone, something, perhaps the author, perhaps God, was providing the sounds.

The footsteps draw nearer and then the door opens and he looks down toward the end of the bed and past it, paralyzed, and sees her hideous face in the entrance. She has never looked like *this*! The image before him is not a ghost, not ethereal and fictional, not translucent and amorphous, but real, three-dimensional and breathing and moving on two solid feet whose treads are audible. The old woman closes the door behind her and regards him. Then she starts across the floor toward him.

"*I will do evil to you*," she hisses, "*and to your friends.*" This time there is no doubt that the words are coming from her. Her face looks made-up, rouged with red, black around the eyelids, white powder in the folds of her skin, her hair dark and long. She comes at him in a sort of glide. He tries to scream but when he opens his mouth, he cannot make a sound. That is the way it has always been, ever since he was a child.

Now she is standing over him, grinning. Then she seizes the covers and sweeps them back, leaving him cold in his nightgown beneath her. *She has never done this before.* She swoops down upon him and he can *feel* her this time, the weight of her torso on him, her body stronger and more powerful than before, her woman's chest on his, her lips close to his mouth, her breath like a strange perfume that makes his head swim. He wants to die. Panic attacks him and his heart pounds so hard that he fears it will burst.

"*I will do evil to you,*" she repeats, "*and to your friends!*" The word *evil* stretches out until it seems to envelop the entire sentence—the *e* long and hard, the rest like a smooth blanket on which it sits.

Then the hag suddenly rises. This time, she does it differently: she does not float away, instead she walks backward, feels for the knob, opens the door and goes out. He hears her footsteps descending the stairs, the front door opening and closing. Then there is silence.

When sound returns, it is Edgar's own breathing he hears, fast and hard. He moves his toes, then his knees, his thighs, his stomach, his fingers, his hands, his mouth. He pulls the covers back up over himself. Then he lies there for hours, unable to sleep. He thinks and thinks. He convinces himself that the old woman cannot be in any way real. This is simply the "hag phenomenon," a psychic reality that descends on some people at night or at dawn, descends on their brains and their imaginations, not a real person upon their sleeping forms. It is in his power to send it away. Annabel is right. He must DO. Whatever it is, he must DO. Go back to work, train for another profession, leave the monsters behind and change his life, stop imagining a devil is nearing.

Then Edgar encounters Beasley.

The butler knocks on his door at dawn. It is an unusual thing for him to do. Beasley is well aware that Edgar never wants to be roused in the mornings or have his clothes prepared or his breakfast brought to him or anything of that sort. He hates all those kinds of services. Yet, there is Beasley, at his room.

"Sir, might I have a word?" he asks when Edgar opens the door.

"Of course, Beasley." The boy smiles at him. He is already dressed for the day.

"I heard something in the night, sir, so I came down the stairs. It seemed like footsteps, each carefully set like those of a thief in the night. When I came to this floor, I had the sense that this intruder had been at your door. Indeed, your entrance was slightly ajar. I followed the sounds down the staircase, as quiet as a mouse, mind you, and saw someone go out the front door."

"Someone?" Edgar's voice is barely audible.

"An old woman, sir."

4

Rich Man

Shaking, Edgar slips past the butler and begins to make his way downstairs, seized by an overpowering need to flee, to run from the nightmare that seems to be alive in his life again. He is anxious not to encounter Annabel, to leave the house before she has the chance to question him again and see his even more unsettled appearance.

"It is likely nothing about which to concern yourself," he hears Beasley say behind him. "Just an old woman, not a threat to anyone, a wandering street person. But I shall ensure that all the doors are locked in the future."

Edgar finds his own quick breakfast of toast and tea in the kitchen at the back, but Beasley intercepts him again as he attempts to slip out the front door. The butler is bearing a card on a gleaming silver tray. It is on the personal stationery of someone whose name he does not recognize, and it requests Edgar's appearance at the London Hospital, where he had worked alongside the monster Dr. Godwin until a few weeks ago. It is as if someone is magically giving him a reason to be somewhere else, to elude Annabel.

His presence is required there in exactly an hour and a half, a perfect length of time to walk through the city to the East End, to calm himself, surrounded by reality, not the dreams swirling in his mind. He tells Beasley to send messages to his friends in Kentish Town and Brixton, asking them to meet him at the hospital in the afternoon—he wants to be sure that they are all right, especially Tiger.

He makes his way through the loud London day as if he were inside a bubble, still anxious about what happened in the night. He tries with his very being to take things in, to concentrate on the real world around him—the sights, the sounds, the smells. He cannot, however, seem to think of anything but the hag. She keeps going round and round in his head. He looks over his shoulder, into the shop windows, down the alleys that he passes.

Eventually, it occurs to him that speaking to someone would be the best way to get out of his bubble and get away from his fears, and even though the matron at the hospital's front desk is as formidable as usual, she is most definitely real. He walks right up to her.

"Master Brim," she snaps, "you are to proceed all the way to the top floor to the chairman's office, where your presence is expected." She looks angry about it.

He wonders why in the world he would be wanted up there where the wealthy and influential people who run the hospital often meet with the powerful man who makes the final decisions. Edgar knows it only as a mysterious place located behind double wooden doors at the end of the upper floor's main hall, an inner sanctum.

The hospital's ceiling fans are little relief against the heat. His shirt soaked through with sweat, Edgar climbs staircase after staircase, gets to the top nearly out of breath, and sees his destination way down the hall. As he approaches, he observes that the doors are wide open and a crowd of doctors and other hospital employees have gathered inside its ample space. Three or four well-dressed gentlemen are settling themselves at a long gleaming table under a huge stained-glass window with an image of Christ looking down upon them. No one seems to notice Edgar as he slips into a chair at one end.

One of the well-dressed gentlemen, a tall, broad-shouldered fellow wearing a monocle, a long black coat, checked waistcoat and gray trousers, rises to his feet. Edgar is surprised to see that his handsome face is tanned, unlike the pasty white visages of his colleagues. "I will be brief," he begins. "As chairman of your hospital board, I have gathered you here today to inform you that we are moving forward on the assumption that our esteemed colleague, the brilliant Dr. Godwin, has met the same regrettable fate as his friend and collaborator, Dr. Vincent Brim. Though the latter's remains were found in the fire that ravaged the Midland Grand Hotel, there was no sign of the former, but his simultaneous disappearance has led the police to conclude that he met his maker in the same inferno. It is a sensible conclusion. Though none of us knew of Godwin's laboratory on the top floor of the hotel, neither were any of us surprised to learn that his dedication to his science, one might even say his art, kept him at his research even when away from this hospital, and also that his dear friend, Brim, would be with him. Medicine has its dangers even to those who are not patients. The fire, it seems, originated in the lab. Some sort of combustion occurred while these two valiant men were at work . . . with the tragic result that they are no longer with us. May God bless them."

There is a murmur of similar blessings from the men at the table. Edgar remains silent, his mind cast back to those terrifying moments in that laboratory. He sees himself and his friends captured and tied to tables so the monster Godwin could experiment upon them, make a hybrid human being out of them, just as Godwin himself had once been made by the brilliant mind and expert hands of another. Edgar thinks of his uncle setting fire to everything, his incineration, and their narrow escape.

"We shall encourage applications for the chief operating surgeon's role here and shall hire another doctor to take the admirable Vincent Brim's place. We shall continue to pursue experimental surgery at the London Hospital and thus will remain at the forefront of advances in our great science. I know it is difficult to go on under these circumstances, but we are meant to be leaders of men, conveyors of succor and aid to the ill, and as such, we shall lift up our chins and proceed. Thank you, gentlemen."

There is an instant of silence and then the grinding of wooden chairs pushing back from the table on the polished wooden floor and a general exodus, which Edgar joins. The chairman, however, calls out amidst the noise.

"Master Brim!"

Edgar turns and regards the man and gestures to himself with a finger.

"Yes, you, Brim, come forward."

The other board members are departing while deep in conversation. In moments, Edgar and the distinguished gentleman wearing the monocle are the only people left in the room.

"I am sorry for your loss."

"Thank you, sir."

Edgar turns to go, but the chairman seems interested in detaining him.

"My name is Andrew Lawrence, perhaps you have heard of me?"

Edgar recognizes his name from the message that Beasley had given him this morning. He turns back to Lawrence.

"No, sir . . . not before today."

Lawrence laughs. "Not a financial man, are you, Brim? I like that." He has a deep voice that in formal speech is elegant and has a slight Irish lilt, but now, in private conversation, betrays a much broader accent. He seems an ordinary man, yet extraordinary at the same time. Edgar imagines him as a father, reading a story to his son in his slightly foreign, down-to-earth baritone and making it sound wonderful. Lawrence takes the monocle from his eye, leans down and speaks softly into Edgar's ear. "They say I am the richest living thing in London, but the Rothschilds and Queen Victoria might beg to differ. They also say that such success is a remarkable thing for a man of my race."

"I . . . I am pleased to meet you, sir."

Lawrence straightens up and pops the monocle back into his eye socket. "And I to make your acquaintance, as well. Do not be swayed by my money or position, my boy, or anyone else's. Most rich folks inherited their wealth and power and deserved none of it. They are fortunate, nothing more. I am pleased to say that I earned my filthy lucre through a combination of brains and effort, but that does not make me anyone special. Take me as I am. Judge me for how I treat you, nothing less. I asked you to come because I was told that one of the gentlemen who died was your uncle and the other was your mentor."

"I . . . I wouldn't say mentor, sir, if I may."

"Of course you may, you may say anything you like."

"He was my superior."

"It sounds as though Godwin was superior to most of us, at least in mental capacity, and his disappearance is a great loss. We were well aware that he was working upon momentous scientific experiments that could have been of lasting benefit to humanity."

"Yes, sir," says Edgar quietly.

"You do not sound convinced."

"Yes, sir, absolutely, sir," he says a little louder.

Lawrence chuckles. "I like you, Brim—a man of his own mind. I thought it right that someone at the hospital, and in a sense I AM this hospital—chairman of the board, chief investor, you know, and the like—should at least say hello to you and offer our condolences."

"That is very kind of you, sir."

There is no response from Lawrence. He is staring over Edgar's shoulder as if he has seen a miracle. The monocle pops out of his eye. Edgar turns and sees Annabel standing in the doorway. She is wearing another black dress, this one remarkably form-fitting for a widow's gown; her blonde hair somehow showing to extraordinary advantage under a bonnet with the word *Love* stitched into it, and her ankles on display again above gray high-heeled boots with white laces.

"Mother!"

"This is your mother?"

Annabel marches forward. There is not a drop of perspiration on her face in this terrible heat, but her temper is heated. "Edgar, I am not pleased with you, no no no! You slipped out of the house this morning without saying a word to your mother. You were to tell me more about your adventures this past week, and then I had to suffer the dreadful news that there was an intruder in our home last night. Another one!"

"An intruder?" says Lawrence.

"SHUSH!" snaps Annabel.

Lawrence glows.

"Mother, you shouldn't . . . do you know who this is?"

"I do not care if he is the Queen of Sheba. I want answers from you, Edgar Brim, answers. Well, young man, what do you have to say for yourself?"

"Mother, may I introduce you to the chairman of the board of the London Hospital, Mr. Andrew Lawrence. This, sir, is Mrs. Annabel Thorne."

"*Sir* Andrew Lawrence, actually, though I would never insist."

Annabel has stopped in her tracks, still staring at Edgar, her back to the chairman of everything at the London Hospital. "Do you mean to tell me that the man I just shushed is Sir Andrew Lawrence?"

"I believe so."

"Well then . . . I should close my mouth."

"Not at all," says Lawrence, "not to worry."

"Oh," exclaims Annabel, turning toward him, "I shan't worry. That is not my way. I move forward, always forward. A smile is always the best remedy." She gives him a dazzling one. "I am never a worrywart, like this one." She motions toward Edgar. "Now, let us start again." She extends a hand. "I am most pleased to make your acquaintance, Sir Andrew Lawrence."

He takes her gloved hand and kisses it. "Andrew will be sufficient."

Annabel pauses for a moment, not removing her hand from the grip of the tall, handsome billionaire with the tanned face and black hair only slightly touched with gray, and a miracle occurs: her face turns red. She pulls her hand back.

"I am a busy woman and I must be going. I am sure you gentlemen have things to discuss, not that I could not discuss them with you. The day shall come, very soon, when not only will this hospital be peopled by female doctors but a woman shall have your place, sir!"

"I have no doubt," says Lawrence, "and I hope to live to see it."

"You do?"

"I do indeed. Especially if that woman were someone such as yourself."

Annabel looks flustered.

"Well then . . . good day to both of you. Edgar, we shall have that talk as soon as you get home."

"Your son, madam," adds Lawrence, "seems like a fine young man."

Annabel pauses. "That is very kind of you to say." She regards Lawrence, who has briefly put his hand on Edgar's shoulder. "Especially since you just met him. Perhaps you have plans for him? I believe he has the ability to go places."

"I see evidence of that already. One cannot have too many fine young men in one's employ."

Annabel regards the chairman again and narrows her eyes a little as if contemplating something. Then she turns and strides from the room, her heels clacking forcefully on the wood floor.

"Good day, Mrs. Thorne," says Lawrence after her, "and my condolences for your loss."

She stops and, without turning completely around, says, "One must go on," and moves off down the hallway.

Edgar turns back to Lawrence to see that he is still gazing at Annabel's retreating back, and smiling.

Edgar spends the day cleaning up his uncle's and his "mentor's" rooms, which have not been attended to for more than a week. Lawrence has told him that he will be assigned as an apprentice to a doctor soon, to help ready him for his medical studies in Edinburgh the following year. Edgar wants to tell Lawrence that he has no interest in being a doctor, and that it is only Annabel's future financial needs that make that profession his only choice. It is books that intrigue him, stories, plays, and works of art, but he keeps quiet.

Just being in his uncle's room and Godwin's laboratory gives him strange sensations. It is as though their ghosts and the ghosts of what happened to them, and what might have happened to him and his friends, linger in the air. The copies of the sensation novels *Frankenstein* and *The Island of Doctor Moreau* are still on Vincent Brim's desk, their presence more poignant now that Edgar knows that his uncle, far from being the villain he had thought him to be, had been studying those texts because he feared what Godwin was planning. Uncle Vincent had given his life for Edgar in that fire.

The laboratory in the basement is more problematic for Edgar to enter. He can barely bring himself to open the door. The operating table with the light above it is there, where Godwin had mutilated animals—Edgar shivers at the memory of what the surgeon forced him to do to a quivering little rabbit. They had also taken apart dead human bodies here, put limbs into formaldehyde jars and kept others on ice, ready for transportation to Godwin's secret lab at the hotel. At the time, Edgar had known nothing of their destination or their fate. He sweeps and cleans up the room like an automaton, trying to resist any emotions, but wondering, again, what in God's name could be worse than a Frankenstein creature.

5

Mad Man

He is glad to see his three friends alive and well outside the hospital and especially pleased that Tiger seems to be more her old, vigorous self again. She is dressed in trousers and appears impatient, her entire leg vibrating as her foot taps the pavement while waiting for Edgar to appear. Jonathan is standing close to her and Edgar wonders if she likes that.

"Edgar!" shouts Lucy as she runs up to him and takes his hand. "I'm so happy to see you!"

"Yes," says Jon, "it must be at least half a day since we saw your shining face."

"Any news?" asks Edgar.

"About what?" asks Jonathan.

"You know."

"No, I don't."

"Creatures," says Tiger.

"Oh God, Brim, that is gone and done," groans Jon. "We have triumphed! Can you never be satisfied? You are such a pessimist! You are not seriously worried about anything the lunatic Shakespeare said, are you? If I had a penny for every brain cell he has that is abnormal, I would be richer than the chap who owns this hospital. I am ready to move forward in life!" He looks at Tiger.

She isn't smiling. "We need to remain vigilant," she says. "I'm feeling better now. I'll spend some time with the Lears over the next while, and we'll keep both the cannon and rifle up there. I'll look out for these two, Edgar."

Jonathan chuckles. "That won't be necessary, though I like your plan of staying with us for a while."

"Just a while," says Tiger. "If nothing comes in a few days, I think the threat will be greatly reduced. The last one attacked right away."

"There was that sound," says Lucy, a hand on Edgar's elbow.

"Sound? What sound?" says Jonathan.

"The one we heard on Spitsbergen Island."

"That was a bear! And we seem to have made it back to England without Satan descending on us."

"I don't like your choice of words," says Edgar.

"You can't be serious. Satan?"

"Something happened last night."

"What?" demands Jon, sticking out his chin, almost challenging his friend to offer evidence of another monster. Sometimes it seems to Edgar that Jonathan is playing at being brave, trying to convince himself of his own courage. Edgar looks to Lucy, then Tiger. He cannot bring himself to tell them. "Nothing," he finally says, "nothing actually happened. I just had a bad feeling."

"Listen, sunshine," says Jonathan, "if you didn't have bad feelings, you wouldn't have any feelings at all."

"No feelings?" asks Lucy. "That sounds more like you, brother."

Tiger takes a step away from Jon. "I would trust Edgar's sixth sense about anything. Always have. But—"

"I like people with feelings," says Lucy.

There is silence for a moment. "As I was saying," continues Tiger, "we have to be realistic. Being too anxious about all of this isn't helpful, being prepared is."

"We should call on Shakespeare and at least tell him what happened," says Edgar. "He's the one who has always claimed to know so much about all of this."

"Oh, Lord," says Jon. "Maybe we should consult Sherlock Holmes and the Hunchback of Notre Dame while we are at it?"

"I'll come with you," says Lucy.

"I will too," says Tiger.

Little William Shakespeare opens his door to the four of them before they have a chance to knock—as always he appears to be ready ahead of time to meet anyone who even approaches his residence. He is dressed in a pair of riding breeches that are so tight as to be obscene as they stretch on his skinny legs and up over his bulging belly. For some reason, though he is not going out (and seldom does, it seems), he is also wearing a tall stovepipe hat, and a jacket, its color best described as pink, without the company of a shirt. The white hair on his naked chest is as furry as a polar bear's; under the absurd hat, his big head is glowing with excitement at the appearance of his four young friends. He is perspiring so profusely in the heat that Edgar almost expects to look down and see a pool of sweat at his feet.

"Enter! Enter, you knights of modern days! It is a glorious morning indeed when I see you upon my doorstep." It is actually late afternoon. "Come, come! Messrs. Sprinkle, Winker and Tightman are present, holding forth on issues of grave importance, pronouncing pearls of wisdom seldom heard anywhere else in the British Empire. We are in full expectation of news that you have conquered the Frankenstein creature, shall be simply thrilled to hear of it, and veritably swollen with enthusiasm to contemplate what might come next." Shakespeare often seems as though he is standing on a stage, projecting his carefully chosen words. He has stepped to the side and is ushering them down the stairs, but as he says his last sentence, he looks closely at Edgar.

In the main room of the Crypto-Anthropology Society of the Queen's Empire, full of masculine wood, rows of novels, severed animal heads on the walls and an enormous painting of Queen Victoria, eight empty chairs sit at the big oak table; four pulled back with blank papers, pens and inkbottles resting on the surface in front of them. A meeting of the mysterious investigators into the existence of monsters seems to be in session.

"My esteemed colleagues, I give you my esteemed colleagues! You all know each other!"

Edgar, Lucy and Tiger dutifully say hello to three of the empty chairs. Jonathan says nothing.

"Well! Well well well well well well well well well well!" exclaims the little man. "A report! I believe we are to be the recipients of an actual report, the story of your manly—and in that adjectival description I include Miss Lear and Miss Tilley—actions in defeating another creature, another aberration! Was it indeed upon the

31

arctic ice floes?" He motions to four of the chairs. "Sit. Sit. Sit. Sit!"

Tiger, Jonathan and Lucy take places, steering clear of Shakespeare's imaginary colleagues.

"As you may have noticed," adds the little man, "Mr. Sprinkle has not yet returned, though he shall be out shortly."

None of the four friends bothers to ask what this might mean. Jonathan rolls his eyes.

"I am in such a state of discombobulated anticipation that—" begins Shakespeare, but he is interrupted by a noise coming from somewhere beyond the door that allows entrance into the rest of his residence. He pauses and looks in that direction, frowning. "As I was saying, I—" The noise interrupts him again.

"SPRINKLE!" he cries. "SILENCE IS THE PERFECT HERALD OF JOY!" He turns back to his listeners and smiles. "Excuse Mr. Sprinkle, if you will. He is within the confines of my apartment employing the water closet."

"Shakespeare has a cat?" mouths Jon silently at his friends, grinning. Edgar, however, is not smiling, and the noise comes again.

"Perhaps you have an intruder?" says Edgar, his voice sounding a little shaky.

"Or a cat?" says Jon, this time out loud.

"No, no, just Sprinkle," insists the little man, "adjourned to make his toilet. He is terribly clean, you know, fixes himself up multitudinous times a day. Tall and spotless, that's Mr. Sprinkle. Let me cast my gaze down the hallway and see if he has completed his hygienic tasks."

An intruder, thinks Edgar, *a creature. Listening to us.*

The little man waddles over to the door that opens into a narrow hallway and peeks in.

"Sprinkle! I say, Sprinkle! Blasted man, are you not done yet?" There is a pause. "Momentarily? I should think so. There is not a man on earth more relieved and more clean than yourself. Sir Edgar Broom and his colleagues are here and you are disturbing us. Come! We are to be entertained with an account of monster hunting!" There is another pause. "What's that you say? One minute and twenty-two seconds and you shall return? A fellow should be more precise than that, but I shall let our guests know." Shakespeare looks back toward the others. "He—"

"There is someone in there," says Edgar.

"Yes, I—"

"Not Sprinkle!"

"Pardon me?" The little man stands there holding the door open, as if inviting his questioner to investigate.

"Don't be ridiculous, Edgar," says Jon. "It could be anything."

Lucy looks concerned. Tiger gets to her feet.

Edgar is quickly past Shakespeare. The door, on some sort of spring, closes behind him as he steps inside. Immediately, he hears the noise again, somewhere deeper in the apartment. He walks toward it, passing the unoccupied water closet just beyond the end of the short hall. As he turns a corner, he sees someone glancing back at him and immediately disappearing around another corner in Shakespeare's labyrinth-like living quarters. The man is tall and lean, dressed in the absurd crimson outfit of someone who is about to ride after the hounds. His clothes are immaculate and his face shining with cleanliness. His shaved head glistens in the dim light.

"Excuse me," says Edgar, his heart pounding, walking briskly toward him. However, the man is instantly gone. "Sprinkle?" he says to himself.

Edgar searches the apartment and finds it empty. When he turns back toward the door, Tiger is standing there, watching. He notices that one of her fists is clenched.

"Everything all right?" she asks. He says nothing and walks past her back into the meeting room. Tiger follows.

There is silence for a moment as he settles into his chair.

"You look as though you've seen a ghost," says Lucy.

"No," replies Edgar, "I'm fine, just a little under the weather. There was no one in there." He glances at Shakespeare, who is staring back at him, examining his expression. Then, the little man lifts his eyes toward the apartment. "On the contrary!" he exclaims, "for here is Mr. Sprinkle, relieved and at the end of his ablutions and ready to hear your marvelous story. I cannot imagine how you did not observe him."

First, I see the hag as real as life, thinks Edgar, *now I encounter one of Shakespeare's imaginary friends. I am losing my mind. But the hag isn't a fiction, Beasley saw it, or did I imagine the butler speaking to me about it too?*

"Cats are elusive," says Jonathan quietly to his friends. Then he lifts his voice. "It is just nerves, as always with our lad."

"Do you want to talk about it, Edgar?" asks Lucy. "You have been through a great deal. I find that talking—"

"No . . . no, I'm fine. We have all been through trials. Let us proceed."

Shakespeare is staring at him again, so intently that there is an uncomfortable pause as they wait for the strangely dressed little man to convene the meeting. Finally, he rouses himself with a start, barks out the society's motto, and sings "God Save the Queen," solo, at full voice. Then he turns to the others.

"So, commence! I shall have Mr. Tightman write everything down." He regards an empty chair with a withering look. "Tightman, you veriest varlet that ever chewed with a tooth, pay attention!" Shakespeare turns back to his guests and smiles.

Tiger holds forth on their adventures over the last weeks, speaking dispassionately, sticking to the facts as they know them, finishing with Edgar's slaying of the monster Dr. Godwin on Spitsbergen Island.

"So, that's that," says Jonathan when she is finished. "Time for a vacation from all of this, I say, time to return to real life. I have just a few weeks remaining before I must be at Sandhurst Royal Military College. Tiger, perhaps you and I could—"

"I have already told you, another will come," says Shakespeare dramatically, his mood instantly changed. He regards the empty chairs. "As you see, my three esteemed colleagues agree."

"Yes," says Jonathan, "and let me guess . . . the next creature will be worse? Perhaps twenty-seven feet tall, emitting flames from its mouth and speaking out its rear end?"

"I am not sure you are quite accurate, Master Lear, though you are making sound points and perhaps painting a picture that is not unlike—"

"This is nonsense! I have had enough, enough of all of this for a lifetime." Jonathan gets to his feet.

"Ask yourselves," says Shakespeare, ignoring him, "what could be worse?"

"The devil," says Edgar before he can stop himself.

"Precisely." The little man's face lights up.

"Edgar," says Lucy, reaching for his hand, "you are tired, over-tired."

Edgar wonders if he should tell her, tell all of them, about how real the hag has become and of Shakespeare's invisible colleague walking about in the flesh in the hallway. The scorn he would receive from Jonathan, the pity from Lucy, the doubt from his dearest friend Tiger would be unbearable. Lucy is right: he is exhausted. That must be the answer . . . or has he really gone mad?

"We are prepared for any attack," says Tiger. "No matter what occurs, we can respond to it."

"You will respond to the devil, will you?" asks the little man, his voice slightly trembling now. Then he mumbles something, barely audible. It sounds, to Edgar, like, "He has been to see me."

"Pardon me?" asks Edgar, leaning closer. Shakespeare does not respond. He sits quietly for a moment, his eyes darting about in his head.

"I have had enough; I'll leave you all to your pressing duty to chase a man in a red suit with a pointed tail," says Jonathan as he makes his way up the stairs and out into the street. The door slams behind him.

"Well," says Lucy, "what if we have a normal conversation? Have you had one of those in the past decade, Mr. Shakespeare? Surely there is more to speak of in our lives than monsters? Dwelling on unhappiness, on fear, just makes things even more frightening than they have to be."

"We cannot ignore reality," says her little host, much clearer this time. "Correct, Master Brim?"

Lucy intercedes. "Reality, my dear friend, is sometimes simply what our minds choose it to be." She smiles at the little man. "Would you mind bringing us some tea?"

Shakespeare shuffles away. Soon, he is banging around in the other room, juggling the kettle and rattling cups. He speaks so loudly to himself that it is difficult for the others to carry on their conversation in the next room. His voice ascends into a high pitch when he is excited.

"Call him Satan, call him Lucifer, or Mephistopheles, or any of so many names, he is not just in the Bible, in the Koran, in the other holy books, he is in *Paradise Lost*, in *The Divine Comedy*, in *Faust*. He is in Byron's poems, in Mark Twain's stories, and between every line in Poe. He is everywhere! Ignore him if you will! Do you think all those authors based their stories on mere figments of their imaginations? The devil is real! It came here to see me! It is coming for those young people. It is! And soon!"

He reappears with a smiling face bringing the tea out on a china tray that looks bigger than he is and is hideously decorated in a combination of garish colors. By this time, Lucy has managed to coax the others into a reasonably cheery conversation, ignoring the ravings from the other room. Edgar is telling them about meeting Sir Andrew Lawrence.

"Lawrence, the billionaire?" asks Shakespeare, sounding temporarily lucid.

"The very one. He is a nice man, kind to me and quite taken with Mrs. Thorne. I believe we may see more of him."

"Romance," says Lucy, "now that's a worthy topic."

The conversation stays on pleasant things for an hour, guided in that direction by Lucy, despite Shakespeare's attempts to turn it to darker subjects. Then Edgar and his friends take their leave and go out for something to eat. He is happy that Tiger will stay at the Lear home that night, helping keep everyone safe. They will have the late Alfred Thorne's remarkable rifle and cannon. His adoptive father's weapons, which he and Tiger stole from the inventor's laboratory atop Thorne House, have been of deadly assistance against both of their monster foes. Edgar lingers near the fountains in Trafalgar Square on his own afterward, worried about leaving himself vulnerable to attack on the emptying streets, but not wanting to get back to Thorne House before Annabel goes to bed, which is usually before ten. He still cannot bring himself to lie to her about what happened in Scotland or in the Arctic and does not know exactly what to say to her about the female intruder. He cannot bring all of this horror into her life.

He unlocks and enters the front door as quietly as possible but is not even to the foot of the stairs when Annabel swirls into view at the top looking very pleased to see him.

"Edgar!" she cries and makes for him, the back hem of her mauve nightgown softly trailing behind her, rustling on the steps as she descends.

"Mother, I, I, I was sent to Scotland on hospital business that really shouldn't be discussed with anyone except medical people! And . . . and word about the fire was late arriving and . . . I was offered a lovely trip in the countryside by the hospital authorities there and took them up on it and came back to Edinburgh to find that the news of Godwin's and Uncle Vincent's demise had been awaiting me for some time. And . . . and I believe the intruder was simply a street person of some sort, a waif, of no great concern."

"Oh, never mind about all of that, do tell me more about Sir Andrew Lawrence! I have heard tell, through the ladies' grapevine, you know, that he is a bachelor. Was he kind to you? Is he a man of morality? How does he treat people in the hospital? Does he truly care for women and their rights? Is he caring when it comes to animals? Is he anti-vivisection? Are his politics Liberal or Conservative, a Salisbury or Rosebery man? Has he ever married? Does he really have all that money? And . . . and what did he think of me?"

"Mother, I know as much about him as you do, though he seemed like a very nice gentleman."

"I felt some electricity."

"I beg your pardon?"

"I felt some electricity between the two of us. He is a fine figure of a man, lovely to look at."

Edgar blushes.

"Oh, don't be such a stick-in-the-mud! One must respond to one's sensations."

Edgar, though, is concerned about more than just his adoptive mother's sensations. He wonders how in the world, despite her liberal ways, she can actually consider affection for another man so soon after the death of Alfred Thorne. It has not even been a full month. This does not seem like her. Her face is lit up even more than usual, as if some sort of medication has seized her mind. Perhaps lingering grief is distorting her thoughts. Perhaps she has been taking more laudanum.

"I am turning in for the night," he says quietly.

"When shall you see him again?"

"I doubt I shall see much of him at all. He is, after all, far above my station."

"Come now, Edgar, there was no doubt that he was impressed by you."

"Nonsense. He only just met me."

"Indeed," says Annabel. "Nevertheless."

"Good night, Mother." He takes a step up the stairs.

"Edgar?"

He stops. "Yes, Mother?"

"Are you all right? You still look too much your . . . old self."

"I am fine . . . just fine."

"Hmmm," says Annabel, remaining on the stairs as Edgar ascends toward his bedroom. When he looks back, she is still standing there in her lovely frilly nightgown, deep in thought.

The hag does not come that night, and Edgar appears at the breakfast table feeling a little better, ready for a day's work at the hospital, though he wishes there was some way to escape his time there, and his dreary future studying medicine at the University of Edinburgh and long life as a doctor. The problem is that Annabel, so loving toward him and the rock of his life, widowed and with an inheritance from Alfred that will be gone inside a decade, needs him to be all of that. He has no choice. He needs to protect her too, from whatever might be after him and his friends. He shudders to think of it.

Annabel enters the room still in her dressing gown. Her blonde hair is a bit of a mess, as if it is attempting to strangle itself in several places, and her blue eyes look tired. She has obviously not slept well. She starts eating the food Beasley has served her—sausages and hard-boiled eggs and tea—as though Edgar were not even there, attacking it absentmindedly, with her thoughts obviously far away.

"Thinking too much?" asks Edgar with a smile.

"Touché," she grumbles.

Beasley appears in the door, bearing another card on the silver plate.

"A gentleman is at the entrance," he says. There seems to be a slight glint in his eye.

"A gentleman? For whom? For me?" asks Annabel. She straightens up and fixes her hair a little.

"No, ma'am, for Master Brim. A Sir Andrew Lawrence, who says he simply wants a word, a quick word."

Annabel glances at Edgar. "OH!" she cries and rises so swiftly that she knocks the chair back and it smacks against the hard floor. In an instant, she is gone, out the door and up the stairs.

Edgar and Beasley regard her flight with open mouths.

"Well," says Brim. "Show him in."

Sir Andrew is dressed to the nines, a pale yellow—one might say even blonde—carnation in his lapel. His monocle is shining. He also seems slightly nervous, not a characteristic Edgar would have associated with such a successful and powerful man.

"Ah, Brim," Sir Andrew says, "thought I might pop by and offer you a ride to the hospital. I was thinking of your future with us and wondered if your career goals might be better served in administration. We need smart young lads to learn how to run our institution, and I asked around and heard nothing but good things about you. Perhaps you can work with me for a short period. A right-hand man? Perhaps help with other aspects of my businesses too. What do you say?" He is glancing around the vestibule and up the staircase.

All Edgar can think of is that Annabel was right about Sir Andrew's interest in him. This offer, however, seems to be more than even she might expect. He and the chairman hardly know each other.

"I . . . I am not sure what to say, sir. I don't know who could have had so many good things to say about me for I have only been at the hospital a short while."

"Never mind all of that. Come with me today and we shall chat. You can make up your mind at some future date. If you'd rather be a doctor and cut up bodies and deal with the dying, that is up to you."

"Yes, sir." Edgar's heart rate is increasing. He imagines, for an instant, a very different sort of future.

"I have brought my horseless carriage with me. Please open the door, butler."

Beasley opens the front door and Edgar looks out into the street. He sees a horse and carriage clop past, and a few pedestrians, some elegantly dressed as is usual on the streets of Mayfair, others in the clothes of domestics or workmen, pausing to look at the marvel parked in front of Thorne House.

"Vauxhall manufacture, Thomas Parker design, engine makes barely a sound, folks call it a 'hummingbird,' you know, electric, batteries in front and back. It is the way of the future! I thought you might like a ride."

Edgar's eyes widen. "Yes, sir, of course, sir. Let me get my hat."

"Is . . . is your mother about?" Lawrence glances toward the staircase that leads to the second floor.

"I believe she is indisposed this morning."

"A shame."

"I will tell her you asked about her. I shan't be a moment." Edgar takes the stairs to his room two at a time.

When he returns, not more than two minutes later, Annabel is in the entrance hall, dressed to the nines herself, in another tight black dress crisscrossed with blonde stitching and with gold jewelry sparkling in her hat. It all works quite well with her hair. How she was able to dress so quickly, to transform herself so magically, is a wonder to Edgar.

She is standing close to Lawrence, laughing at something he has said. They are a striking couple, Edgar thinks—he so dark and intriguing and she like a beacon of light.

"Ah, my boy!" she says, turning to Edgar. "How marvelous that Sir Andrew would fetch you to work, and in a horseless carriage as well. A motorcar!"

"A voyage in it could be arranged for yourself as well, Mrs. Thorne."

"Really? How exciting!"

Annabel soon bids them farewell, taking Edgar into a warm embrace, an even more dramatic hug than she often delivers. Then she offers her hand to Lawrence, who kisses it and backs down the front steps as he says good-bye, almost stumbling on the bottom one.

"Oh, Edgar," says Annabel, "might I have a word?"

He slips up close to her.

"I am mortified," she says. "Me, a new woman, an independent thinker, a proponent of suffragettes and the vote, rushing off like a schoolgirl to appear attractive to this gentleman. And Alfred so recently passed."

That is more like it, thinks Edgar. He pauses. "Not to worry, Mother."

"He is rather charming though, wouldn't you say?"

"I do not have a thought on the subject."

The ride through London in Sir Andrew's horseless carriage is like something from a fantasy story; Edgar feels as if he were in an exhilarating scene from one of H.G. Wells's futuristic novels. They seem to fly through Mayfair, quietly humming along. Surprisingly, Sir Andrew has no driver with him. He is handling the steering mechanism himself, wearing goggles, monocle still in place underneath, his jet black and silver hair shimmering in the wind. Edgar grips the rail in front of him and is sure they are about to crash at any moment.

"At least thirteen miles an hour, my boy!"

My boy, thinks Edgar. Annabel addresses him in the same way.

Sir Andrew sits on the front leather bench, steering the machine wildly at times, a grin fixed on his face. They have to slow a little in busy Piccadilly, but pick up the pace again through the Circus, down Haymarket, whizzing through Trafalgar Square, then swerving in and out of the paths of horses and carriages (the animals' eyes bulging at the sight of this contraption even under their blinders) and pedestrians crossing the street in every direction. It is mob rule as usual when it comes to traffic on the London arteries. They have to slow again on Fleet Street, and as they near St. Paul's Cathedral and then swing north through Aldgate toward the East End, Edgar can see the two towers of the Tower Bridge looming over the gray Thames—just two years since its opening, it shimmers like a modern, double-headed monster in the already hot July morning.

They move onto Whitechapel Road, the crowds still thick, peopled with a tougher-looking sort. But Sir Andrew is so fascinated by the startling conveyance he is operating that he doesn't seem to see any of it, nor does he appear to be aware of all the vehicles and animals and human beings into which and whom he nearly collides. A man of muscle and quickness, he somehow evades all disasters with a dexterity that is thoroughly admirable.

Edgar is impressed beyond words, but his interest in their journey is suddenly overshadowed by something he sees when they are only minutes west of the hospital.

It is a man, a small one, rushing along the street amidst the hordes of mostly working-class East End folks. They have reached the center of criminal London, near the alleyways where the infamous murderer Jack the Ripper struck less than a decade ago, and might, some are sure, still be about. The diminutive man looks intent on his errand, wearing a plain gray suit and a black cap pulled down over his brow. He does not even glance up when the motorcar passes, his business apparently much more important than such a marvel.

It is William Shakespeare.

6

The Devil and Andrew Lawrence

S ir Andrew pulls his machine up close to the side of the hospital on narrow Turner Street, where the carriages are sometimes left, and leads Edgar through the back door, straight up
to the top floor and into his spacious office. He tosses his goggles
onto his desk and turns to Edgar, motioning for him to sit.

"So, how long has she been widowed?" He leans against the
huge desk and crosses his arms.

"Just a month, sir."

"Terrible thing, to lose a husband." Sir Andrew regards Edgar.
"And a father, of course."

"They adopted me, sir, when I was nine."

"Nevertheless, his loss must have been a trial for you too, my
boy. May I ask how he died?"

"He . . . he was murdered."

"My Lord, murdered?"

"Yes, sir, by an intruder in our home."

"Dear, dear." Lawrence pushes himself up from the desk. His
ornate office is spectacular. The walls are red and gold, and its

47

latticed windows, reaching almost from floor to ceiling, offer a view of Whitechapel and the River Thames, with the Old City of London in the background. "She seems to be bearing up well."

"Yes, sir, that's Annabel Thorne for you."

"Remarkable woman."

Edgar is uneasy about Sir Andrew's interest in his recently widowed adoptive mother and wonders when he will turn the conversation to business and to what he will have Edgar do, but the billionaire seems to have almost forgotten about all of that. He continues to talk incessantly about Annabel Thorne. It is a conundrum for Edgar. Despite this off-putting obsession, Lawrence is offering him an enticing opportunity, and he is an easy man with whom to converse, gracious and warm. The fact that his office is lined with bookcases filled to the brim, the books looking worn and read, many of them fiction, makes Edgar feel surprisingly relaxed too, as if he is in a home rather than an office, his sort of home.

"It would be improper for me to ask her to dinner so soon after her tragedy, but perhaps I might dine with both of you. What do you think, Edgar?"

It takes him a while to respond. "I don't know, sir," he finally says. "I suppose that would be acceptable, though Mother doesn't worry very much about what is acceptable."

Lawrence smiles. "Indeed. Remarkable woman."

As you keep saying, thinks Edgar.

"What do you think she thinks of me?"

"I don't know."

"Surely you could ask her." He pauses. "Though that is tricky, isn't it, getting into the area of feelings with a woman, not our territory, is it?"

"I believe we have feelings too, sir. They aren't so unlike us, in many ways."

"Quite so, good point, Brim. We are so often not fair to them. The genders are perpetually judging one another . . . and races and nationalities do too. I certainly should know better. I am of rather low birth, you know . . . and a dark-skinned Irishman, Black Irish as some put it." He pauses. "But . . . ask her, will you?"

Edgar takes a mental note to make up something the next time he sees Lawrence.

The conversation continues in the same vein for what seems like nearly an hour before Sir Andrew finally addresses Edgar's new role at the hospital, a vague sort of job description that seems to entail mostly his reporting to this office and helping with whatever business emanates from it. He covers the subject in a few sentences before returning to Edgar's past.

"So, how about your own background, Brim? How did you come to be adopted by the Thornes?"

"Well, sir, my mother, my real mother, was an American, and she died giving birth to me."

"Goodness me. Another very difficult thing for you, I am sure, my boy."

"My real father was a squire, though he fancied himself a writer, and Raven House, our home, was falling apart because he spent so much time reading and writing books rather than paying attention to his duties."

"Well, authors, good ones, do not write for the money they will make from it."

"We lived alone, the two of us, and he died mysteriously . . . of a heart malfunction." Edgar can barely get the words out. He still vividly recalls that night when he, just a little boy of nine, found his father dead on his bed in Raven House, in that room from which Allen Brim had read the horror stories that had crept down the heating pipes and entered the infant Edgar's brain, the stories that had seemed so alive, that had infused his soul with fear and anxiety. He also thinks of what he now knows was done to his father, of the vampire creature, the revenant, puncturing a hole through Allen Brim's breastbone and sucking out his blood.

"Are you all right, Brim? You look pale."

Edgar realizes he has been grimacing, pulling his lips back from his teeth. He grips the arms of the chair. "I am fine, sir."

Lawrence pours him a glass of water from the jug he keeps on his desk, walks over to give it to him and puts a hand on his shoulder. "It is all right, my boy. They are memories, difficult ones to be sure, but just memories, the past. One must make one's peace with the past. You are safe here."

Edgar takes a drink. "I have a sort of nervous disorder," he blurts out, shocked that he would say such a thing to a relatively new acquaintance. "And I have had strange experiences."

"What do you mean?"

"Strange things have happened to me." His voice sounds almost foreign to him. "Perhaps I have imagined some too."

"Imagined?" Lawrence pauses for a moment. "Delusions?" He takes a long look at Edgar. It is almost as if he is not sure if he wants to say more about this. "I . . . I have learned about such things of late. We have a new doctor here . . . a psychiatrist, an alienist, a specialist in nerves. That profession is the coming thing in medicine these days. This person helps with mental disorders of all sorts; though I am told such problems are rarely seen in men . . . perhaps men are not coming forward, being honest." His voice drops lower and he hesitates for a second. "There is no shame in it," he adds, much louder. "None whatsoever. But I doubt you—"

"I believe there are monsters."

Lawrence says nothing for a moment. "How do you mean, monsters, Brim?"

"Well, perhaps not monsters. It's just that . . . when I read, when I look at a painting or see a play . . . I saw Henry Irving once, playing the devil at the Lyceum Theatre . . ." Edgar's eyes enlarge.

"Brim?"

". . . when I read a book I enter it."

"Enter it?"

"I feel like I am really there in the story, and I can hear the things that go on and see them and smell them. They are very real. The characters are alive for me. Perhaps the villains, the creatures, are the most vivid."

"That is extraordinary . . . so do I."

Edgar cannot believe it. "You do?"

"Don't tell anyone, that's not the sort of thing a man of industry wants to be known for, but it is true nevertheless. It was not until later in life that I became an avid reader, but when I did, I took to it like a duck to water. Now, when I read the likes of Dickens or Collins or most anyone who is good, I can actually feel as if I were a boy meeting a gruesome man in a graveyard or a chap seeing a ghostly woman walk past his house. It can be ghastly, though at times it is marvelous. We are sensitive sorts, you and I. Let's not spread it about!"

They both laugh and Edgar is suddenly exceedingly happy, a joy that feels like it infuses his whole body and soul. He wonders how much he can tell this man. Can he reveal that he helped kill two monsters who veritably seemed to rise up from the pages of famous novels? Can he tell him that the last one was Dr. Percy Godwin? He decides that all of that is for another time, if ever.

"Sir, I could ask my mother what she thinks of you, but . . . I already know."

"And?"

"She calls you charming, which I believe is a word that women use when they mean a great deal more. She also said you were a fine figure of a man."

Lawrence had sat down in his chair. He leaps to his feet.

"Heavens, what good news!"

"And your offer of a ride in your motorcar and dinner would be met with acceptance. Just a friendly ride and dinner, though, sir, with me along as well, as you suggested."

"Why, yes, of course. Well, that is fine indeed, but I am still somewhat concerned about staining her reputation, with you in tow or not, and doing harm to Annabel Thorne would be the last thing in the world I would want. What will people think if they see me running about with her, and you, in my horseless carriage and squiring you two off to dinner a scant time after her husband's death? To say nothing of my being a foreigner!"

"Like I said, sir, her reputation is not important to her. She likes you. She wouldn't care a fig how others view it."

"Are you sure?"

"Yes, sir."

"Remarkable woman."

"You've said that, many times."

"Yes, I suppose I have."

"I admire her a great deal, sir. Imagine not caring at all about your reputation, especially being a woman and feeling that way, with all that society says they must care about. She believes in happiness, in kindness, and in being true to yourself, and that is it. Take her for a spin in your car. She will adore it."

Edgar spends the rest of the day doing odd jobs for Lawrence—carrying messages for him, bringing papers to sign—then says good-bye for the day around four o'clock. As he reaches the floor directly below Lawrence's, he notices a room with a blind fully drawn on its door. That is unusual. The entrance bears the name DR. BERENICE and under it the words ALIENIST—NERVE SPECIALIST. He wants to peer inside. He nears the door and pauses. He can tell that the lights are dim inside, and there is some sort of indistinguishable sound, a moan at first and then a voice speaking in a monotone. It makes his heart rate increase. "Why did Lawrence mention the person in this office to me? It was out of the blue, almost like a warning," he says under his breath. He puts his hand to the knob but then chastises himself. "I am being ridiculous." He thinks again of the billionaire's smiling face.

He goes out the entrance of the London Hospital with a spring in his step, feeling as though he hasn't been this happy since the days when his own loving father was alive, or at least since Tiger befriended him and stood by his side like a lioness while Fardle and those other morons bullied him at the College on the Moors. Then he catches himself. He stops dead on the street. "What am I doing? What have this man's generosity and fatherly ways done to me? Has he drugged me! He has convinced me to offer my grieving mother to him. And she, somehow, is a willing accomplice!" He puts his hand to his forehead. "Accomplice? What a word. There is nothing wrong with this. It is innocent. Two people attracted to one another simply desiring to be friends. Surely Alfred would want her to be happy."

Then he sees William Shakespeare again.

Edgar is on the south side of wide Whitechapel Road at the far west end of the hospital across from a spot where two small streets, the first no more than an alleyway, run north from Whitechapel, knifing into the wicked slums of Spitalfields. Buck's Row, where the Ripper took his first victim, is no more than two minutes into that rookery. Carriages are passing and pedestrians are going about their business and dirty-faced boys and girls are standing around in ragged clothes and bare feet staring aimlessly or looking for opportunities. Through and beyond them, Edgar sees Shakespeare come into view out of a doorway a good distance down the second of the two alley-like arteries. As Edgar watches, the little man looks both directions, then starts moving toward Whitechapel Road at a good pace, his big head down, but his eyes up, looking deadly serious. Edgar turns around so Shakespeare cannot spot him, and when he turns back, the little fellow is out on the main road, hailing a hansom cab. In moments, he has one and is gone.

It is difficult for Edgar to imagine that the little lunatic would ever even step outside his enclave in Drury Lane let alone be this far away from home, looking so grave, as if intent on some sort of mission. Edgar darts across Whitechapel and into narrow Thomas Street. There are only a few pedestrians on these footpaths and before he is more than a dozen strides down the road, a sense of foreboding fills him. Buck's Row is nearing. He can hear the screams of Mary Ann Nichols, the woman the Ripper butchered there. He can see her lying on the street near a brick wall not far from the Broad School, her image not black and white like the drawings he saw in the papers when he was a child, but in color in the dim alley light, her throat slit in a smile, her abdomen mutilated. He shakes his head to expel the scene from his brain and rushes along Thomas past a man in a sweat-stained kerchief, eyeing him, and a woman with an ugly bruise on her face, watching him too, her dress obscenely low around her chest. He comes to the door from which Shakespeare seemed to have exited. It is large and wooden with a big black handle, two sharp points on it like devil's horns. Edgar tries the door and discovers it is unlocked. On the outside, the grimy nondescript brick building appears to be just three stories high. Inside, he finds a dirty winding staircase that looks like it goes up many flights. There are no inner doors on the ground floor, just the stairs. He starts to climb but then feels a hand on his shoulder, a big one with a firm grip. It violently turns him around.

"Might I 'elp you?"

The face is broad, the nose squashed into the cheeks, the black beard obscuring most of the face. The head, under the woolen cap, looks shaved.

"I . . . I noticed an acquaintance come from this building, a little—"

"Been no one 'ere all day."

"But—"

"Been no one 'ere all day!"

The big man spins Edgar around and shoves him down the four steps he has ascended, knocking him face-first onto the stone floor. He barely gets his hands up in time to save his teeth from being knocked from his mouth. Two gleaming boots step right up to his head, resting below the well-tailored cuff of navy-blue, pinstriped trousers.

"A good day to you," says the man.

Edgar gets to his feet and leaves without another word.

By the time he is on Fleet Street, he is wondering if he imagined the whole scene, just as he imagined the Ripper mutilating his victim. It could not have been William Shakespeare in that alley. Not just because of the look on his face but because he was walking about in this neighborhood and, more importantly, how he was dressed—in a dull gray business suit. As Edgar thinks about it now, Shakespeare moves in his imagination in slow motion, spectral and unreal, floating down Thomas Street toward Whitechapel Road.

He is scared, but this time not because of an imminent threat— he wonders if his mind has truly become unhinged. *What sort of fantasy world am I in?* he asks himself. *What sort of reality is my fevered brain creating?*

I imagined that the hag was real, that one of William Shakespeare's ghostly friends inhabits the interior of his apartment, that the little lunatic himself has dealings in the East End . . . and that the DEVIL IS AFTER US! He realizes it is all absolute insanity and that the existence of the vampire and Frankenstein creature is just as absurd.

How much of my life am I imagining?

He stops suddenly and bends over, hands on his knees. Even in the bustle of the London crowd on the footpath on Fleet Street, people hear him cry out. For a moment, several of them stare at him.

Edgar straightens himself to a standing position, and then picks up his pace and almost runs all the way home to Mayfair.

Annabel is singing, loudly, as Edgar climbs the stairs and passes her room, belting out "Love's Old Sweet Song," a melody generally meant to be a good deal more sedate than her robust rendering. Her lovely voice often filled the house when he was younger, but he has not heard her in such fine form for a long while. Every word sparkles. It makes him smile and he needs that. He steps up to her door, but as he raises his hand to knock, he pauses to listen for just a little bit longer. The singing suddenly stops. He hears soft footsteps padding in his direction and the door flies open.

"Edgar! My dear, you will not guess what has happened!"

She stands in front of him in bare feet and underclothing, her slim figure fastened into a girdle and petticoat that leaves little to the imagination. He looks down at his feet.

"Mother!"

"Oh, don't be such an old lady, dearest. I have news! Lawrence of London has sent out an invitation!"

"An invitation?"

"I am to be his guest at the Café Royal on Regent Street, just me and him, ushered there in the terrifying Vauxhall horseless carriage. He said I might even pilot the thing! A dangerous offer, that one. He shall soon learn not to be so careless, for I will take him up and we shall see what speed that miracle can actually achieve!"

"But . . . I was supposed to . . . just for you? You and Mr. Lawrence, alone together?"

"Well . . . I believe we are adults. Why, do you want to chaperone?" She lets out a belt of a laugh.

"Should you really accept a dinner date, Mother, so soon after Father—"

"Oh nonsense, Alfred would want me to enjoy myself. And I can assure you, Edgar, I will!" She raises her eyebrows to depict a sort of enjoyment her adopted son would prefer not to imagine her experiencing.

"But I was just with him, not more than an hour or so ago."

"Well, he works with great haste then, doesn't he? He is obviously a gentleman who knows what he wants. There was a boy here with Sir Andrew's card a half hour ago. The message also said that our man might squire me over to see his lovely home in Kensington! Edgar, I have just another two hours to dress! I cannot wear these horrible widow's weeds simply as they are. I shall color them up a little."

Lawrence lied to me, thinks Edgar. "Should you? Perhaps a little restraint would—"

"Yes, my son, I should. I am not Alfred Thorne's possession and neither shall I be a chattel to the chairman of the London Hospital, though I would not mind being a slave to some of his money. This idea that we women must mourn our deceased men for months and years on end is positively medieval. I do not see widowers with nearly the same dedication. No, sir, their eyes begin to wander before their wives have even begun to rot in the ground!"

"I—"

"I have no time to dawdle. I must make myself presentable. His motorcar will arrive at half past seven sharp. Beasley will have your supper for you. Wish me well! Good night!"

The door closes but then opens again.

"I shall tell you all that transpires on the morrow."

The door closes once more and she launches into another parlor song, this time a very sprightly version of "Beautiful Dreamer."

At precisely half past seven, Edgar is in his room when he hears Beasley receiving Lawrence at the door, taking his hat and cane, a pause while the butler ascends the stairs, another pause, then the sound of Annabel descending in her heels, exclamations of admiration from Sir Andrew, the door closing, another pause, the lurch of wheels, the shriek of Annabel Thorne and the horseless carriage beginning its sprint out of Mayfair toward Regent Street.

———

Alone and unsettled, Edgar climbs the stairs to Alfred Thorne's laboratory on the top floor. The NO ENTRY sign is still affixed to the door from the days—and nights—when his adoptive father worked up here on his mysterious inventions in weaponry. Inside, the blinds are drawn open, as always, on the huge window that almost fills the room's ceiling. The stars are sparkling in one part of the black sky and a gentle rain is beginning to fall from the other. Edgar advances toward Alfred's well-stocked bookshelves, containing all those novels whose presence used to surprise him. He sees *Dracula*, *Frankenstein* and *The Island of Doctor Moreau*. He lingers a little over *An Antarctic Mystery* by Jules Verne and the terrifying *The Beetle*, about an Egyptian insect creature that comes to London in murderous pursuit of an Englishman. Such books remind him of his father, his voice reading grim tales. Tonight, however, Edgar is thinking about even darker creations. Terrified by what may be after him and his friends, imagining the worst, he is looking for stories that feature the very devil himself.

As he slides his finger further along the spines, he soon realizes that gathering up all such tomes is an overwhelming task. Whether known as Satan or Lucifer, as Beelzebub or by a myriad of other names, the devil is everywhere, just as Shakespeare said. Edgar knows it looms in every sacred text, in all kinds of novels, in countless poems.

The Bible, he thinks, *would be a good place to start*. He finds himself shaking as he reaches for it, knowing that if the truth is indeed in these pages, it may actually give him a description of their next monster. He hesitates, pulls his hand back, and instead takes up a thick dusty volume of Adam Clarke's commentary on the holy book, searching for the page that notes the references to the devil in scripture. He finds a long list: the evil one, the serpent, the beast, but mostly Satan. It makes his heart thud. He reaches out again and grips the black Bible, then slumps down in the chair with it behind Alfred Thorne's desk. He starts to read the part in Genesis where the dark one slithers along on its belly through the Garden of Eden and tempts Eve and then, through her, Adam. Edgar is instantly back there at the beginning of time in that garden. He feels hot, the humidity so thick that it seems like the air is water, and drips of perspiration run down his forehead and into his brow. He hears strange animal sounds, and yet, somehow, here in paradise, a sense of peace slows his heart and his fears subside a little. It does not last long. Soon, he senses that something evil is approaching and a feeling of impending doom comes over him: a slithering and rustling in the leaves. He cannot stand it.

He escapes by skipping to the New Testament to find the place in Matthew where Satan tempts Jesus in the desert. He hopes he will be able to read it, but here too, he finds himself horrified. The devil is invisible, not a single feature described, as if Satan were not flesh-and-blood but inside Christ's head! *Our Lord confronted by a power that could actually overwhelm Him!* Edgar flips further into the good book, hoping to find a creature he and his friends might be able to confront. He finds 1 Peter 5:8, "Your adversary the devil, as a roaring lion, walketh about, seeking whom he may devour." *Is that what is after us?* he asks himself. *A lion . . . that eats human beings!* He moves on to Revelation. Instantly in a dream world, he sees an enormous dragon descending from black skies and a beast with many heads, three numbers carved into its pulsing body!

He hears a sound in the lab and looks up to see a human being on the glass ceiling above him! It is soaked by the rain now pelting down and splayed there like a giant spider, dressed in black, his face red, the skull shaved. Edgar cries out and stands up. The thing vanishes. He shoves the Bible back onto the shelf.

"I'm seeing things again!"

He knows he must deal with monsters, though, real or imagined, just as his father said. *Do not be afraid.* Humanity must attack evil, not run from it. He looks back up to the glass and sees his father there, prone on the ceiling the way the evil man was, but smiling at him, dry as an angel in the rain. Edgar smiles. He knows Allen Brim is not there, but he imagines his father as a sort of guardian spirit, his god of books, protecting him here in this laboratory of literature. Edgar shakes his head, steels himself, and glances at the spines on the shelves again, intent on picking out another book that will give him a believable clue, help him know what may be in pursuit. His eyes rest on the two most revered secular texts that feature the devil: *The Divine Comedy* and *Paradise Lost,* both briefly discussed in his literature class at the College on the Moors. Surely, there is truth there, if it is anywhere! He selects the first, which is the older of the two, takes a deep breath and reads. He enters its opening section, *Inferno.* He remembers some of this story—the tale of an anxious writer named Dante, descending into hell, accompanied by a great poet. The memories come back like a nightmare. Instantly, he is inside the book and the poet has him by the hand, guiding him downward, crossing burning rivers, going through circle after circle of horror where sinners are boiled in blood, chased by black angels, pursued by serpents, hanged upside down, their bodies cut open, one holding his severed head in his hands. Down, down he goes into the abyss, all the way to the bottom. There, in a frozen lake, his guide brings him to a hideous giant who stands eternally locked in ice from his waist down. The demon has three heads and enormous black wings! Each mouth is eating a human being, the legs squirming from the lips. *SATAN!* Edgar shuts the book. He looks up to the ceiling again. No one is on the glass now. Just rain.

He takes out *Paradise Lost.* He remembers some of it too, a complex story the professor had simplified for them. Alfred Thorne's edition is thick and brown, with terrifying illustrations by a man named William Blake. Edgar flips through the text, looking mostly at the pictures. Satan has huge wings here too, but he starts out as good, an angel in fact, then he rebels against God, descends to earth to infest the souls of human beings, turns into a creature and slithers into the Garden of Eden.

Edgar slams the big book shut. He does not want to enter any more of these stories: to descend into another hell or to become the devil or bear an attack from him. He has had enough. He puts *Paradise Lost* back and gets to his feet.

He looks for his father again—up on the glass, in the room, on the shelves. Edgar is alone.

What is this monster, really, if it exists? he asks himself. *What is Satan? A three-headed creature at the bottom of an abyss that is the opposite of heaven? Is he an angel, a fallen one who disagreed with God and opposed him?* Edgar gulps as the full force of what that means comes over him. *The enemy of God!* He takes a step away from the table. *Is that really what is after us?*

He shakes his head and says aloud, "This is insanity. Perhaps I should go back to the hospital and seek help from that nerve specialist."

He cannot stop thinking of the devil though, no matter how much he tells himself to calm down. He is obsessed with the idea. He starts to pace in the lab, wondering how a demon like this would come after them, what form of the incarnations he has read about would it take were it to pursue him here in London. Would it be one of these horrible creatures in flesh and blood or some sort of invisible power? Would it attack them in the streets and tear them limb from limb or invade their minds and destroy them from within? Might it take up residence inside him like a disease? He sits down in an attempt to stop himself from thinking like this. At first, his mind keeps racing and that terrifies him because it seems to be gaining momentum, but after a while, his heartbeat begins to slow and with it, his thoughts. He closes his eyes.

He isn't sure if he has been asleep when a sound at the door downstairs rouses him. It is Annabel and she is singing even louder than before, something about holding a man from heaven in her arms.

"Edgar!" she cries from down below. "He has the most gorgeous home in Phillimore Gardens! The largest on the street. I could marry him and I know he could marry me! He had a desperate look in his eyes. That's when you know you have them!"

7

Visitations

Edgar comes suddenly out of a deep sleep in his bed that night, but the culprit is not the hag or a sound at the door or even a jolt of fear. It is almost as if someone has entered his room and shaken him by the shoulders to bring him to consciousness. He lies very still, imagining that his door is opening and then closing, that footsteps are traveling very softly down the stairs. He is not sure though. Then he feels something moving in his bed. It is down near the bottom, accompanied by a strange rustling sound: his blanket is quivering, as if its flesh is crawling. Something is coming toward him.

In the dim light, he sees the snake in the covers: gigantic and lurid green.

Edgar leaps to his feet in his bed. The snake's huge head is emerging from under the blanket, its forked tongue darting toward him. He steps back to the wall and throws his arms flat against it and the creature pauses. It regards him silently and appears to smile, but the tongue reaches out again and the big serpent makes for him. Edgar jumps to the floor, runs out the door and slams it behind him, crying out for help.

Instantly, the house is alive.

"EDGAR?" shouts Annabel from down below.

"MASTER BRIM!" cries Beasley, who sounds like he is running.

Seconds later, Thorne House is full of people carrying lanterns and charging up the stairs, quickly surrounding Edgar in the hallway outside his closed door. A male and female servant, known to be sweet on each other, are part of the rescue party, somehow dressed and awake at this hour.

"What is it, Edgar?" asks Annabel. "You look terrified!"

"In . . . in there!" he cries, pointing toward his door.

"In your bedroom?" asks Annabel.

"A snake! A giant one! Green and horrible!" He feels ridiculous saying this—his voice sounds like it belongs to someone else again, this time someone who is falling apart.

"I shall survey the room," says Beasley.

"No," says Edgar, "no, don't go in there!"

"I had occasion to meet a good many snakes in India, sir," says the butler. "One must not be frightened. It does not help, for they sense it. One must do as is required. If I can throw a blanket or sheet over it, then it will likely settle nicely."

He opens the door gingerly, inch by inch, and it creaks as he peeks into the dim room, shedding light around it with his lantern. He steps inside and closes the door behind him. There is silence. It goes on for a good two minutes. Edgar is ashamed that he is simply standing there doing nothing and wonders how he could have let the butler go into the room on his own. He reaches for the doorknob, but the door opens and out comes Beasley, holding on to a blank expression.

"There is nothing in your room, sir. Or at least, no snake."

"But that can't be."

"I'm afraid, sir, that it is."

Annabel frowns at Edgar. The other servants drop their gazes to the floor.

"I'll show you!" says Edgar and rushes into the room, turns on his electric light and regards his bed. Nothing. He opens his closet door and searches inside. Nothing. He gets down on his knees, looks along the floor from one end of the room to the other and sees only the gleaming hardwood planks and his rugs.

"Well . . . it was here."

"If . . . if that is the case, ma'am," says the young female servant to Annabel, "then might it be on the loose in the house!"

"Nonsense!" says Beasley. He glances in Edgar's direction. "Nonsense, that is, that it might still be slithering about the house . . . do not worry yourself, my dear. We have had enough excitement. Let us make our way back to our rooms."

As the others depart, Edgar and Annabel remain outside his door.

"You know, my son, those books by this Freud fellow are translated into English. You can find them in the British Museum Library. He has invented something called psychoanalysis . . . and you can do it on yourself!" She lets out a laugh, slaps him on the back and makes her way downstairs too. When she reaches the next floor, however, she looks back up at him with a worried expression.

Though Edgar doesn't sleep another wink that night, by the time the sun has risen, he has convinced himself that the snake was a figment of his imagination, and that fact scares him almost as much as if it had been real.

There are two messages on Beasley's little silver plate in the morning and both are for Edgar. He reads them as he and Annabel take a quiet breakfast, during which he several times catches her examining his face.

The messages are strangely similar.

Could we meet sometime today? reads the first. *Something happened last night. Lucy.*

The second says, *I went home last night. Something happened. Come to the Lears' today if you can. Tiger.*

"Anything of interest?" asks Annabel.

"Uh, nothing, no, just social notes from friends." He wants to tell her more, but right now, his adoptive mother does not seem like an ally.

When Edgar arrives at the hospital that day, he finds a note saying that the chairman will be away for the day. Lawrence, however, has left a good deal of work for Edgar to do, mostly involving his carrying signed papers to various locations in the city, among them banks and insurance offices. His shortest trip, however, intrigues him the most—the delivery of a thick, sealed brown envelope to Dr. Berenice, one floor down. The package is not stacked with the other items, but it seems evident that it should go out, so he descends to the alienist's office, intrigued by who will answer the door and what he might see inside, and immediately notices the blinds drawn down on its door again. As he approaches, he hears voices on the other side, speaking in low tones. He could swear that one of them belongs to Sir Andrew Lawrence.

"I must stop being ridiculous," he whispers to himself, "imagining things. I am letting the fears in my mind control my nerves."

He knocks.

The voices stop.

Suddenly, someone speaks to him, a woman, from right at the other side of the door, though there was no indication that anyone had approached.

"Yes?"

"I have something for Dr. Berenice."

"Slide it under the door."

He jams it partway through and then feels it pulled the rest of the way by a strong hand. The woman does not say another word.

Edgar finishes the rest of the work set out for him, and about three o'clock, an hour before he is scheduled to leave, departs the hospital and almost runs all the way northwest to Kentish Town, making the ninety-minute walk in less than an hour, perspiring in the heat.

The first thing that strikes him when he enters the quiet home is the presence of William Shakespeare sitting in one of the big comfortable chairs in the living room, his feet dangling well above the floor, his big face beet-red with sweat. The others look stone-faced.

"Why is he here?"

"Well, Edgar Brim, Broom, Brim! It is indeed a pleasure to see you as well! I just happened to be about the neighborhood and thought I might stop by and see our inestimable acquaintances, when what should I be told but that you were going to make your glorious presence felt as well. I thought I should stay to greet you! And I have been informed of some rather disturbing occurrences in the residences of our friends this past evening."

"I thought you didn't get out much."

"I don't."

"Are you sure? Do you have business in the East End, in Whitechapel?"

"OH! Whitechapel! Such a mess in our multitudinous and meretricious metropolis, such a scandalous and scurrilous section of squalid sprawl! . . . Never been."

"I thought I saw you there, yesterday."

"You were mistaken."

"And yet, here you are, far from home, at just the right moment to hear whatever news we might have."

"Edgar," says Jonathan, "what are you talking about? The little boob just happened to drop by."

"Boob?" says Shakespeare. "You must have me confused with another gentleman. I knew a Boob once, two Boobs, in fact, three, now that I think of it!"

"I had a visitor last night," says Tiger.

"And so did we," says Lucy.

"Snakes," says Jonathan.

Edgar, in the process of sitting down, straightens up. "I beg your pardon?"

"We both had snakes as guests," says Tiger. "One in my bed in Brixton, another in Lucy's here in Kentish Town. Not very friendly chaps."

Edgar falls back into the chair. "There . . . there was one in my bed too! I didn't think it was real!"

"This isn't good," says Shakespeare, "not a good thing at all!"

"Such brilliant analysis," says Jonathan.

The little fellow smiles. "Thank you, Master Lear. You see, I just put together three intriguing facts that—"

"What is after us now?" asks Lucy, her trembling hand reaching out for Edgar's. "I cannot go through this again. I cannot."

"I told you all it would be worse! And now, it has come!"

"Hold your tongue, little man," says Jonathan.

"It isn't his fault, Jon," says Lucy. "He is just telling us the truth, like he's done all along. I have to escape from all of this and you three must come with me! We must flee and get as far away as we can, to the continent, maybe to America."

"The devil is everywhere," says Shakespeare in a dramatic voice. "You will not be able to elude him, no matter where you go." He stares off into the distance as if he were seeing something horrific. Edgar has never seen the little man look so distraught.

"I told you to be quiet!" Jonathan is pacing now.

"What happened to the snakes? Are they still loose in your homes?" asks Edgar, rising and stepping toward the hallway and peering down it. "The butler did a thorough search at Thorne House but found nothing. What were they like?"

Lucy speaks in a monotone. "It was gigantic and green, like a monstrous worm in my bed. I screamed when I saw it and ran from my room, and Jonathan met me outside my door. He went in with his cricket bat, but could not find any sign of it, though the window was slightly ajar. It has not come back. At least, we don't think it has."

Edgar is wondering about the window in his own room. He will have to examine it when he returns.

"Anacondas, squeezers, lethal," mutters Shakespeare.

"How do three gigantic snakes suddenly appear in our homes on the same night?" asks Tiger. "Is there an *army* of monsters against us this time?"

"Satan," says Shakespeare. "He can take any form, be in many places at once!"

Edgar tries not to react. He returns to his chair and sits down, holding himself rigid.

"There goes my vacation," says Jon. His smile is forced.

Tiger scratches her chin. "How do we fight this?"

"We don't," says Lucy. "We must pack our things tonight and get across the channel . . . to France."

"The home of the devil," says Shakespeare.

"We can't run, sis. We have the cannon and the rifle, and we have our brains and our resourcefulness. Grandfather killed Grendel; we eliminated the vampire and a Frankenstein creature! We can do it again. We have a responsibility to protect others too. We know about the creatures, what they have done in the past, about our loved ones whom they killed! I will employ the weapons myself!"

"To shoot at what? Three giant snakes in three different places at once? An evil, a force as powerful as God?" says Lucy.

"I don't think that's quite—"

"You could . . . negotiate," says Shakespeare.

"Ah, yes, a deal with the devil," snaps Jon.

"It has been done before. In the *Faust* story for example, and in many other tales," says the little man.

Edgar remembers the great actor Henry Irving portraying the devil so convincingly in the *Faust* play at the Lyceum Theatre, he and his friends and Professor Lear watching as if entranced from the seats . . . the night the vampire creature first appeared to him, right on that stage. He remembers murdering it just a few days later.

"Exactly. Stories!" shouts Jon.

"And what did the devil want in *Faust*?" asks Edgar in a monotone. He knows the answer.

"I believe it was a soul, Master Broom."

"Ah, yes," says Jon, "a small price to pay." He strides to the fireplace and seizes Alfred Thorne's remarkable rifle from the mantel, the one with the expanding bullets, the one that took off three-quarters of the vampire's neck. He snaps the chamber open and sees that it is loaded. He smiles. "Let's stop talking nonsense. I am not running away. If it can incarnate itself as something, then that something must be made of flesh and blood, a visible living being of a sort, and that means we can kill it. An anaconda, big as it is, would not react well to one of these bullets exploding its head into a million pieces." His face is flushed. "Let it come, I say!"

He points the gun at the door, then down the hall. Edgar, however, can see the fear in his eyes, doubt behind all the bluster, doubt that is creating the bluster.

Edgar lowers his head into his hands. "I'm not sure what to do. I do not think fleeing is the answer either. It wasn't the other times we were pursued. They keep coming. We simply have to figure out how to defeat it."

"Or them," says Shakespeare. "As Miss Lear pointed out, there were three of them in your beds!" His foot is tapping wildly, as if someone else were controlling it.

"Three or six hundred and sixty-six, we'll be ready!" says Jon.

Edgar lifts his head. "I'm going to stay here tonight and maybe tomorrow, maybe all week. I think it is best we are together with the cannon and the rifle. Tiger and Lucy should share a bed, and Jon and I another."

"I thought you'd never ask," says Jonathan.

"Every precaution, everyone alert, every weapon primed."

"I have seen him," says the little man under his breath.

"What did you say?" asks Edgar.

"We've all seen him," mutters Tiger. "One way or another."

"It will not work!" screeches Shakespeare. "OH! We are all doomed!"

"We?" says Jon. "You haven't been a target yet."

That is true, thinks Edgar, *very true.*

Edgar leaves for the hospital the next day with some trepidation. He wishes he could remain with his friends all day. He sends a note to Annabel, telling her that he has decided to stay at the Lears' home for a few days and that Beasley should send some clothing to the Kentish Town address for him.

When Edgar reaches the second-to-top floor, he sees that the blinds on the nerve specialist's door are down once more and the lights dim again too. He rushes past it without pausing.

When Edgar is shown into Sir Andrew's room, the chairman is too wrapped up in the invisible woman he is squiring about the floor in a waltz to notice his assistant. He is singing too, just as Annabel did, though he is butchering his song, an operatic piece sung at an ear-injuring level. His happiness makes Edgar feel as though they are living in different realities. The chairman is positively floating on air, a man unquestionably in love. It is such a contrast to the evil that Edgar feels is closing in on him and his friends.

Edgar stands quietly inside the office door until Sir Andrew comes to the end of his dance. "Ah! My boy!" he finally says. "Sit down."

"Thank you, sir."

Sir Andrew takes the chair behind his desk and Edgar the one in front of it.

"How is your mother? You know, I am not quite myself when I am with her. I feel a sort of intoxication, almost. It is very strange. I know I should have told you that I asked her to walk out with me, alone. I am sorry for that, not like me to do that, normally, but she seemed so accepting of it when I asked. How is she, indeed?"

Edgar wonders how he could have doubted Sir Andrew Lawrence. "She is well, sir." He pauses. He thinks of the fact that there is not a single man left in his life to whom he can talk. "I have something of pressing importance to share with you."

"Well, no beating around the bush, I see. If it is a bad thing, then let us hear it. I think I could bear anything right now, even about your mother, though I shan't believe it if it is too unsavory."

"It is bad, yes, but it's about me. It is something that I must tell you. I desperately *need* to tell you . . . because I believe I can trust you." Edgar's hands are shaking and Lawrence notices.

"This sounds serious indeed. You have my full attention. Whatever I can do for you, I shall."

Edgar pauses again. "Do you recall that I said something about monsters the other day?"

"Yes, yes. You and I share a vivid imagination. We enter the stories we read, the plays we see, and the paintings we regard. Though I do have the sense such experiences are more intense for you. So . . . monsters? You have encountered them in the sensation novels that are about these days. That is nothing to be ashamed of, even if it upsets you greatly. It is not unmanly. It shows you have feelings and that you care. It might actually be a good—"

"They are real."

"I beg your pardon?"

"I should not say that. They are not all real. I don't mean that . . . but some of them are."

"I don't follow you. What is real?" Lawrence's light tone is diminishing.

"There are aberrations in the world, sir."

"Aberrations?"

"There are monsters; there are creatures alive on this earth like one might find in our imaginations, in their darkest corners. Some have appeared in famous stories."

"Whatever do you mean? Are you referring to the beasts in fairy tales? Surely you—"

"I mean like Dracula."

"Dracula?" Lawrence sits back. "Isn't that the repulsive character which that fellow Stoker, the manager at the Lyceum Theatre, Irving's man, put in that trash of a novel he wrote this year. There is a lascivious tone in it, lascivious indeed! Look here, I do not recommend that you read such things. I saw a review of it in the—"

"The monster in it was real."

"Surely you can't mean—"

"But we killed it."

Edgar's voice has dropped low, and though Lawrence barely hears him, he hears enough.

"Edgar . . ."

"I don't mean to suggest that Mr. Stoker found a Count Dracula living in a castle in eastern Europe. Nor do I mean that he knows of a revenant that sucks blood from women's necks, taking their essence from them in their bedrooms while their husbands are absent. And I am not suggesting that he knows of women who have been infected by such a beast and thus had to be staked through the heart by men with iron—"

"Edgar!"

"That is not what I am saying."

"Then what, in God's name, *are* you saying?" Sir Andrew is sitting bolt upright now.

"Mr. Stoker accidentally stumbled upon an aberration, one he didn't know was a monster, and it found its way into that novel."

"And . . . you killed it?" Lawrence pushes his chair back from the desk.

"Not just me. Me and three friends and a professor who destroyed Grendel."

"Grendel? From the story . . . *Beowulf*?"

Edgar is not listening. He speaks as if in a trance. "A professor, a dear man, and a brave one, with just one arm . . . who is dead now . . . his throat crushed by another aberration . . ."

"Edgar, get a hold of yourself."

"Frankenstein!"

Lawrence gets up from his chair, walks around his desk and puts a hand on Edgar's shoulder. "Listen to me. You are suffering from delusions, a phobia of some sort, some neurasthenia, or nerve problem. I . . . I know about those things. I told you we have someone here now who can help with such difficulties. There, now, I won't judge you."

"Frankenstein's creature . . . we murdered it too."

"That is not something you—"

"We had to, sir. We had to!" Edgar is shouting now. "It was coming after us! I killed it with a harpoon gun from a whaling ship. It had gone north to the Arctic . . . like in the novel. Mary Shelley had seen it, though she was not aware she had. She put that thing into her novel and did not know that it really existed. Can you imagine that?"

"No, Edgar, no I cannot. You are in a real place here, right now. Look around this room, an office, my office, in the London Hospital in London, England. You are not in a novel, a play or a painting. You are here with me."

"Dr. Godwin . . . he was Frankenstein's creature!"

Lawrence's eyes widen. "All right, Edgar, you really need to come with me."

Edgar leaps to his feet. "I can prove it to you! Godwin was trying to make another creature just like himself. He was trying to eliminate us because we knew. That is what he was doing in that laboratory at the top of the Midland Grand Hotel! The reason he wasn't found was because he escaped; his face burned off, yellow and scarred, stitched up, a marvelous brain placed in his skull. We chased him, though! We tracked him and destroyed him! They believe they cannot live if people know about them! There may be more of them. Who knows? Someone told us that if we killed one, another would come after us. I see a hag, sir, an old woman. She sat on my chest as I woke in the mornings when I was a child, but now she comes all the time . . . the hag phenomenon, sleep paralysis . . . no, it isn't that . . . it is real! It talks to me now! My father read horror stories when I was a child; he did not know that I heard them. They came down through the heat pipes! They electrified my brain! . . . Find out where Godwin came from, sir. You will see. Because he came from nowhere and was not born of a woman. Find out where he was before he took up residence here, what hospital recommended him, and where he was before that! We dropped the dead vampire into the basement of the Lyceum, buried him in a grave along with his severed head— we cut it off in a guillotine—yes, put his head in there with him! Go there, sir, dig up the earth in the basement of the Lyceum Theatre! You will see!"

"Edgar, I am going to take you by the hand and lead you to another room now, a special room one floor down. I have mentioned it before." Lawrence's hand is shaking as he takes a hold of

Edgar. "I will inform your dear mother of your situation." His voice sounds choked.

Edgar pushes him away. "Shakespeare says that the next one that comes after the likes of us is always worse!"

"Shakespeare?"

"Do you know what is after us now?"

"Edgar, I—"

"DO YOU KNOW?"

"No."

"There were SNAKES in our beds! SNAKES!"

"Edgar—"

"The devil! SATAN himself!"

Lawrence stares at him. Edgar Brim is quivering from head to foot.

"You must . . . God, SOMEONE must help us!"

Edgar runs from the room.

8

The Alienist

"Stop him!" cries Lawrence as he rushes to the door of his office and sees Edgar racing down the hallway. Two burly men who drive delivery carriages for the hospital have just appeared at the far end. They seize Edgar before he can get away.

"Take him to Dr. Berenice," says Lawrence sadly, and then watches as the two men guide Edgar, struggling in their arms, out a door and down the stairs to the floor below. Realizing how powerful they are, he stops resisting.

That room with the blinds drawn down.

Edgar wonders if these men are working for *him*, for the devil. Perhaps Lawrence has a similar allegiance. *They have me now!* he thinks.

One of the men knocks on the alienist's door and the same woman's voice that Edgar heard the day before calls out for them to enter. They lead Edgar inside. All the lights are on in the room now, all the blinds on the tall windows pulled up, giving the sparse interior a stark brightness. It is almost cold in here, remarkable in the middle of another stifling hot day. The woman is sitting behind a desk near a sofa and when she notices the distraught expression on the face of the young person ushered in, she motions for the men to put him on a bed across the room. There are straps on it and they tie him down. She is past her middle years, wearing a plain brown dress without a bustle, that fits her unusually snugly, as if to accentuate her shape. Her stomach is flat, her arms muscular. She stares at Edgar with wide eyes and intrigue, almost as if she recognizes him. He wonders for an instant too, if he knows her. There is a scent in the air around her, the mild aroma of a strange perfume. It too is vaguely familiar.

"Dr. Berenice?" says Andrew Lawrence, who is now standing at her door looking nearly as distraught as his young friend. "Please do not tie him to the bed. He is simply upset and I would like you just to speak with him. May I have a moment?"

"Of course, sir," she says, nodding to the men to untie Edgar. Then she steps out into the hall and closes the door. Lawrence is a big man but Berenice is nearly his height. Edgar can hear them speaking in low tones for a good five minutes. "This is him?" she seems to ask at first—Edgar is not sure—their other words are muffled.

The burly men stand over the bed, looking down at the patient as if he were an animal. As the door opens, they begin to make their way out. Edgar glances toward the door and is shocked to see the doctor just leaving Sir Andrew Lawrence's embrace; her hand going up and affectionately caressing his cheek as she steps away from him and re-enters the room. Edgar blinks. *I cannot have seen that,* he tells himself. *The door was only open for an instant and there was barely a glimpse of them. I made it up in my distress.*

The men depart and Berenice closes the door behind her without even glancing at them. She walks over to the bed, striding like an athlete, her feet making no sound on the floor as if she were not wearing shoes, or were gliding on air. She pauses for an instant above Edgar and then sits beside him, her wide hip under her thin garment touching his. He is trying not to struggle and lies there as limp as he can. She brings her face up close to his, examining him. She is quivering, her skin perspiring. He is surprised at how old she is—an aging visage on a fit and voluptuous body that she seems to make no bones about displaying. Her long hair is raven black, though it does not appear dyed.

"My name is Hilda Berenice," she says in a quiet tone. Her eyes are black too. There is some sort of slight accent in her voice. Edgar wonders if it is German. She is attempting a smile but it appears as though mirth of any sort does not come naturally to her. She fidgets, first holding her hands together, then setting one on the bed near Edgar, then sliding it along so it touches him, then pulling it back. "So, Master Edgar Brim," she finally says, "how are you feeling, now that we have you lying down and unrestrained?"

"I am fine now. I believe, in fact, that I am ready to leave." He begins to sit up, but she puts a strong hand on his chest and presses him back down.

"Tell me about the monsters."

"I was mistaken."

"I see. Well then, at least tell me what you told Sir Andrew."

Edgar repeats parts of what he said, but qualifies every comment, saying that he was upset when he was talking to Lawrence and that he realizes now he was simply reacting in an extreme way to a very bad day, that he has had some tragedies in his life, a terrible one recently, and the problem is simply his nerves. She follows his story with her eyes, in pursuit of his when they turn one way or the other. "A temporary malaise," he adds. "I am not mad."

"Well, Master Brim, I must tell you that is for me to decide." Though her voice is soft, her gaze is intense. "And I shall."

Edgar wonders if she too is working for the devil, then realizes that he cannot even think something like that, even if it is true, since his face will betray him, and this woman will see that he is afraid of her, and absolutely no good can come of that. He pictures himself either locked up somewhere or sent south of the Thames to Bedlam—the Bethlem Royal Hospital, to which lunatics are confined, never to see the outside world again.

"Yes, Dr. Berenice, you will decide."

"That is an excellent start, acknowledging my position and your situation."

"I understand. I am beginning to have a clearer picture of what was plaguing me." Edgar is now using every fiber of his being to appear calm.

"Most would say that you experienced a brain fever. Do you believe that to be correct?"

"Yes."

"Or do you think your condition more than that?"

"What do you mean?"

"Never mind, for now. You may indeed have just a temporary problem, but if your difficulty is deeper, there are many ways to proceed. Conventional wisdom is that the miasma in the air or problems with your brain from birth or a growth on it cause conditions that have symptoms like yours. That or any of a number of material origins. In my days as a neurologist, I believed that sort of thing too. We in my new world, the one to which I have ascended, the psychological world, have different views. We study the soul. Psychology is a science of the soul and psychoanalysis is a voyage into one's mind. We can adjust the mind and heal it. We can navigate within your unconscious. It takes time, however. If it were up to me, I would have you committed for at least a short while to the Bethlem Royal for observation. The lunatics who are kept there are well looked after and some of them are able, after a good deal of rest and treatment, to resume ordinary lives."

Edgar holds his face firm.

"I do not think Mr. Lawrence would allow that, though. He wants a quick analysis. He wants you released and back to your mother, Mrs. Annabel Thorne, if at all possible."

Edgar relaxes a little, although he is surprised to hear that Lawrence has mentioned his adoptive mother to this woman, revealed her full name too. He is still hoping that he imagined that embrace.

"Sir Andrew wants to know if your mind is in trouble and is dearly desiring that it isn't. What do you think?"

"No." It is all he can muster.

"Look at me," she says.

Edgar looks into her eyes with what he hopes is an expression of sanity.

"What do you see?"

The black eyes are mesmerizing. They peer into him.

"I see you, Dr. Berenice."

"Not a monster, not someone who could turn into one?"

"No, nothing like that, just an ordinary person, though I know you are extraordinary in your ability to help people like me who have had . . . temporary problems."

She seems pleased with this answer.

"Is the devil in pursuit of you?"

"No," says Edgar, and attempts a laugh.

She looks at him again for a while. "Come with me." She gets to her feet and takes him by the hand. Her grip is strong but her hands soft. She presses his hand and guides him toward her desk and the sofa, moving silently again. She is at least his height, perhaps a little taller despite possibly being in bare feet under her long plain dress. "Lie there," she says.

"On the sofa?"

"Yes. I am a quasi-devotee of young Professor Freud of Vienna and I have my patients lie down while I investigate them."

Edgar gets on the sofa.

Dr. Berenice glides around the room turning off electric lights and lowering blinds. Then Edgar hears her opening a drawer at her desk. She returns to him in the dark and switches on a dim lamp over the sofa. Then she pulls up a chair and sits close to him, behind his head, a pad and pen in hand. He can smell the perfume more now, as if she has just added some. Its strange scent invades his nostrils and for some reason seems to relax him a little.

"Are you comfortable?"

"Yes."

"Are you calm?"

"Yes." That lie seems like the right answer.

"Good. You will talk and I will listen. That is always the best way. Tell me how you found yourself in this situation?"

Edgar begins to talk, almost against his will. Somehow, nearly everything flows out of him. He tells her many secrets. He starts with the death of his mother at his birth, his father's dreams of being an author, writing unpopular happy stories while harboring a love of the darkest ones and their truths. He speaks of Allen Brim's belief that the monsters in stories are real, his time with his father in broken-down Raven House, his father's death at the hands of something sinister, his struggles at the College on the Moors and with the bully Fardle and the menacing teachers. He tells of Tiger, how she was once a he, how he loves her, of Professor Lear and how that one-armed gentleman slew the creature Grendel, and lays out in detail how he and his friends killed the vampire monster and Dr. Godwin, the Frankenstein creature, of Lucy and how he loves her as well, and Jonathan Lear, of his own intense interest in books and writing. He tells the doctor that he is being pursued by the devil, forgetting that he had told her the opposite.

"Now we are getting somewhere," she says. He looks up at her and sees her face glowing in the dim light. "You believe that the devil is real. Is it Satan?"

"I don't know."

"Your life is dominated by fear, Edgar."

"Yes."

"It is important that I tell you the truth about your mind. That will help you heal. Fear is indeed a great power and fearing the devil is the ultimate terror."

"Yes. I know that." He almost feels as if he were in a trance.

"You *should* fear him. We all should. Whether he exists as a living thing or not."

"Yes."

"I will not discount your belief that there are monsters, in general. It is not my place to do that. You tell me that you saw them in flesh and blood, so who am I to contradict? You must not run from your fear of them or of anyone or anything else."

"Yes, I believe that. My father told me that—"

"You must struggle with your monsters. Then, you and you alone must decide whether the world they are giving you is real or a delusion."

"Yes."

"Delusions are powerful. The mind is the most powerful force in the world. It can even make you believe that fiction is reality."

"I . . ."

"Struggle with it, Edgar Brim. Do not attempt to destroy the devil before you, not yet. Experience it!"

"Yes."

"I know about fear," she says suddenly.

"You do?"

"I was once afraid, but I have learned that there is nothing to be afraid of, there is just life. I have lived a full one. I have explored my own mind and its potential. I have summoned the courage to experiment. I have met extraordinary people and they have taught me to take pleasure in everything." She sits erect in her chair, caressing her thigh with one hand, gazing off into the distance. "Do you think that your solution might be to accept the devil in your life?"

"Should I?"

"Satan is omnipotent."

"Pardon me."

She hesitates. "At least, the thing that we say is the devil has indescribable power. Perhaps Satan is merely part of us, something we need to reject or somehow embrace. The classic story of him is that he was a dark angel."

"I know."

"An angel who quarreled with God and became his opponent. Perhaps our wise forebears made up that story to tell us that evil is part of us, not some man dressed in red."

"Or perhaps that isn't just a story," says Edgar. "It has been told so many times in books! What if the devil is among us? What if he is real and walking the streets of London?"

He was hoping for a quick rebuttal, but she does not say anything for a while.

"Dr. Berenice?"

He hears her sigh. It is almost a moan. "Monsters are one thing, but what you just said, at least to my way of thinking, is not a sane idea. Is your mind unhinged, Edgar Brim?"

He can feel her staring at him. He turns toward her. "No. I don't think so."

"You don't think so?"

"I—"

"I want you to struggle with all of this. Explore your madness, your fears, this devil who is in pursuit of you and your friends."

"Should I not resist?"

"That will not heal you, not in the long run. I must tell you that you are on the brink of a great danger and running from it will make it worse." She is quiet again for a while. "I am going to turn off the last light and leave you to your thoughts for a period of time." She caresses his shoulder. "I want you to try to relax every part of your body, from the top of your head to the tip of your toes. Concentrate on your breathing, slow and relaxed breathing." She gets up and switches off the lamp. Edgar closes his eyes but hears her settling into her chair at her desk and then there is silence. He continues to concentrate on being quiet and calm, effecting a silent sanity, though his mind is still boiling underneath. He cannot decide if he should follow her instructions and is fixated on the fact that she seems to think that he is in deep psychological waters. He tells himself to trust her. She is a professional.

The lights stay off for a long time, perhaps half an hour. Dr. Berenice shuffles in her chair from time to time and occasionally sighs. Suddenly, she rises and turns on the dim light, which seems bright now. She sits on the sofa beside him this time, her hip touching his again.

"How are you feeling now?"

"Calm," he says in his very best imitation of a normal, quiet voice.

"Hmm," she says. She gets up and walks around the sofa, glancing at him from all angles.

"I feel well now, quite well, very calm. Do you think, ma'am, I might go?"

"Are you ashamed of yourself?"

"Pardon me?"

"Are you ashamed of being weak and thinking such ridiculous things?"

Edgar is not sure how to answer this. He has the feeling that what he replies may be the deciding factor in this examination.

"Yes," he finally says, "I am ashamed. I was unmanly, I was fearful, and I do not like myself for that. I believe it was a passing fit."

"I must tell you that I know now that it was *not* simply temporary," she says, "and you must not think that. You cannot oppose your own mind that way."

"Yes," he replies.

"I am going to allow you to leave, but I am doing it with some reservations and because you are a friend of my superior. I would like to see you again. For now, take with you the things I have told you."

Edgar nods.

"All right, then. You may proceed to Sir Andrew Lawrence's office and bid him farewell. If you can do that and not break down, then you may leave the hospital."

Edgar gets up from the bed and walks toward the door. "Thank you," he says just before he goes out, but when he turns to see her, she is rolling up a blind and staring out the window into the distance. She hasn't heard him.

Sir Andrew Lawrence races across his room and answers the door when Edgar knocks. He looks terrible.

"Edgar! Are you well? Are you all right? Perhaps I should not have sent you to Dr. Berenice, but I was so worried. Those things you said! I thought she might help you get over that little fit. It can happen to anyone."

Edgar knows now that he could not have seen Lawrence secretively embracing Dr. Berenice and her caressing him, for the billionaire's concern, his look of deepest sympathy, is genuine. Sir Andrew is a good man, not a liar. Edgar summons every power he has within him and musters a smile. He holds his hands in fists behind his back. He can still smell Berenice's perfume on his clothing.

"I am fine, sir, just a few personal difficulties were influencing my behavior, things which perhaps I may share with you some day. I realize now that what I said to you in this office was absolute nonsense."

"Was it?"

For an instant, Edgar wonders if he can be even more frank with Lawrence than he was with Dr. Berenice. In measured, not hysterical terms. Something tells him he needs to do that. However, when he looks at the chairman's pleading expression, he sees a stranger who really knows nothing of what is going on inside his head, and realizes that he actually has few real friends in the world, and this apparently kind man isn't one. Despite Lawrence's apologies, it is still true that he walked out with his bereaved mother, sent him to the alienist, and embraced her . . . Edgar stops himself. *You imagined that.* He still cannot trust him, though, not now, not anyone, really. Not even Tiger or Lucy, not completely, or even Annabel Thorne. He could never bare his soul to any of them the way that he did in that downstairs room. *Why did I do that?* The insane idea that everyone around him is working with the devil slips into his mind. *Is everyone I know manipulating me,* he asks himself, *driving me insane?* It is beginning to feel like it.

"Yes, it was all nonsense indeed. I think I should go home now. I may take a day away from here, if that is all right?"

"Yes, yes, absolutely."

"But I shall see you the next day, sir, bright and early, ready for work." He tries the smile again.

Lawrence does not appear convinced. For a moment, it looks like he wants to embrace Edgar, but he settles for a handshake.

When Edgar turns away, his face crumbles. He wants to run down the hallway. *Flight!* He has no idea where he wants to go, but he needs to get away, from Berenice, from Lawrence . . . from everyone and everything.

2

Visions

Shaken, Edgar descends the stairs as quickly as he can, though he cannot resist glancing down the hallway on the next floor, looking toward Berenice's office. He sees someone entering it, so tall that he has to lower his head to get in, but Edgar keeps moving, down three more sets of wide stairs, taking several steps at a time, until he reaches the basement, and enters the dark hallway near Godwin's laboratory, which is now empty. There is no reason for anyone to be down here. He staggers into a dark corner to hide, curls up into a ball on the stone floor and stays there throughout the rest of the day, and long after evening has fallen.

Finally, Edgar struggles to his feet and goes out the back door, walks up Turner Street and moves quickly under the dim lamps in the black night along Whitechapel Road, looking back, wondering if Berenice or Lawrence have sent anyone after him. The sky is like a dome, like a false ceiling on the world. Jack the Ripper is passing by him in the darkness, many Rippers, one after the other, and so are his victims, in legions, bleeding and disemboweled. He stops, shuts his eyes hard and holds them shut. Then he opens them and glances back again toward the regal brown-brick hospital, so out of place in this desperate neighborhood. Something catches his eye on the roof. It is on all fours and barely visible since it is as black as the night. It comes to the edge of the roof and looks down on him, its dark shining eyes staring out at London. It has the face of a black ape and the body of a panther.

He turns and runs, racing blindly, knocking into the few pedestrians who are out in Whitechapel in the night. The unusual ones have left their lairs at this witching hour—drunks, prostitutes, people with diseases and deformities. Some curse at him, others try to seize him but he keeps running.

Then someone has him in a grip, an iron grip, a gloved hand over his mouth, ushering him down the street just past the Pavilion Theatre and into an alleyway. When they are a good dozen strides down it, in a spot where it has narrowed almost into a V, whoever has him throws him to the cobblestones. The surface smells of urine. Muffled sounds from Whitechapel and other nearby streets are all he hears—a distant shriek, horses, carriages and the pop of a gun. His attacker stands over him, blocking out much of the light. Edgar dares to look up.

The man, if it is a man, stands eight feet tall. His face is red, his eyebrows thick and black, every inch of his visage caked with some sort of makeup. A crooked stovepipe hat sits at an angle on his shaved head and he wears a navy-blue peacoat and twirls a huge cane in his hand. He holds it high in the air as if he is preparing to strike. Edgar is sure he is about to die.

"I won't hit you, sunshine, if you don't open your gob!"

Edgar cannot talk anyway.

"My name is Mephistopheles. Heard of me?"

Edgar nods. *A character from a story!* He remembers Henry Irving playing this devil on the stage at the Royal Lyceum Theatre again.

"Otherwise known as the servant of Satan, and I am here to tell you that you are going to die. So are your friends, one after another. My boss is fixing it as I speak to you. You have crossed the devil you have! Prepare to perish! You cannot stop my boss, no one can, not God Himself."

He pulls the cane back and swings it down at Edgar with a mighty swipe. There is a great whiz in the air and the cane connects with the brick wall just over Edgar's head, chipping a big piece out of it that flies off and smacks Edgar in the cheek. Pain shoots through him like an electric shock.

"Fear us! Fear him! Let it be all around you and inside you! Until it destroys you!"

He glares down and brings his face within inches of Edgar's. Then he tosses his cane high into the black sky, pivots, and catches it as it drops. He strides away, laughing. When he is out on the street, Edgar can hear him growl at someone, the whiz of the cane and a cry of pain.

Edgar lies in the alley for a long time, trying to stop his heart from smashing against his ribcage; he is certain it will explode. He stares up at the walls of the dirty buildings until his gaze reaches the heavens. He wonders if any of it is real: the walls, the sounds, the ground he lies on, the air, the sky. There cannot be eight-foot men who work for the devil walking about London, he tells himself. *Yet, I saw him*, thinks Edgar, *I heard him and felt him.* Edgar knows that if there are creatures such as that, then he is in deep trouble, as Dr. Berenice said, and if there are not, his situation may be even worse.

The alienist had told him to explore his fears, investigate the devil, but he just wants it all to go away.

Then he thinks of his friends, fears for them and gets to his feet.

He stumbles toward Kentish Town, holding his face, dreading what he will find at the Lear home.

Everyone, however, is in one piece there, at least until they see him.

"EDGAR!" cries Lucy when he fumbles his way through the door, bleeding from the wound on his face, now risen into an ugly lump. That, at least, is certainly real.

They set him down in a chair with a cold compress on his face. It is only then that he realizes someone is missing.

"Where is Jonathan?"

"He went out looking for—" begins Tiger.

The front door opens and closes, then Jon walks into the living room. He appears strangely serene, a blissful expression on his face.

"Jonathan?" asks Lucy. "What took you so long?"

"I went all the way to the hospital, inquired about our lad with someone there, wonderful lady. Walked home." There is a faint whiff of perfume in the air. He only now seems to notice Edgar and a slight expression of relief comes over him, but then he sneers. "Took in a few pubs on your return home, did you? Run into a door on the way out of one of them?"

Edgar ignores him. He turns back to the others and begins to tell them what happened in the alleyway. He tries to speak with conviction, though it sounds preposterous as it comes out of his mouth. As his story unfolds, Jonathan begins eying the rifle, leaning against a wall nearby. Eventually, he picks it up, snaps it open to make sure it is loaded and listens with it pointed toward the door.

There is silence for a while after Edgar finishes.

"So," says Tiger finally, ". . . what do we make of that?"

"That I am mad. I was raving like a lunatic at Lawrence before I left the hospital, and he had to have someone talk to me about it."

"What do you mean?" asks Lucy.

"A nerve specialist, an alienist, a psychiatrist. She talked about having me committed!"

There is silence again in the room.

"And I imagined I saw that half-panther and half-ape that Godwin made, looking down from the roof of the London Hospital!"

"You could have," says Lucy. "It got away."

"And this wound on your face," says Tiger. "It's real, as real as the flesh and blood under it."

"But the man was eight feet tall and said he was Mephistopheles, and he looked like something from a nightmare. Perhaps I had a fit and struck myself or fell on my face in my madness . . . I've been imagining things."

"What do you mean?" asks Jonathan.

"The hag, she—"

"Not that again."

"She seems real now."

"Edgar," says Lucy, "you don't have to—"

"The hag phenomenon isn't something to be ashamed of," says Tiger, "and as vivid as it is, it's only in your mind, a bad dream.

It isn't chasing us in the streets." She looks calm but glances toward the cannon, just down the hallway from where they are sitting.

Edgar shakes his head. "But she appeared SO real the last time."

"And there are a good many things that are real right now that we never imagined could be," says Lucy quietly.

"Shakespeare used to ask people on the street if they were afflicted by the hag phenomenon because he wanted to catch the old woman. I'm as looney as he is!"

"Never mind all that, Edgar," says Lucy. "I don't know about the hag, whether she is real or not, but these other things, you're seeing them, I'm sure of it."

"The eight-foot man?"

"Yes."

"Are you being serious, sis? Are you that intrigued by our Edgar that you honestly believe he was accosted by a gigantic man who works for the devil?"

"Was there a snake in my bed and one in Tiger's?"

Jon has no answer and that obviously bothers him. He looks down at his feet.

"I . . . I left out something," says Edgar.

"What is that?" asks Lucy, though she appears as though she does not want to hear it.

"That grotesque man in the alley . . . he said that his boss is going to kill us all and soon, that we are doomed."

There is another silence.

Jon looks up. "Sounds like more of the tripe the lunatic Shakespeare goes on about. *The next one will be worse!*" He offers a chuckle, but no one laughs with him.

"Why would our enemy warn us?" asks Tiger. "Why not kill you in that alley, Edgar, and then come after the rest of us?" She immediately appears as though she would like to take her words back.

"Good question," says Jon.

No one speaks for a moment.

"Never mind," says Lucy. "Maybe there is some reason why this creature didn't kill you, Edgar . . ." She does not look convinced. "Maybe you exaggerated his appearance a little, but we know something is after us, something very different than we have experienced before. Something harmed you." She puts a shaking hand gently on Edgar's wound.

Jonathan cocks the rifle. "Maybe he wounded himself. But no one is coming in here and harming a single hair on any one of your heads. I'll see to it!"

Lucy steps away from Edgar and reaches for her brother's hand. "This thing may not be that sort of creature, Jon. It may not be something you can shoot, not even with the cannon."

Edgar notices that as Jon's hand accepts Lucy's, it is shaking slightly too. She squeezes it tightly.

"Who did you speak with at the hospital?" Edgar quietly asks Jon a few moments later, after Tiger and Lucy have left the room.

"A woman."

"What woman?"

"A very interesting one, actually." He smiles at the memory. "I enquired about you at the front desk and they said you might be on the top floor in Andrew Lawrence's office, but when I reached the floor right below his, a woman appeared almost out of nowhere and asked if she could help me. She said she knew of you but that you had been gone for some time. She seemed concerned. I liked her a great deal. She was one of those people whom you feel, upon first meeting, to have known for a long while. She had a way of looking at me, sympathetically, had the most amazing black eyes. She was different, quite striking, actually embraced me. Do you know her . . . long dark hair, wearing a long brown dress?"

"I am . . . not certain," says Edgar. He is not sure why he says that.

They all stay close together from morning until night the next day, every one of them more anxious than before. Jon trying to appear strong, though at times just as jumpy as the rest. Edgar stays with them, taking his day away from the hospital. They keep the cannon ready in the hallway, its business end pointed toward the front entrance.

Late in the afternoon, Edgar finds himself alone with Lucy in the parlor, Tiger and Jonathan out in the little, walled-in backyard working together in the Lears' garden. He stands at the open window and watches them digging, raven-haired Tiger with a shovel, the dark-blond Jon with a big fork. They have the rifle nearby, lying on the grass. It is hot work and Edgar can see that both of them are perspiring a great deal: Jon in a white shirt that forms a thick, wet V on him as his powerful upper torso bends to his work; sweat soaking Tiger's white blouse to her back and her black trousers to her legs. Edgar can see the sinewy muscles in her arms and shoulders striving to keep up with Jon's pace and doing well. He keeps wiping his brow, often smiling, talking, glancing at Tiger every now and then, which she notices, though when she glances back at him, he never seems to catch it. Edgar loves Tiger more than anyone on earth, and in a manner of speaking, loves Jonathan too, despite his bluster. He knows Jon is softer underneath than he says. He recalls the notebook his muscular friend took with him up to the Arctic, with its surprisingly good poems, most of them odes to Tiger Tilley.

Edgar hears Lucy sigh at the table behind him, reacting to a story she is reading. She always sounds so lovely to Edgar Brim. He starts thinking about her, something he does often, something he cannot stop himself from doing. "She has intoxicated me," he whispers. "She is like an angel." He does not know what he would do without Tiger in his life, but not to see Lucy for even a very short while would be like torture.

"You are very strong," says Jon to Tiger.

Edgar turns his head back toward the open window and listens.

"Thank you," says Tiger, quietly, not looking at him. "So are you."

He smiles and thrusts his big fork into the soil, wipes his brow and strips off his shirt, peeling it from his sweaty back and chest. He starts working again, naked from the waist up. Tiger stands still for a moment, gazing at him, but returns to her task before he notices.

"You are a different sort of girl," he says between grunts.

"I know, I know. I'm pushy and don't know my place."

"I think you are fine, and you are not a girl, I used the wrong word. You are a woman. Exceptional would strike me as the best word for you."

All the way from the window in the parlor, Edgar can see Tiger blush. He has never seen her do that. Ever. He has a sudden desire to walk out there and interrupt them, but he knows it would not be right. Tiger's strong arms are relaxing now as she engages Jon in conversation, her fingers playing on the handle of her shovel. Edgar thinks of Lucy reading her book near him, so different from Tiger. At this moment, gazing out at the scene in the backyard, the very thought of her comforts him.

"I must admit," Jon tells Tiger, so quietly that Edgar can barely hear, "that the thought of the devil himself rather . . . rather . . . scares me." Then he speaks up. "But we are going to stop the thing that is after us, I don't care what it is. You and I will make the difference. We have what it takes. You, actually, probably more than me." His last few words are barely audible again.

That night, Edgar calls them together in the living room to talk about their situation.

"I have another admission to make to you all. I'm telling you this because we are in a desperate dilemma and have to look at all our options."

"Confessions of Edgar Brim, by the young lady herself," says Jon.

"Sod off and listen!" says Lucy.

Her words and tone give Edgar a start—*Lucy said that?*—and it takes him a few seconds to begin. "A few days ago, when I saw William Shakespeare in the East End, I noticed exactly where he'd been and I went there, into a strange building down one of those frightening little streets across from the hospital, near where the Ripper struck."

"Why didn't you tell us?" asks Tiger.

"It just seemed mad to me that he was there and mad to have followed him, and what happened in there seemed insane too, but now that I've told you the other—"

"Ah, yes, the alienist and the eight-foot man who—" begins Jon.

"Hear him out," says Tiger, and she puts her hand on Jonathan's. Edgar cannot believe she is doing that, right in front of the others. Her touch, however, stops Jon's sarcasm in its tracks.

"I . . ." continues Edgar, "inside that building, I was attacked by a man of good size but not superhuman and he threw me out, as if he had something to hide."

"William Shakespeare barely leaves his cave. He wouldn't even know how to get to the East End." Jon smirks.

"I saw him."

"Are you certain, Edgar?" asks Lucy.

"As certain as I am of anything that has happened over the past few days."

"All events as real as those in a storybook," says Jon.

"What if Edgar didn't imagine any of this, none of it, what if it all actually happened to him?" asks Lucy. "What does that mean? Why would Shakespeare be in the East End? Why in a building that is being guarded?"

"What did Shakespeare say to us last time about the devil?" says Tiger. "He said that it would destroy us and that our only option was to negotiate."

"I'll negotiate . . . with the cannon!" Jon's last word sounds shrill.

"Remember who the little man is," says Edgar. "He is the first person your grandfather went to many years ago when he first grew concerned that an aberration existed. Professor Lear said Shakespeare was sane in those days, went by a different name, and did not really believe in monsters, that he just had concerns that there were strange semi-human beings on earth. Shakespeare has known about this sort of thing longer than all of us put together, and he is the one who keeps predicting what will come next. Maybe he knows something, even in his madness. Maybe he is fumbling his way toward helping us . . . attempting to meet with this thing. Maybe there is something or someone in that building that we need to see."

"I'll go back there with you," says Tiger. "Just you and me, late at night, tonight, armed."

"I should come too," says Jon. "Or just you and me, Tiger." He steps toward her, his eyes looking uneasy.

"Edgar has to be there. He knows where the building is, which door to enter, and he has a feel for all of this. We can't leave Lucy alone either."

10

What They Found in Whitechapel and When They Returned Home

They decide to head out in the small hours of the morning when the skies are black and the lights are dim, when much of London that sleeps is still in bed. They leave the weapons behind for the other two to protect themselves.

"Tiger!" calls Jon when they are about to leave. "Take this and use it well if you have to. I know you can."

He is gripping his wooden cricket bat, flat like a shovel at the business end, holding it so tightly that his knuckles have turned white.

"I have my pistol," she says, patting the side of her coat. She somehow always makes it disappear in there.

"This can be even more effective."

She smiles and takes the bat from him, making sure that her hand touches his as she receives it. They stand there for a moment, close to each other, her hand lingering on his.

"We must be going," insists Edgar.

"Thank you," says Tiger, still looking at Jon.

"See you shortly." He gently squeezes her fingers as he releases her.

Edgar and Tiger do not speak for a while as they walk along quiet Progress Street toward Mansfield Road. They have a long trip in front of them. They aren't bothering with finding a hansom cab, especially since there are not many in this area at this hour. They are moving down Highgate Road before either of them says a word.

"He is developing quite an interest in you."

She merely grunts.

"And you in him."

"I wouldn't say that. And why would you care, anyway, if it were true?"

"I don't."

"Really?" She looks over at him, but he is not looking back.

"Yes."

They walk on in silence, but after they reach the bottom of Kentish Town Road and near the St. Pancras Railway Station and the Midland Grand Hotel, Edgar's nerves start to bother him and he needs to talk.

"Do you believe the things I've been seeing are real?"

"I'm here, aren't I?"

"That's not what I asked."

"I believe in you, yes, always have."

"That isn't what I asked either. Tiger, Lawrence sent me to a mind doctor and the chairman of the London Hospital is a reasonable man, wouldn't you think?"

She hesitates. "Are all the things that have happened to you real? I suppose we will soon find out."

It almost sounds like a threat. An overpoweringly dangerous thought flashes through his mind, a thought about Tiger Tilley. He pushes it away.

Edgar would prefer to stay to the main roads, but once they are through Clerkenwell and moving down wide Commercial Street on the edge of Bethnal Green and into unsafe Spitalfields, Tiger wants to cut through the narrow streets to get to their destination faster. This means walking right into London's worst rookeries, through the tight alleys populated by wizened old prostitutes who look like witches and carry cutthroat razors to protect themselves, and past greasy thieves, and starving children. Stinking pubs and tawdry rooming houses line these roads. Tiger doesn't seem to care, in fact, she appears to be seeking the most frightening arteries to see what she can face, readying herself for what they are about to encounter in Thomas Street. She gives Edgar the pistol and instructs him to hold it in his coat pocket so part of it is visible and she swings the cricket bat as she walks, letting one-and-all know she can use it.

A drunk approaches. "I'll play cricket with you! In me bed-room!" he shouts at Tiger. He has a leering expression on his face that would suit Mr. Hyde and a staggering young woman on his arm who is dressed in little more than rags, just a few teeth in her gummy mouth. There is a knife gleaming in the waistband of his trousers. He reaches for Tiger. She steps back and cracks him so hard on a kneecap with the bat that the sound echoes up and down the street, and the man drops like a rock onto the cobblestones, howling. "Well struck," she mutters to herself. They move on.

They get to Baker's Row, pass a workhouse and the Broad School, slip onto Thomas Street and turn south, Whitechapel Road looking well lit and like an oasis at the end of this tunnel-like street. There are not many people here and the only ones who are about seem to be minding their business.

"It's about ten doors down," says Edgar.

Tiger pulls her lock-springing tool from her trousers. As Edgar learned when they were at the College on the Moors together, she can break into anything.

Edgar finds the building and that wide wooden door with the big black handle with the two sharp points on it like horns. He swallows and tries it. It opens.

"Not bolted? It must be three in the morning," says Tiger, putting her tool back into her pocket, and gripping the cricket bat tighter.

The door creaks as they push it farther open.

It is difficult to know if they are alone inside the building's nearly pitch-black confines. They start walking up the staircase, feeling their way, their footsteps whispering and echoing on the gritty steps. They are all the way up the first flight before their eyes begin to adjust.

Suddenly, he is there.

"You is back, is you?" says the big, bearded thug to Edgar, his thick, shaved head like a dark pumpkin and his wide body a wall on the dim landing.

He can see Tiger but merely sniffs at her and reaches for Edgar, so she pivots and swings the bat even harder than her last effort, as if she were striking a six for England on a cricket field, and it connects with that big skull, which might as well have been sitting on the wickets for her. Edgar is tempted to look up the stairs to see how far the head will travel. The sound is like a gun going off and the rough becomes instantly limp and falls in heavy thumps nearly a dozen steps down the stairs to the bottom.

"He won't bother us for a while," says Tiger.

Edgar stands there with his mouth open as she continues to stride up the stairs. Tiger Tilley still surprises him. He wonders what it would be like to oppose her.

"Let's sneak up to the top as quietly as we can and investigate the floors from there, downward," she says. "That way, if we encounter something else, it won't come at us from either above or below."

Edgar does not want to think of what "something else" might be.

As they step quietly upward, though, all is eerily silent, and they have the sense that the rooms on the lower floors are unoccupied. At the top, five floors up, they can see a dim light in the cracks of a big door. Tiger touches the knob and the entrance swings inward.

As Edgar takes out the pistol, Tiger lifts the bat into striking position and pushes the door all the way open.

Nothing comes at them, but what they see is breathtaking: a large, strangely cold room lit with candles. In fact, there are candles everywhere, even surrounding the big black throne that sits at the front of the room on a stage. It has red horns on the top of both sides of its back and on its arms. There is a red trident painted on the seat and carved green snakes curl up the legs. Arranged on the room's floor, as if looking up at the throne, are more than a dozen rows of large and elegant wooden chairs. Painted images of pyramids and staring eyes with light rays emanating from them decorate the walls. There are just a few stained-glass windows, and large jars rest on the floor on either side of a center aisle. Edgar and Tiger walk toward the stage and pause at the first jar. It has something in it: a red liquid.

Blood.

It is up to the brim in every jar.

Then there is the sound of something moving along the floor on the other side of the wall beyond the stage, thudding forward, moving in two beats at a time—boom, boom . . . boom, boom. Whatever is there seems to be on two feet, but they are not foot-steps like any sort Edgar has ever heard. They sound unbooted and loud, striking the surface with the force of a large animal with *hooves*. He dare not look at Tiger, who has gone silent. "This does not make any sense," he says so quietly he can barely hear himself. "We are at the far end of the building and up above the two beside it. Are those steps coming from mid-air?" Tiger does not respond, and when he turns to look at her, she is gone. He frantically sur-veys the room and finds her on the stage near the throne gazing upward. He wonders if she heard what he heard.

"Look," she says, still staring up. There is a dark column, smooth as marble, ascending to the ceiling, so dark that it was not visible from the back of the room. Up at the top there is some sort of big box, oblong shaped, carved and decorated with more pyramids, eyes, snakes and horns.

Edgar walks toward Tiger and feels something underfoot. He reaches down and finds a feather. He lifts it so it is between their faces, and cannot believe its size: large and black, it is more than half the length of their bodies.

"A dark angel's wings," says Tiger. He can see fear on her face, which is remarkable to observe, since he has never seen it there before.

"We should leave," says Edgar, and surprisingly, Tiger does not offer resistance.

The two friends instantly turn and walk out of the room at a brisk pace. Edgar has never known Tiger to flee from anything, but she seems to be doing so now. They pound down the steps without speaking, descending all five flights of wide, winding stairs in a minute. As they reach the bottom, the big rough with the squashed nose and pumpkin skull is just getting to his feet, staggering, shaking that wide head, bringing the two young people who assaulted him into focus. Tiger smacks him again, another batter's blow across the face, and he drops to the floor once more and lies still.

It takes them half the time to get out of the seedy neighborhood that it took to get into it. Edgar looks back several times as they move, imagining the devil on the loose in London and chasing them through its streets, his mind reeling with vivid, changing images of something large, something red, black, grotesque, slithering, hobbling, flying, howling. Nothing, however, seems to be following and they slow a little as they progress. They go the safer route: down to Whitechapel Road and through Aldgate and the more frequented parts of the city. They say nothing. Only once they are past the Midland Grand Hotel do they start to talk.

"Perhaps we should have stayed longer, investigated more," says Edgar. "The candles were lit, so someone must have been there recently."

"Perhaps," says Tiger, and when she turns to him, he can see that she does not look frightened at all. It is the old Tiger. He wonders again if she heard what he heard, saw what he saw. He realizes that she has not said a word to confirm any of it. She bears the expression of someone who has simply made a prudent decision.

They walk on in silence, going up the hill along Kentish Town Road toward Highgate and the Lear home. The sun is just beginning to come up, casting a warm, foggy glow over London. They stop on Mansfield Road.

"What are we going to do?" asks Edgar. "We are in much deeper trouble this time."

"So it appears."

Did she really say that? he asks himself. *Simply that? We were just in the devil's room!*

"We need to stick together," he says. "That's the first thing. Any one of us alone would be an easy target. We do everything together now, until we figure out how to survive . . . or kill it."

"Stick together . . . yes." He thinks he detects a slight bit of suspicion in her face. Tiger is so good at being strong, even emotionless, so it is difficult to read her sometimes.

They don't say anything again for a while, trudging along Mansfield Road until they come to Progress Street. The Lear home is just a dozen houses away.

"At least we came out of there unscathed," says Edgar. "When we get to the house, we'll have the weapons and be on our home ground."

Tiger does not respond.

Then they hear a shriek. It takes them a moment to realize that it is Lucy's voice.

They run toward the house. She is sitting on the front walkway near the little brick wall that separates their tiny front lawn from the street, rocking a lifeless Jonathan in her arms.

11

Devastation

There will be no miraculous recovery this time.

Jonathan's heart has stopped. There is no apparent reason. Though he is pale, there are no signs of violence on his face or anywhere on his body, not a tear in his clothes, no traces of blood. Age eighteen, as healthy as a bull and with a young bull's physique, he has simply dropped dead. Lucy looks up, still shrieking. She stares right at Edgar and Tiger, but does not see them. People have come out of their houses to gaze at the strange scene at the Lears' house.

Tiger faints, falling hard onto the brick walkway leading to the front door. It is difficult for Edgar to believe that she is even capable of such a thing. For a moment, he doesn't know what to do, whom to go to, how to even form a word, but then he sits Tiger up against the house, ascertains that she hasn't struck her head, takes Jonathan gently from Lucy, and lugs his heavy body into the house and onto a settee, and covers it with a blanket. Lucy follows in tears, her whole body quivering. Edgar goes out to revive Tiger.

He does it all as if he were a walking dead man. He kneels down to his dear friend, takes her face in his shaking hands and strokes her cheek. She comes around and seems immediately to remember what has happened. She locks her face into a tight grimace and there isn't a trace of a tear in her eyes. It is heartbreaking. Tiger cannot cry, cannot collapse, though it seems she desperately wants to.

"He is dead," she says bluntly, and gazes into the distance. "There is no use in falling apart about it. Let us tend to Lucy and then make plans. We are now under attack and we need to find out what happened here and respond."

She pushes Edgar away and gets to her feet, staggering for a moment as she seeks her equilibrium. Deep pain still written on her face, she marches into the house.

It takes an hour before Lucy is even capable of speaking. She tells them what happened in sobs and convulsive heaves. Shortly after she and Jonathan had risen early that morning, as they were in the kitchen about to make breakfast, there was a knock at the door. Jon picked up the rifle and went to the front hallway, telling Lucy to stay in the back. He looked through the window next to the door, seemed to relax a little, set the weapon down inside and went out. She could hear him talking to someone and then there was silence. It lasted for a long while. When she finally went outside, she found him lying on the walkway, pale and still. Whoever had come to the door was gone.

"He wasn't himself when he rose from bed. He looked exhausted; I don't think he had slept at all. He was worried about you, Tiger. He kept talking about the devil. It was as if everything he was holding inside, everything he had held inside forever, was trying to get out. It almost seemed like he was about to cry, but he was trying not to with a terrible effort. That was just before the knock came." Lucy breaks down again.

They find some laudanum, make Lucy take it and get her into bed. They stay awake in the sitting room, the cannon and rifle near them, not wanting to summon a coroner until the morning. Edgar is shaking, and Tiger is holding her hands together in a tight lock. They sit on the sofa, but a good three feet apart. She has the vacant look of someone in shock.

"It couldn't have been a creature," she finally says. "Jonathan must have known whomever was at the door, that's why he went out. That's what puzzles me."

"Or at least whoever it was seemed so harmless that he didn't sense any danger."

"We could go around to the houses on the street and ask if anyone saw this person."

"Maybe it wasn't a person."

"But it had to have been!" Tiger shouts at Edgar and gets to her feet and turns on him, her face filled with anger. "Did you not hear what I just said? Are you a fool? Have you lost all sense of reason? Are you as mad as your alienist said?"

"Tiger, there's no need to—"

"Do not say anything if you cannot say something helpful!" She looks like she hates him for an instant, then her face falls and she sits back down. "He's dead," she says softly, burying her head in her hands.

"Maybe he or she or it, at the door . . ." says Edgar softly, "just looked human."

"Jonathan had no injuries," says Tiger through her hands. "What could make someone like him drop dead, just drop dead for no reason?"

"Whatever was at the door made it happen . . . a look from it, a touch?"

"How, in God's name, will we fight this thing, Edgar, this being that must have seemed normal, this force that took Jonathan from me . . . from us . . . without any effort? How do we fight it?"

He does not have an answer or even any sort of consolation for her, but he pulls one of her hands out of the other and holds onto her. He cannot remember whether he has ever done this in any sort of earnest way. Her hand feels smaller than he thought it might, and softer, and cold, but there is undeniable power when she grips him back.

"I loved him." Tears well in her eyes, but do not drop.

It is not what Edgar wants to hear. He wants her to say that she loves *him*, not Jonathan, that they are still together as a team and that he and she care for each other like no one else does, and that they will survive this even if it is indeed the devil himself who is after them, the two of them working in tandem as they have almost since the moment they met at the College on the Moors long ago. But Tiger does not seem like his ally right now.

"I know," he says.

They speak to the neighbors, but the incident happened so early in the morning that no one actually saw the mysterious visitor, and the few who were about did not notice anything unusual on the street at that time.

Then Tiger and Edgar go indoors and stay there for the next two days. They try to keep alert but are barely able to speak to each other, and Lucy is inconsolable. They all put on dark clothes. Tiger doesn't eat much though she makes sure both the cannon and the rifle stay in good working order and insists on taking a longer shift on watch at night. Beasley comes with Edgar's clothes but they say nothing to him about what happened. They do not even ask the Thorne House butler indoors and send him home with a note saying that Edgar will be staying at the Lear home for a couple more days, and instructions to tell the hospital that he will not be coming in for that time either. When the coroner comes to examine the body, they make up a story of heart troubles in the family and early sudden deaths and dissuade him from a close examination. Edgar is not about to tell him that he fears the devil killed his friend. They do without a funeral and simply hire a gravedigger and have Jonathan buried, not in Highgate Cemetery near his grandfather but in a smaller graveyard near a little church nearby. When they go through Jonathan's things, Tiger finds his notebook and reads his poems. Edgar hears her stifle a sob and walk out of the house, the book in hand. He never sees it again.

They wait—for what, they aren't sure—cowering in their house. Edgar dreams of the hag at night. When he is awake, he veers between believing that everything that has happened over the last few days is fictional, and a debilitating, mind-bending fear so extreme that he constantly wants to run from the house, run away, even though he has nowhere to go. He has spells where he has difficulty breathing. Tiger is no help. As the two days pass, she remains almost completely silent. Lucy is different—when Edgar goes into her bedroom to see her, she is honest and expansive about her feelings and cries a great deal. Edgar wants to ask Tiger about the sounds he heard in the devil-worship room on Thomas Street— was that just in his mind? She does not say anything about it, as if it never happened. He cannot bring the subject up: both his pride and his tenuous grip on reality will not allow it. They sit in the house for long stretches, barely moving.

On the third day, Lucy suddenly appears in her bedroom door first thing in the morning with her dark dress on, her face cleaned and wearing a determined look. She comes into the living room and addresses her friends.

"I am not going to lie here anymore and live in fear. Jonathan would not have wanted that, not in the least. This thing is after us and we have to fight it. Fight it or die trying. I do not care what it is! I'm not cowering for another second."

Edgar stops feeling sorry for himself almost the moment she speaks and her words seem to affect Tiger too. She gets up and is soon pacing, muttering, as if trying to find the old Tiger inside and drive herself into action. She stops and stands before them with her legs wide apart and her hands on her hips in old Tiger style. "If there is anything we can do, absolutely anything, even if it seems almost useless," she says, "then let us do it, now. We cannot worry about leaving ourselves vulnerable. That simply is not a good tactic. It is getting us nowhere."

"We could go back to the room in that building on Thomas Street," says Edgar, "all three of us this time, with the rifle, maybe even the cannon." He thinks he sees fear flicker across Tiger's eyes.

"All right," she says, and then pauses. "Do you think we missed something? I thought we looked through it thoroughly."

Edgar evades her glance. "Maybe that would be a waste of our time." He wonders, however, why she is resistant to exploring one of their few options.

"One of us could go on watch outside the building," adds Tiger quickly. "When we see anyone suspicious enter, we could alert the others and investigate. Remember, someone must have lit those candles."

"What about Shakespeare?" asks Lucy. "Perhaps he knows more than we imagine. He has been insisting that our enemy is the devil all along. We have some reason to believe he has been visiting Thomas Street too."

Something that has been bothering Edgar for a while comes back to him. He remembers the little man saying that the devil had visited him. Now that Edgar thinks of it, he realizes that Shakespeare said it twice. He wonders if the other two heard it. They have never mentioned it. Edgar asks himself if Shakespeare *really* said that. He wonders, for a split second, if only he can hear some of the things the little man says.

There is a knock at the door and Edgar and Lucy freeze. Tiger picks up the rifle and aims it at the entrance. Lucy moves toward the cannon.

"I'll answer this," says Edgar. "Keep the rifle trained."

He walks slowly toward the door and glances through the window. He immediately recognizes the face.

"Oh!" says Edgar with relief, "it's just a friend of mine, the chairman of the hospital board. I mentioned him to both of you—Andrew Lawrence." Edgar is about to open the door.

"Stop!" shouts Tiger. "Open it slowly. I'll keep the gun trained at his head."

"Tiger, it's my friend, one of the wealthiest and most respected gentlemen in London!"

"You mean someone who doesn't *appear* to be a threat? We should have been cautious with Beasley too. I'm not letting anyone else approach this door without protection."

Edgar knows she is right. He opens the door slowly and Lawrence smiles at him. Then he sees Tiger pointing the rifle at his head.

"Edgar, what is going on?" Edgar does not respond at first. He is thinking about how this man lied to him and sent him to a mind doctor. *Did I really see them embrace?* "Why are you staying away from the hospital?" continues Lawrence, his eyes right on the end of the gun barrel. "Are you ill? Those demon thoughts are not still driving you mad, are they? I understand your concerns, I really do . . . I have looked into things. But—" Lawrence glances at Tiger. "Are you going to shoot me?"

"That depends," says Tiger. "What do you want?"

"I just want to speak to Edgar."

"You can speak to all of us. You keep your distance and you do not touch anyone. I want to see your hands at all times. Those are the only conditions under which you can come into this house. Do I make myself perfectly clear?"

"Absolutely."

Lawrence enters the house and sits down on the settee. Tiger stands against the wall with the rifle still in ready position. Lucy is down the hall near the cannon.

"Who are these people?" asks Lawrence.

"They are my friends."

"Lovely friends."

"We have reasons to act this way. We have had a terrible few days. We are under siege."

"I am sorry to—"

"What do you want?" snaps Tiger.

Lawrence turns to Edgar. "I have come to inquire after your health, to ask you to return to the hospital and to apologize to you."

"About what?"

"About the monsters."

"What do you mean?" Edgar sits on the settee.

"Well . . . I've been having a marvelous time with your mother, saw her twice in the last few days, though I did not say a word about the state you were in when you last left my side and the fact that you have been away from the hospital for so long. I did not want to upset her. As my fondness for her grows, I see her deep love for you and my heart has been going out to you and the state you are in. I felt that, rather than simply thinking you deeply troubled, I would look into things, give your perceptions, however strange, some consideration. I had several people pursue research on our Dr. Godwin: where he came from before he was with us at the London Hospital, where he was before that, and before that. I had different individuals do the research for each institution, so they could not connect any dots should any irregularities turn up."

"And?" asks Lucy, stepping forward and sitting next to Edgar.

"Our Dr. Godwin, a man who appeared to be barely forty years old, had been at some dozen hospitals as a surgeon . . . over the past seventy-five years."

"He was *made—created*—by a human being," says Edgar. "He would never have died of natural causes."

"That is sounding less insane to me than it used to." Lawrence sighs. "I have friends at the Royal Lyceum Theatre. I have funded many of their enterprises—Irving's productions are very expensive, as you well know, everything needs to be lifelike for him. I am seeking permission to have a little digging done in the basement of the theatre, where the soil is piled deepest."

"You will find a decomposing body there," says Edgar, "a large one with an astonishing tooth in its mouth that can puncture a breastbone to allow its owner to suck out blood . . . you will find half of its neck shot off, the work of an extraordinary weapon." It all sounds mad as it comes out of his mouth and he glances at Lucy. To his surprise, she is looking down, almost as if embarrassed by his words. No one says anything for a moment.

Lawrence turns to Tiger. "Can you set down your gun now, if you please?"

She keeps training it on him.

"Tiger," says Edgar.

She hesitates, then lowers her weapon and sits on the settee not far from Lawrence, eyes on him.

"The devil is after us now," says Edgar.

"Or something very much like him," adds Tiger.

"I am less inclined to disbelieve that too," says Lawrence. "In fact, I am also here because I would like to know what I might do to help you. I have money and many other assets at my disposal. If you need protection, I can hire people to watch over you twenty-four hours a day. I can hire investigators or speak to friends at Scotland Yard, whatever is needed."

"They would laugh you and us out of their offices," says Edgar. *Why is this man suddenly so much my ally concerning all of this?* he asks himself.

"And one wonders what protection might accomplish," says Tiger.

"What do you mean? Don't you think that—"

"My brother was killed a few days ago," says Lucy in a monotone, "right outside our door here, without a single mark on his body. How do you protect someone from that, from such evil power?"

Lawrence goes pale and does not say anything for a while. When he speaks again, his voice is low and measured. "You know, I was born into poverty. My father was a laborer in Ireland. My mother sewed clothes for pennies. They worked hard and I was proud of them; I still am proud of them. I vowed, however, that I would have more than they had, and never suffer the abuse that they did, that I would fight with my very soul to make something of myself and not let anything, my heritage, my social standing, stop me. I came to London as a young man with little more than the clothes on my back. There was nothing for me at home: no secondary schooling, no reputation, nothing, and I had no choice but to come to the city to seek my fortune. I was afraid of my very shadow in those days, though I had an inner strength. I summoned that strength, the power we all have inside us, and I built a tool-making business and then a textile company and then another and another. I am respected now, revered, in fact . . . money will do that." He pauses again. "You *have* to face this, whether it is indeed the devil himself or not. Satan takes many forms, my friends, I know. I will help you. Now, what is to be done?"

"We have discussed a couple of possibilities," says Lucy.

As she seems poised to reveal the plans they had made in private, Edgar remembers again that Lawrence is inappropriately courting his dear widowed mother, and sent him to see Dr. Berenice the instant he appeared to be having nervous troubles . . . that embrace. He also thinks he can smell a whiff of perfume on the chairman. "Perhaps there might be a better time to—" Edgar begins to say.

"No," says Tiger, "we need to do this now. We are in a desperate situation and maybe this man can truly help us. He has the motivation and funds to do it. Who else can we go to?"

Edgar wonders how Tiger can so suddenly be on Sir Andrew's side. *Is it just desperation?*

"We are considering questioning our friend Shakespeare," says Lucy.

"I thought you truly disturbed, Edgar, when you mentioned that name in my office," says Lawrence, "but I sense now that you weren't really referring to the great bard, were you?"

Edgar does not respond, but Lucy speaks up immediately, revealing everything about Shakespeare to a man who was a stranger to her just moments ago.

"He is a lunatic," she says, "who lives here in London: a little man who was of eccentric ways to begin with and lost his mind as his years progressed. He was a scholar, a person of some wealth, and he believed that it was possible that some of the creatures that are part of our folklore and our novels and poems might, in some ways, really exist. He wrote papers about it. My grandfather went to see the little man when he was still of reasonably sane mind, and Shakespeare helped fund him when terrible circumstances in his life put him in pursuit of something that seemed very much like the monster Grendel from the great legend *Beowulf*."

"Edgar said something about that. Was it really—"

"Grandfather killed an aberration."

"What does that mean?"

"He killed something on the moors in northern Scotland that looked like a huge ape, a strange being that walked on two legs, had killed my grandmother and had been murdering children in Scandinavia."

Lawrence looks like he does not know what to say.

"Shakespeare told my grandfather he was worried that some aberrations might keep track of each other and know if harm came to one of their number and seek out anyone who might be aware of them and want to eliminate them. All for self-preservation. So, after my grandfather killed Grendel, the little man was frightened that something worse would come after him up at the College on the Moors."

"And it did," says Tiger, "or so it seems. The thing you will unearth at the Lyceum. Then Shakespeare warned us again, after we killed that revenant. He seemed frantic about it that time. Something even worse did come. It killed Professor Lear, but Edgar slew it on Spitsbergen Island about two weeks ago . . . Godwin, the Frankenstein creature."

Lawrence looks from her to Edgar. "It is just as you said during your ravings, my boy. This is incredible. It truly is." He shakes his head. "And imagine—these great works of literature have contained such truths all along."

"Think about it, sir," says Lucy. "What could be coming for us now? What could be worse? Mr. Hyde? Witches? No, not anything like that. None of those creatures are worse than what we have already encountered."

"The devil," says Tiger. "Shakespeare said it himself."

"But why would you believe an insane old man?"

"Because he has been right, twice . . . three times if you count now," says Lucy.

"When I asked you about what we might do, you mentioned his name."

"It is because we are grasping at straws, trying to find some sort of starting point for fighting back. Edgar says he saw the little fellow in the East End, going up Thomas Street near the hospital the other day and entering a building. He apparently did not look like himself that afternoon. He always wears flamboyant clothes, says bizarre things and has a lunatic look in his eye. He has three imaginary friends with whom he meets on a regular basis to discuss the existence of human aberrations. He calls it the Crypto-Anthropology Society of the Queen's Empire. So that is the sort of person we are talking about, as strange and unique as that, yet when Edgar saw him in the East End, he was wearing a gray suit and appeared very serious. Earlier, he had spoken to us about negotiating with the devil."

"So, Edgar and I went there," says Tiger, "to Thomas Street in the early hours of the morning. We were accosted by someone, a large man whom I was able to quickly incapacitate." Lawrence raises his eyebrows. "And we went upstairs in the building and found a place that looked like it was the throne room of the devil. There were jars filled with blood on the aisles. We saw other things too." She does not elaborate, perhaps wanting to spare Lucy, or, thinks Edgar, because the hoofed footsteps were a figment of his imagination. The story makes Lawrence shift uncomfortably on the settee.

"Someone attacked Edgar near the East End too," says Lucy. "He . . . was eight feet tall and spoke of the devil and said it would kill us all."

"My God," says Lawrence. He sighs and rubs his face. "Have you confronted this Shakespeare fellow about his presence in the East End?"

"Yes," says Lucy, "Edgar asked him about it once, but didn't pursue it since he denied it. That denial probably should have made us suspicious. We have no way of fighting back, it seems, but we know about that building and that room . . . and what was in it."

"Where is this Crypto . . . poly . . . morph . . ." Sir Andrew frowns. "Where does the little man live?"

"In Drury Lane."

"We need to pay your friend a visit," says Lawrence, getting to his feet. "Now."

"Not now," says Edgar, who has remained silent for a long while, his heart thumping. Something tells him that he should keep Lawrence away from William Shakespeare. "We cannot be too rash about this. We are exhausted, excited about a couple of possibilities that seem far-fetched. Let us gather ourselves today. We shall speak to Shakespeare tomorrow. We need to think carefully about what we ask him, in case he is hiding something and we alienate him."

"Really?" asks Lucy. "You want to wait, with this thing at our door?"

"That's all right," says Lawrence. "It will give me time to marshal some resources and to excavate that body in the Lyceum. Who knows, it may tell us something."

"It was good to see you," says Edgar, getting to his feet, extending a hand toward the door.

"Yes," says Lawrence. "Yes, of course. It was very nice to meet you all, even under these circumstances." He shakes hands with the others, who are now smiling at him, and moves to the door. "And Edgar, you should speak to Dr. Berenice again. She is the best there is at what she does, the top of her class when she was studying medicine and psychology. I believe she can help you a great deal, whether these creatures exist or not."

12

Navigator of the Mind

Edgar goes that same afternoon. Lawrence seems to be directing him to this mind doctor and he needs to know why. The moment Tiger and Lucy are in another room, he slips out the door without telling them and heads south. It is just past noon and the sun is straight above in another unusually hot London day. The heat feels positively unnatural. Edgar does not want to encounter Lawrence, so when he gets to the hospital, he sneaks up to the third floor and knocks on the alienist's door, perspiring inside his black suit coat and trousers. She opens it immediately, almost as if she had been expecting him.

"Edgar Brim," she smiles. "How nice to see you. Come in and lie down."

He goes into the room without comment, but when he gets to the sofa, he sits on it instead of reclining. It is cold in here again.

Berenice stands at the door for a moment regarding him. Then she strides across the room in her silent way, swaying her wide hips under her tight brown dress, the same one she had worn the last time Edgar was here. If it is a uniform, it is a very strange one.

Her face looks even older today, but her body somehow younger. "How have you been?"

"Not well. There are more problems."

"I see." She looks at him intently. "So, you do not want to lie down and tell me. You want to sit?"

"I have come here as part of seeking the truth about myself and my situation. In order to do that, I must ask you some questions first."

"Are you sure you would like the truth, even if it is difficult to bear?"

He clears his throat. "Yes."

"Ask me what you will."

She sits on the sofa beside him, very close. He can smell her perfume again, but this time it is different, or at least, much stronger. It is unlike any he has ever smelled before.

He gathers himself. "Tell me more about yourself, who you are and how long you have known Sir Andrew Lawrence. He has not been entirely honest with me and I believe it is part of his plan to have me speak to you again. I want to know why. I need to know more about both of you before I can allow you to probe my mind or before I do anything more with him. A mysterious caller murdered my colleague and good friend a few days ago without laying a finger on him . . ." He regards Berenice. "I believe you met him."

"Oh?"

"A young man, late teens, dark-blond hair, came here looking for me?"

"Oh . . . yes, I recall now. Handsome young man. He was murdered? How terrible." She says it without much emotion, a doctor's clinical response, fixing her hair as she speaks.

"Things are becoming awfully strange and desperate," says Edgar, "and suddenly, Lawrence is offering to help me find the creature. In fact, he seems extremely interested."

"A creature? The devil?"

"Yes. I will say it no matter what you think of me. Lawrence is going along with that idea, came over to my side without giving it much thought, in my opinion."

"Your side? You really should lie down."

"Tell me who you are."

"I am Dr. Hilda Berenice, as I said. I was a neurologist first, studied at the London University. I have always been fascinated by the human brain."

"The top of your class?"

"Yes. Did Lawrence tell you that?"

"He made that clear."

"Well, he had the final word in hiring me. It was a bit of a risky thing, though, bringing me in to head up a psychiatry department, one dedicated to the sort of new work beginning to be practiced by the likes of Professor Freud, involving psychoanalysis and investigating repression, the unconscious and dreams."

"Where did you practice neurology?"

"I never did. I met someone while I was in school and he influenced me to take up psychology. He was a marvelous man, with the most powerful brain I have ever encountered. I am gifted, but he is more so. He was an explorer, not afraid to look into things that others feared to investigate. He was magical. He and I became . . . very close." She runs her hands along her thighs and her mind seems to drift. "Have you ever met someone you feel you have known for a long while, since before you met, before you were born?"

"What was his name?"

"It is immaterial. He showed me that psychology was the proper field for someone in search of the absolute truths about life."

"And Lawrence?"

"I likely know little more about him than you do. He is a wealthy man, a kind man, who has built himself up from humble beginnings in Ireland. He is of an open mind too. He has submitted to psychoanalysis."

"With you?"

"Of course."

"So, you must know more of him than you are saying."

"I cannot—"

"What did you learn when you analyzed him?"

"My dear boy that is none of your business. I could never divulge such things, but I can assure you he is a good man and you have nothing to fear, directly, from him. Might you lie down now?" She speaks the last sentence in a different sort of voice, a quiet, almost husky one, somehow soothing. Her perfume is now engulfing Edgar. He lies down.

"Let us seek the truth and see if we can help you." She gets up, shuts off the lights, and returns in the dark to turn on the lamp above the sofa. She sits in her chair behind him and says, "Relax."

The word seems to take five minutes to leave her mouth. Edgar feels himself drifting. He hears her voice as if it is coming to him from a great distance, though it is clear and warm. "The last time I saw you, you left out important things, didn't you? You mentioned your parents but you did not say anything about how you felt about them. Nor did you say a word about your dreams. I sense that dreams are very important to you."

"Yes." He pauses. "Dreams. My parents. I lost my mother on the day I was born."

"How do you feel about that?"

"I hate it."

"You hate your mother."

"No."

"I believe that, in some way, you may. What about your father?"

"He was everything to me."

"Both mother and father to you?"

"Perhaps."

"He looms large in your mind and in your unconscious."

"He told me not to be afraid."

"But it was he who brought fear into your life. You told me last time that he read dark, sensation stories to you. It was he who first brought into your mind the idea that the monsters were real."

"Yes. It was not his fault though. He did not know I could hear the stories. He read them out loud in his room up above and they came down the heat pipe—"

"Into your brain."

"Yes."

"So, he put them there. You have issues you need to resolve with him. You need to encounter him, psychically, and chase this fear. Do you dream about him?"

"No, I dream of monsters."

"So, you have nightmares."

"Yes, many."

"For how long?"

"Since the day I was born, it seems."

The alienist does not say anything for a while. Edgar lies there under the dim light, hoping for her voice to appear again out of the darkness. She has done this before.

"Dr. Berenice?"

"I am here. I am here for you." Her voice sounds almost seductive. "The monsters in your dreams are the incarnations of your fears. Do these monsters ever start out as friendly and then turn against you, attempt to kill you?"

"Perhaps once or twice but—"

"Then, it is evident that you perceive your friends, at least some of them, as your enemies, as monsters. Do you have friends, close friends, whose loyalty you have recently begun to doubt?"

Edgar thinks of Tiger's strange behavior at the devil-worship room on Thomas Street, of the hatred in her voice for him after Jonathan's death, of Lucy's willingness to tell all their secrets to Lawrence and immediately take his side.

"Yes."

"I suggest, then, that you investigate that concern. You must stay away from these friends until you are sure about them. It will not help your state to fear them."

"I don't think I—"

"You must protect yourself at all costs. We do not want to increase your paranoia. A paranoid mind is a diseased one."

"Paranoid?"

"Now, let us address the devil issue. As long as you are calm and intelligently questioning your fears and keeping away from those who in some way frighten you, you should be able to differentiate between the devil inside you and one that might actually exist in flesh and blood and be in pursuit of you."

"The one inside?"

"Your mind turning on itself."

The thought terrifies Edgar. A devil inside him—living in his mind. He thinks of Satan in the Bible trying to infiltrate the soul of God.

"I am sure you have no evidence of an actual living devil pursuing you . . . do you?" Her voice seems closer, as if she is leaning down toward his head from behind.

He thinks of the big black feather he found in the devil-worship room, the sounds of the hooved footsteps. He thinks also of Grendel, the vampire creature and Dr. Godwin, made by the hand of man, all monsters alive in flesh and blood. He thinks of Shakespeare saying that something worse, as real as the others, will come for him.

"Edgar? Do you?"

He wonders if Tiger, Lucy and Lawrence, if Professor Lear and Shakespeare are all in this together, always have been since the start, taking his mind apart, slowly leading him into the arms of Satan, their final goal. He wants to see his father.

"No. No, I do not. That would be madness. And I am not mad."

It takes Dr. Berenice a long time to respond. "Good," she finally says. "To finish, let us do something called free association. I will not belabor it. I will merely ask what comes to your mind when I say a few different words. Are you ready?"

"Yes."

"Your mother."

"Love."

"Your father."

"Love."

"Fears."

"Do not be afraid."

"Dreams."

Edgar says nothing.

"Dreams?" she asks again.

"The hag."

"Pardon me?"

"I have not told you about my most important dream, a recurring one that I have had since I was a child."

"Well, that omission is itself interesting. Does this dream contain an old woman who sits on your chest when you try to wake in the morning? Do you feel paralyzed and cannot move your limbs?"

"How do you know that?"

"Surely you know why, Edgar. You know that such a dream simply has to do with sleep paralysis, an easily explained phenomenon where the subject wakes suddenly and the body, doing its job in the way it should, has merely put its functions to sleep too, so that the subject does not get up during a dream and injure himself.

This sleep paralysis, known to some as the hag phenomenon because it sometimes involves the fear-induced delusion of someone, often an old woman, sitting on the chest, is actually nothing to fear." Edgar glances up at her: her old woman's face and her intense black eyes. "The only thing you have to fear in this situation," she continues, "is the fear itself. That, in the end, is really all you have to combat. Our bodies are helping us in these moments, keeping us safe. Again, it is only when our minds turn on us that we have true problems. Our bodies are generally wonderful things, Edgar. It is a good idea to explore your body and its potential too, as well as your mind. I was taught that by my mentor." She says the last word as if she were speaking of God.

"The man you knew in school, who pushed you into psychiatry and magic?"

"A great man," says Berenice, and her voice sounds distant. "You have nothing to fear, as long as this hag does not come to you in situations other than waking from a deep sleep. She never does that, does she, Edgar Brim?"

"No," says Edgar quickly. "No." He thinks of the hag appearing on the boat on Spitsbergen Island in the north, of it attacking him before he can fall asleep in his room at home. He thinks of it calling out to him, telling him that it is the devil, seeming as real as his own flesh and blood.

"I have one last word for you in our free association exercise."

"Yes."

"Satan."

It takes a few beats before Edgar replies. "Nothing," he finally says.

"Well, that is an interesting response indeed. I should tell you that we psychiatrists understand that patients often answer the opposite of what they really know is the truth. They repress the truth. Take care that you have not done that. As I have said before, it is better to battle your fears than to run from them."

She switches off the dim lamp, walks silently across the floor and turns on the bright lights. Edgar has to put his hand over his eyes to shield them from the glare. He sits up. Dr. Berenice is standing close to him. He can smell her perfume again, like an intoxicant in the air. He feels almost giddy. He looks up and sees that aging face, obviously once beautiful, dark featured and exotic, sitting on top of her young body.

"Perhaps Satan is real, Edgar Brim, as real as my hand." She places her left hand on the side of his head at his temple, its soft, warm surface feeling as though it is touching his brain inside his skull. She runs it down his cheek to his chin and removes it. She smiles.

"Life is to be embraced in all its possibilities. Perhaps the things we think are evil are not so terrible, and the things we think are good are not so wonderful. I was taught that too and I keep it close to my heart to this day." She puts her hand on her chest and moves it to a place over her heart. "Go out now and grapple with these fears, avoiding those whom you suspect, and embrace the devil if you must."

When Edgar reaches the street, he has no memory of leaving Berenice's office, though he thinks he can still smell her perfume. He is sure he was on the lookout for Lawrence as he came through the hospital, trying to avoid him, and certain too that he was being followed or at least watched, but that is all he remembers. It is as if he wakes up on Whitechapel Road. He actually considers, for a moment, if he was ever in Berenice's office, ever spoke to her, or if she even has an office at the London Hospital . . . if she exists at all. He still feels a little lightheaded, and surprisingly, very good.

Edgar walks all the way to Kentish Town. Just as he turns into the Lears' street, he sees his father walking toward him.

13

Last Ally

It is so hot all the way along his walk that the pavement, the horses, carriages, buildings and even the people look like they lack solidity. They are wavering in the heat. His father appears to bend like everything else, but as Edgar nears, there is no doubt it is Allen Brim. His disheveled hair, flaming red like Edgar's, marks him from a great distance. They lock identical blue irises onto each other, all four the color of stormy English skies. The squire has aged a great deal since Edgar last saw him lying on his bed in Raven House seven years ago, those eyes wide open, his face as pale as the pages in the mountains of books he had read. Though Allen is beaming, he walks slowly and gingerly, like a man with a heart problem. They fall into each other's arms. A few pedestrians stop and stare.

"My son, how you have grown!"

"Father, it cannot be you," he whispers into his chest. He can smell him, though, that same father smell. He can feel that same thin chest. When they pull back and look at each other, Edgar can see the familiar circles under his father's tearing eyes, now much darker.

"Oh, but it is me, Edgar. I know you have seen remarkable things since we last embraced, especially over this past year. You have seen monsters come to life from the great books, alive just as I said they were. Well, I am a monster too."

"A monster?"

Allen Brim smiles. "Of a sort. I lived through something that should have killed me. I had stopped breathing, was presumed dead." He holds his hand to his heart and coughs.

"But . . . but when you were well enough, why did you not come to Thorne House and take me back?"

"It was not that simple. I sneaked away. Coming to see you was not something I felt I should do, a dead man should do. I have lived as an outcast, my story unacceptable to others. I saw that you were well looked after, well loved, in fact."

"But why have you come now?"

"Because you need me. I have followed you over the years, usually from a distance but sometimes closer, and I know that you are now truly in dire trouble. There is a hellhound on your trail."

"The devil," says Edgar.

"We shall defeat it."

"I don't believe this is you. It cannot be. I am making you up." Edgar notices more pedestrians staring at him. "How could you have—"

"Believe it or not, I am with you."

Edgar eyes him carefully. His father keeps standing there, not fading, not even a little. "Tell me how you survived, what happened? It seems impossible. Tell me everything!"

"There is no time for that now. I will explain later. You desperately need to do something now to escape your fate, to elude the dark angel. It is life or death. You have no allies. I will be that eternal friend, true to the end, that comrade in arms."

"But I have—"

"Tiger Tilley? Lucy Lear? Andrew Lawrence? Annabel Thorne? William Shakespeare? No, Edgar. I have observed them in action when you were not with them, and I can tell you they are not your friends. You know that yourself, deep down. It is you and I again, Edgar, against the world."

"But—"

"Do not be afraid."

Edgar's knees almost buckle when he hears those words. He has been hearing them in his imagination ever since he saw them written in his father's journal. They have given purpose and meaning to his life. To hear them now, direct from the source, fills him with hope.

"Your friends are plotting against you and it is because the evil one has entered their minds. They are in league with the devil. Satan lived in the Bible, in *The Divine Comedy*, in *Paradise Lost*, in so many other stories, and he is in the world today too, as real as the other monsters but so much more powerful. He is slippery. He can live inside us, if he so chooses."

"How do we fight that? What do we do?"

"Interrogating this Shakespeare chap is indeed a good idea, as I believe you have considered. As you know, he has not only been in that building on Thomas Street, but he has twice mentioned that the devil actually visited him."

Edgar wonders how his father can know all that, but he does not question it. He is in too much danger to do anything except move forward and cling to the dearest person he has ever known.

"As has been suggested too, a return visit to the devil-worship room would make sense. There must be more to learn there. Let us act."

"Wait a moment!" says Edgar. He is looking over his father's shoulder toward the Lear home, which is near the end of the street, and has spotted someone standing outside it, looking at it, sizing it up. Edgar begins to run.

He slows a little as he nears, seeing that the man has not noticed his approach. *I can take him by surprise!* thinks Edgar. He can hear noises from inside the house, raised voices, Lucy and Tiger arguing. He hears his name shouted.

"See," whispers his father into his ear, sounding a little out of breath. "They are not your friends."

The intruder seems to have had enough of surveying the house and starts to approach the front door. He is dressed in a frayed tweed suit and cloth cap. *An ordinary man,* thinks Edgar, *approaching the front door, appearing benign, about to call one of us out!* Edgar seizes the man from behind, placing a hand on his mouth and whirling him around and pulling him back out into the street.

The intruder's features are in the glare of the hot late-afternoon sun glinting off the street lamp and he appears dark-faced and horrible, slashes of black mark his cheeks, his eyes peer out from deep, gray sockets.

He and Edgar stare at each other. Edgar slides his hand from the man's mouth but keeps him in his grasp.

145

"Oh!" exclaims the stranger. "Don't hurt me!"

As the man pulls his head back, his face comes clearly into view. Edgar can now see that he is a slight, middle-aged fellow, and the darkness that was on his face and the slashes across it were simply shadows cast by his standing between Edgar and the sun.

Edgar loosens his grip a little. "Why are you snooping about?"

"Snooping?" says the man. "I merely came to pay a call on the Lear home in order to tell the folks here something." He is trembling.

Edgar releases him but keeps him within arm's length.

"Perhaps you should not be quite so aggressive, Edgar," says his father. "You might get more from him that way."

"Good idea," says Edgar.

The man regards him with a questioning look.

"I am sorry," adds Edgar. "I have been living in this house and thought you meant us harm. Do you . . . mean us harm?"

"My Lord, no," says the man. He straightens his collar. "Well, I suppose your actions are understandable, after what you have been through."

Edgar wonders if he should seize him again. "What do you mean? What do you know of my situation?"

"Nothing, really, young sir, except that an acquaintance of yours or perhaps your brother was killed here not long ago."

"An acquaintance."

"I live just down this street and I happened to be about early that morning in the wee hours. My wife told me she had heard you were inquiring if anyone had seen anything suspicious at your door that morning. Neither she nor I were at home when you were asking."

Edgar steps close to him again, lowering his voice. "Did you see something?"

"Yes, I did, my friend, though it seems of no consequence. I would certainly not employ the word *suspicious* in connection to it. I told the wife that, but she made me come to speak with you anyway. I saw an old woman at your door. That is all."

Edgar staggers.

The man steadies him. "Are you all right?"

I am the devil. I will do evil to you.

"Yes, I . . . I am fine . . . tell me more."

"She was dressed plainly, nothing remarkable about her, certainly of no threat to the young man of a good physique who came to the entrance in answer to the knock."

"Jonathan."

"Is that the deceased?"

"Yes."

The man removes his hat. "That was all I observed, just an old woman at the door and your acquaintance opening it to her. Oh, that is not quite correct. He opened it to a child first. She had a child with her too."

"A child?"

"Yes, which makes it even less likely that it was they who harmed your friend. An old woman and a child? They killed that powerful young man?" He laughs. "No, something else must have bedeviled the deceased that morning. I keep unusual hours and I was on my way into the city, so I did not linger to watch them.

There was no reason to. I moved on. I did not see anything more. There was no noise, no gun shot, no one crying out, as I walked away. It was as quiet as heaven."

"Can you describe the little one? Was it a boy or a girl?"

"Oh, it was a boy all right, but a strange looking one, wearing unusual clothes, bright in color, a pillbox hat, sky-blue coat and scarlet trousers that appeared to billow like a Zouave military getup. Perhaps he was dressed up for a play. Perhaps she was his grandmother."

"A Zouave? You mean like a French soldier?"

"Yes, sir," the man responds. "I must be on my way. I hope I have been of some help, though I cannot imagine how." He excuses himself and is quickly off down the street, glancing back a few times.

"The hag, my boy," whispers Allen Brim.

"But this man saw her! Alive on the streets? That is not how she comes. It must be wrong. There was a child with her too, dressed as an old-fashioned French soldier. What sense does that make?" His head turns left and right, his gaze darting up and down the street. "This is what is after us, in flesh and blood?"

"Do you think Satan will approach you wearing a red suit and sprouting horns from his head? That may be the way he is played in a farce at The Gaiety, but not in the Holy Book or in most of the great poems and novels."

"But her and a child? *They* are connected to that building on Thomas Street?"

"It is all a puzzle at the moment, indeed, but let us store this information in our minds and move forward."

"If this thing can take the form of an old woman and a child and kill without a mark or a sound, and it can enter our very brains, then we are doomed!" Edgar glances up and down the street again.

"Do not be afraid."

Edgar swallows and straightens himself. "Yes," he says, "keep telling me that." His mind is swirling though, images flashing through it. He sees Jon's dead face, the vampire creature, Professor Lear's last gasp, Godwin with the harpoon in his chest and the large dark feather in the Thomas Street building. Now, this.

"I shall, Edgar. That, after all, is the sort of thing for which a father exists." Allen Brim smiles. "Now, where to start, my boy? A return to the Thomas Street building or Drury Lane? I suggest we visit Mr. Shakespeare first—the Crypto-Anthropology Society of the Queen's Empire! Even if that strange little fellow can tell us nothing, bear in mind that he knows as much about these monsters as anyone and encourages and funds pursuit, and yet miraculously seems to be immune from attack. Nothing has ever pursued him. That is a stone-cold fact. His lair may be the safest place in London for you."

"Let us go in and speak to Lucy and Tiger first, tell them what I know, what that man meant to say to them, or at least where I am going."

"No, I don't think that is wise. We must go alone."

Allen Brim takes Edgar by the arm and leads him south toward Drury Lane at a brisk pace.

They walk silently. Edgar wants him to explain how he survived his death, but feeling warm in the clutches of his dear father and not wanting to disturb that feeling, he says nothing and they continue to walk on in silence. There will be time for such questions soon.

Pedestrians pass by on all sides of them as if they were floating along in a dream, he and his father not even moving their feet. He watches everyone carefully—for faces resembling the hag's, quick movements from hands in his direction, signs of dark wings sprouting from backs, but held close by his father, he reaches his destination safely.

14

A Different Sort of Visit

"This," says Edgar to William Shakespeare when the strange little man answers the door, "is my father, Allen Brim."

"Where?"

"This gentleman beside me."

"I see," says Shakespeare. He stands there in another display of colorful clothing, looking up to Edgar's right.

"Over here," says Edgar.

Shakespeare looks to Edgar's left and regards Allen Brim with a blank gaze. For an instant, Edgar wonders if the little lunatic cannot see his father, if he is so mad that nonexistent people like his three invisible friends are real to him and certain real people fictional.

"My my my my my my!" the little man suddenly exclaims. "Mr. Brim, it is! MR. . . . SIR . . . LORD . . . KING . . . BARON . . . Brim . . . you are most welcome here! You, sir, the sire of our own Edgar Broom, in MY humble abode, my residence, my hut, my shack, my lean-to, my living quarters of Spartan surroundings! ME, Sir William Shakespeare himself! Hosting YOU! You who knew of the monsters! Just wait until Messrs. Sprinkle, Winker and Tightman set their gaze upon you, until they train their deep-thinking cranial sponges upon the wisdom you are surely to disperse for their benefit! LORD Brim, you are most welcome!"

"Allen will do fine," says Edgar. "We have some questions for you."

"For ME? You have questions for ME? Let us descend to the august meeting room of the Crypto-Anthropology Society of the Queen's Empire and direct said questions in my direction, whereupon I shall field them and consider them and send them back to you in the form of answers, audial articulations, that I am sure will satisfy. OH! Let us descend!"

Shakespeare's eyes are nearly popping out of his head; his lunacy appears to be seizing him more thoroughly than it ever has.

"You seem especially nervous," says Edgar.

"HA!" cries the little man, and he quivers as he scurries down the stairs in front of them.

The place settings for his three imaginary colleagues rest on the big table, as always, and Shakespeare gestures for his visitors to sit in other chairs, leaving those three spots open.

"Mr. Winker, wake up!" he shrieks. "Can you not see we have visitors of the highest standing, you poisonous bunch-backed toad!" The little man turns to his guests. "Where, may I ask, is Master Lear and Mademoiselle Lear and the Tigress, Master Tilley?"

Edgar and Allen sit without answering, their faces grim.

"What? What is wrong?" The little man is so taken aback by their expressions that he does not sit. He is at eye level with Edgar.

"Two of my friends are at home. Jonathan is dead."

"DEAD!" shrieks Shakespeare. "Not by the hand of a monster, my dear! Assure me that it was NOT by the hand of a monster! A particular one!"

Edgar does not want to reveal everything he knows to the little man, not yet. He is not in a trusting mood, especially concerning someone whose activities are now suspicious to him. "We do not know," says Edgar, "though we think it likely. Someone, some thing, came to the Lears' door and merely interacted with him . . . and he is no longer with us."

Shakespeare bursts into tears. "Oh, it is my fault! I led you all into this!"

"And you may help lead us out of it," says Edgar.

The little fellow stops sobbing as if he were a tap that someone has turned off.

"Whatever do you mean?"

"Not long ago," says Edgar, leaning toward Shakespeare and regarding him closely, "I asked you if you had visited the East End recently and you denied it. I have reason to believe you are lying."

"That is perhaps harsh," says Allen Brim quietly.

"It is time to be."

Shakespeare's head swivels back and forth, regarding Edgar, then his father, then Edgar again.

"Your father concurs?"

"Answer the question. The building you visited there is of interest to us."

Shakespeare pauses for a few seconds, opens his mouth to speak, closes it, opens it again, closes it and then bursts into tears once more.

"How, Edgar Broom, could you accuse me of such a thing? Mendacity!" He reaches into the pocket of his tight little orange suit coat (meant to complement his scarlet-and-green checked waistcoat) and pulls out a handkerchief. He holds it up to his substantial nose and blows hard and long. The sound is like a trumpet, a high-pitched note of tenor or perhaps even soprano tone.

"What were you doing there?" demands Edgar.

The little man blows his horn again. "Oh! I have denied it and yet you persist with a corollary. Do you make it a habit of poking fun at lunatics?"

"Do madmen know they are mad?" asks Allen Brim quietly again, into his son's ear.

"A very good question, Father."

"What . . . question is that?" asks Shakespeare.

"Are you indeed mad, sir? Or is this a game you play?"

A strange look comes over the little man's face. "I . . . I . . ."

"We are in a desperate situation and we must have allies. It is time for you to stand up and be counted."

The little man straightens up. "ONE!" he cries.

"That isn't good enough, Mr. Shakespeare, not anymore," says Edgar. "Tell us what you were doing in the East End or we will take you home with us tonight, strap you to the mouth of our cannon and blow the big bullet through you."

"Dear, dear," says Shakespeare. "Might you do that?"

"Speak!" says Allen.

"Well . . ." he begins, "you see . . . I . . . is it hot in here?"

"Come with us," says Edgar.

"NO! . . . No, I shall tell you." He pauses.

"Yes?"

"In a moment." He pauses again. Edgar reaches out for him and he pulls back. "No! I shall be frank with you, as frank as a madman can be." His voice drops lower and it quavers as he speaks. "I have not been visiting the East End. I barely leave this august room, as you know. I have struggled with my sanity for some time, as you well know. What you may not know is that I used to have lucid moments, but they are fewer and fewer these days. I will admit to you that there was a time when I exaggerated my illness, in order to keep the monsters from me. What enemy would seriously consider a lunatic like me a threat? I broadcast my insanity, wore strange clothes, still do, but now, my friends, I have no idea how mad I am. It has all caught up with me. Am I sane now, for example, at this instant? I feel different. I do not know!" He slumps into a chair and looks distraught, then breaks down and cries again, this time intensely, his shoulders heaving. "My God, young Jonathan dead!"

"No monster ever came here?" asks Edgar.

Shakespeare sits bolt upright. "Certainly not."

"But you said, while you were airing your latest threat about another creature pursuing us, not only that it was the devil—"

"It is," whimpers the little man.

"—but that the devil had been to visit you. You said that twice."

Shakespeare stares into the distance. "No I didn't, I didn't I didn't I didn't I didn't I didn't I didn't I didn't!"

"What did you mean when you said the devil had been here?"

The little one puts his hands over his ears. "I . . . DID . . . NOT . . . SAY . . . THAT!"

"Perhaps you merely meant that an evil feeling has come over you in these rooms, the presence of an evil force, twice?"

Shakespeare removes his hands from his ears. "Yes, that is it! I merely meant that!"

"But he denied ever having said it at all," whispers Allen. "He is lying again."

"You are lying, William Shakespeare, or whatever your name is."

"Don Quixote."

"Pardon me."

"My name is Don Quixote, not William Shakespeare! Where did you get such a nonsensical idea, you bolting-hutch of beastliness! Thou art a boil, a plague sore!" He glares at Edgar with his eyes on fire, as mad as King Lear.

Edgar will have none of it. "The devil came to see you . . . didn't he?"

15

What Shakespeare Knew

William Shakespeare stands transfixed in front of Edgar, then stares back and forth between him and his father, and then falls on his knees in front of his accuser, clutching at his shoes, his face to the floor.

"Long ago, I, Don Quixote, was visited by a devil-man! Yes!"

Edgar swallows. "Not Don Quixote, you. What form did it take? Was it Satan in the flesh?"

"I don't know." His voice is barely audible. "But I can tell you that I was not insane then, that much I know."

"Tell me about this person, if that is indeed what he was. Or was it a she?"

Shakespeare lifts his face from the floor and, still on his knees, looks up at Edgar. His eyes glaze over. "It was a man. He first came many years ago, about the time I met Professor Lear, but before he had actually killed the Grendel creature, when, as I said, my mind was better and I was merely investigating the possibility of the existence of human aberrations and dark forces. I was still writing literary criticism, intrigued by the monsters inside some stories, who seemed so terribly real! I had inherited a good deal of money, as you know, and had given Lear funds to do his researches. This devil person had seen one of the pamphlets I distributed on the streets asking anyone who had experienced the hag phenomenon to come to my residence to converse about it, for a fee."

"What did he look like?"

Shakespeare's voice is shaky. "A large man with a shaved head, dressed in black, wearing a crucifix and in possession of the most penetrating black eyes I have ever seen on a human being. I have been too frightened of him to ever tell anyone!"

"What did he do and say that day?"

"He asked me why I was distributing the pamphlets, what I knew about the hag phenomenon, what I thought the human mind could be exploring as it conjured such a creature, and if I thought that creature might be real."

A shiver goes down Edgar's spine. He has the sense that his father has left the room but he does not take his eyes off the little man.

"What else?"

"That was all, at first. I answered as best I could. He came back."

"How much later?"

"About a year later. He had a way about him." Shakespeare quivers.

"What do you mean?"

"He got things out of me. Just like you!"

"What things?"

"About Professor Lear."

"What do you mean?"

"Lear was in London at that time, recovering from the grievous wound Grendel inflicted upon him, and had come to see me about his situation, and I was petrified by it all. It unhinged me and began my steep decline. Am I making sense?" A tear rolls down his cheek.

"Yes, go on."

"I seem to have lucid memories of these things." He pauses. "The devil-man, he then got it ALL out of me! He had been telling me about his own studies, his researches, his fascination with religion, with the occult, with the extraordinary power of the human brain. He told me, that second day, that he suspected he had unlocked some of the secrets of the mind, of existence, of God and of evil. It frightened me so, and I responded with a veritable flood of details . . . he asked me with his beckoning eyes and I told him. The story of Professor Lear and Grendel riveted him. I even added that I wondered if there were other monsters about, human aberrations, some of them captured in the great works of literary art. The idea excited him so much that I thought he might fly about the room!"

"Was that the last you saw of him?"

"No, he returned another time."

"Once more?"

"I . . . I must admit . . . I must tell you it . . . has been . . . many times . . . and on each occasion everything feels darker."

"What do you mean?"

"He looked different as the months and years passed. His face grew grayer, the shaved dome on his head more like leather, and his eyes somehow more intense. He would come perhaps once every three months or so, talking more and more of his accomplishments, his knowledge of human life, of his mastery of black magic, of evil, of secret societies, of the mind. He pressed me more about the monsters. As Lear began to speak to me about a presence near the College on the Moors, which he feared was a new monster in pursuit of him, I told my visitor all about it. It excited him to no end too! He asked me if I thought that the greatest monster in existence might be the devil, alive and living in London." Shakespeare pauses and looks pleadingly at Edgar. "So, that means it isn't HIM, is it?" He does not wait for an answer. "After you came here with Miss Tilley the first time, I told him about you as well, your remarkable dreams, your unprecedented hag phenomenon. He often asked about Lucy Lear and Jonathan too. He followed you, all of you, and observed your efforts as you destroyed the revenant-vampire creature, and possibly your elimination of Dr. Godwin, the Frankenstein monster, in the Arctic." The little man puts his hands on either side of his head and looks at the floor.

"This devil-man adored fear. He kept speaking about it. He said it was like an electricity, a power beyond anything else that one might harness. He said it was like the waters of an unimaginably large Niagara Falls. He would talk for hours and I would just sit here as if mesmerized! He gave me his card, told me to report to him, but I never did . . . because . . . because he always came here."

Edgar's heart is pounding. He gets to his feet.

"When was this man last here?"

The little lunatic does not respond. Edgar can see him swallow.

"When!"

"A few days ago." Shakespeare stares up. "Edgar, his eyes were on fire!"

"I doubt . . ."

"I, Don Quixote, shall now get upon my noble steed, Rocinante, and ride off into the sunset, going in all directions at once!" Shakespeare leaps up and rushes around the room in circles, seizing chairs and side-tables, putting his hands and even his feet on the walls, as if he were contemplating climbing them. "Pay no attention to the things I say, Edgar Broom, no attention at all! Such concerns will kill you! They shall kill us all! Fly away from the devil. That is what you must do! Flight! It is a simple matter!"

"My name is Brim."

"Yes, indeed, Sir Edgar Brim, my dear, dear, dear, dear, dear, dear . . . acquaintance. That is all you are, you know, we have no real connection; do not say we do if asked! In fact, you may not even be real!"

Edgar sighs and sinks into a chair.

"OH!" shrieks the little man, leaping to his feet. "You elvish-mark'd abortive, rooting hog! You have sat upon Mr. Winker! I shall extricate him from beneath your girth and relocate his posterior into another chair!" He seizes Edgar and lifts him with remarkable strength and then grunts as he pulls on an invisible form that had apparently been beneath him, finally getting it out and depositing it into another chair.

"Master Broom, why would you—"

"You know very well that my name is Brim, sir! You must stop talking nonsense! We are in desperate need of sanity. There is no one here but us!"

"Yes . . . yes, Brim." He sits on the floor and becomes very, very still, holding his breath. His face begins to turn purple.

"You have to breathe."

Shakespeare lets out his breath. "Thank you, Broom." He clams up, staring down at the floor. "What will we do?" he whispers. "What if this man is truly a messenger of Satan?"

Edgar hears a noise and sees his father at the door that gives passage into the inner portion of the apartment where Shakespeare lives. Allen Brim must have been poking around in there. Now, he is beckoning Edgar to him with a finger, an excited expression on his face.

"What, Father?"

Allen keeps motioning.

"I have more to inquire of Mr. Shakespeare," says Edgar.

His father, however, does not stop.

Edgar gets up and heads for the inner door. "What is this about?" he says. Allen Brim has already vanished back into the apartment.

"Mr. Tightman is in there," says Shakespeare abruptly.

"No he isn't."

Edgar pushes the door fully open and goes through it into the narrow hallway, Shakespeare quickly in pursuit. Edgar stops for a moment and listens for the sound of someone moving around farther in the apartment, but he hears no one. Shakespeare almost runs into him from behind.

"What are you doing?" asks the little man, his voice shrill.

Allen goes right by the water closet and heads down the hallway and past a couple of rooms. There is a desk in one, with old-fashioned feather-pens and inkpots; another is set up as a small sitting room with an ottoman that looks like it was once the property of an Arabian sheik; and then, at the end of the hall, he encounters a bedroom. There is not much in it other than an elaborate bed with carved bedposts that nearly reach the ceiling and a silky white mosquito net covering it. There are closets taking up almost every inch of the walls, and one of the closet doors is open, and Edgar can see a spectacular array of clothing inside. He recalls with a slight smile the time the little man had provided him and his friends with a remarkable supply of clothes, after they had survived the terrible fire in Dr. Godwin's laboratory at the top of the Midland Grand Hotel. Allen goes into the room and motions for Edgar to follow.

"You cannot enter my inner sanctum, Edgar Broom! You cannot!"

An idea has seized Edgar and he moves into the room and over to the closet as fast as he can. He begins to look through the clothes hanging there.

"What are you doing, Brim?" shouts Shakespeare. "This is outrageous!"

Edgar soon finds something that almost stops his heart: there is a sky-blue coat and billowing scarlet trousers hanging in the closet and up above them on a shelf a pillbox hat . . . like a Zouave soldier would wear.

"What are you doing?" repeats Shakespeare, sounding perfectly sane.

"I have more questions for you." Edgar's face is red as he turns to the tiny man.

Shakespeare pauses for a moment and then his eyes light up with a lunatic's gleam. "Lovely! We shall adjourn to the meeting room and entertain them!"

Allen Brim follows silently behind them.

When they are back at the table, Edgar makes Shakespeare sit and stands over him, his hands on the back of the chair next to him, the one usually reserved for Mr. Sprinkle. The little man is squirming in his seat.

"Broom . . . Brim, you are, uh, crowding Mr. Sprinkle. Please—"

"Hold your tongue, you little fool!"

Shakespeare starts, but recovers himself quickly, squeezes his thumb and forefinger together and runs them across his lips as if sealing them.

"We are at the end of games, Mr. Shakespeare, or whatever your name is. You need to be straight with me!" Edgar lets go of Sprinkle's chair and passes directly behind the little man. "You, sir, were seen at the Lear home, in the company of a particular person, wearing those ridiculous clothes you now have in your closet, that Zouave costume, in the early morning hours when Jonathan was murdered. In fact, it was you, sir, and the person who was with you, who were somehow the agents of his death!"

There is a long stretch of silence. Edgar cannot see the little man's face, but when he comes around the chair and looks at him, the expression upon it has changed. He looks deadly serious. Edgar keeps quiet and sits in Sprinkle's spot, directly upon him, and Shakespeare says nothing for a long while.

"I was not responsible for the death of Master Jonathan Lear," he finally says. He speaks in such a calm, collected voice that it startles Edgar. "I know little of that, nor am I aware of this particular person you mention. Jonathan was an admirable young man! The clothes you refer to are not 'Zouave' as you say. If you examine them closely you will see that they are merely rather loose pantaloons, the kind of habiliment, along with riding jodhpurs and ancient breeches and outrageously bright jackets and coats and blouses, that I have employed publicly over these last years as a means to accentuate the appearance of my lunacy. When you accuse me of murder, you are jumping to conclusions based on something someone else has told you. You have been exaggerating everything of late, Master Brim. You are in danger of losing your mind too! In fact, that may have already happened." He glances toward the inner door where Allen Brim had stood. "I have had deep concerns about you over these past few weeks. You must remain calm in our hellish situation, though I must say that serenity will do nothing to save you from your fate."

"Which is?"

"Certain death; that will also be the fate of your friends."

Edgar swallows. "How can I trust you when—"

"Who told you about me and my supposed companion appearing at the Lears' home, Edgar? Have you ever seen this so-called neighbor before in your life? Do you really believe that this informant lives on the Lears' street? Why is he suddenly materializing with this story?"

Edgar wonders if he told Shakespeare that the witness lived on the Lears' street.

"The devil," continues the little man, "who may be the power behind the person who came to see me, or even the actual individual himself, is in pursuit of you. He or it possesses an evil beyond our comprehension; he may have the ability to infiltrate your very soul, sir. Now, do you think this demon would have any trouble assuming the role of an informer, neighbor or not? Do you think he would not consider it best to have you accuse me, add to your paranoia, perhaps harm me, when I am your only ally left? He has likely been in the back rooms of my apartment, seen my clothing. Why would I intend any harm to Jonathan Lear! Who did he say was with me? Some demon from your dreams? The hag? That would be perfect! Be careful what you are thinking, for your mind may now be working for your enemy."

"Do you really believe we have brought the devil himself down upon us?"

"I fear we have. I have been trying to warn you!"

Edgar is shaking. "What do we do now?"

"We? Very different things. I remain mad. My visitor, or his leader, does not fear ME or intend ME harm. I am not in pursuit of monsters in any real or threatening way. I have made sure that is the perception. You, however, must flee. To where, I do not know, for if this demon is whom we fear he is, he will track you to the end of the earth. In fact, it seems he has already begun to accompany you inside your brain! You believed that I, William Shakespeare, came with a figment of your imagination and murdered Jonathan Lear! Remember, it is written that he is capable of all such powers and more in the Bible itself!" The little man is beginning to sound shrill again.

"Surely, you don't believe—"

"Why would such great men, why would God, write of such a force, over and over and over, if it does not exist?"

"I must get away," says Edgar to himself and his heart pounds.

"Do not be afraid," says his father from somewhere behind him, but for the first time, Edgar thinks those words nonsense.

"Yes, flee, and do not return here!"

Edgar starts for the door but turns back. "I don't know where to . . ."

"It is the devil!" shouts Shakespeare. "It is Satan himself! RUN! FLY AWAY! HIDE SOMEWHERE EVEN GOD CANNOT FIND YOU! FEAR YOUR ENEMY IN A MANNER YOU HAVE NEVER FEARED ANYTHING BEFORE! AND MAY GOD BE WITH YOU!"

Allen Brim turns back to William Shakespeare. "If we discover that you had anything to do with the death of Jonathan Lear, it is YOU who had better run, for we will come back for you!"

Deep in his terror, Edgar has the very same thought.

16

First Disappearance

"I need to see Tiger and Lucy," says Edgar.

"That is not advisable."

Allen Brim is trying to keep up to Edgar as he rushes along Drury Lane bumping into gentlemen and brushing past ladies' billowing dresses and sending goods flying from mongers' hands, drawing shouts and curses. He does not so much as even look back.

"This is the devil, Father. I cannot do this alone. I have to try to trust them. I have to trust someone."

"You have me."

Edgar stops and regards his father. He reaches out and touches Allen Brim, caressing his face. "Yes, I do," he says. A man in a tall black top hat and his purple-bonneted wife stare at them. A string of schoolchildren hand-in-hand with their teachers, notice too, and giggle.

"We must pursue Satan and this devil-man before he or they pursue us," says Allen.

"But we really know nothing about him. Even his appearance!"

"You must face him, no matter what."

"So, all the better to be with my friends and with the rifle and the cannon too. We have more chance of survival in greater numbers."

"Those are merely earthly weapons and your foe is supernatural. This is not just a mere revenant or a creature made by the hand of man. And how can you survive if your allies are your enemies?"

"I do not know that for certain."

They argue all the way to Kentish Town, the elder Brim beginning to fall behind as they near. When they finally reach the house, Allen stays out on the street. Edgar approaches the door, and then turns back to his father.

"I won't remain with them for long if I suspect anything," he shouts. "You know where to find me."

The door opens. Tiger is standing there, rifle in hand.

"Who are you shouting at?"

Edgar watches his father move backward down the street and out of sight. He hears Dr. Berenice's voice saying: *Do you have close friends whose loyalty you have recently begun to doubt? You must stay away from these friends until you are sure about them.*

"No one."

Lucy appears at Tiger's shoulder and her face glows when she sees him.

"Edgar! We were worried sick. Where did you go?"

It is time for supper, almost past it. The sun will soon set. Edgar has been gone since just after the noon hour.

"I . . . I went to the hospital to speak with Lawrence, to tell him we are ready to team with him and make use of his assets," Edgar lies, "and he wasn't there."

"That wouldn't have taken five or six hours," says Tiger, who is almost pointing the gun at him now.

"I . . . I went to see Shakespeare too."

"I thought we were going to do that together," says Lucy. She looks at him with a longing expression.

"It turned out not to matter," says Edgar quickly. "Shakespeare does not know anything. The devil-man visits were imaginary. He is a lunatic."

Lucy looks down, as if she knows he is lying.

"Shakespeare is mad? Thanks for the news," says Tiger, and she sounds just like Jonathan when she says it.

Edgar decides not to tell them about the woman and child at the door, not yet.

"May I come in?"

"Why did you do all of this on your own?" asks Tiger. "We know something awfully powerful is pursuing us. Why risk being out on the streets alone?"

"I don't know, I just went, perhaps it wasn't rational, perhaps I thought that if our enemy got to me then that would be just one of us, better one than all three."

"How noble of you," says Tiger.

"Thanks, Jon."

Tiger glares at him.

"May I come in?" he repeats.

"Of course," says Lucy, who takes him by the hand and pulls him indoors.

They eat in near silence, only asking each other to pass the salt or pepper or the boiled pork and bread and butter that Lucy cooked for them. They sit on the settee afterward, Tiger at one end and Lucy beside Edgar but her hand cold where it touches his thigh.

"We should go to that room on Thomas Street again," says Tiger, getting to her feet and taking up the rifle, which she has kept cradled on her knee.

"I thought you were against that, Tiger. Besides, we've already been there," says Edgar. "What else could we learn from—"

"You claim Shakespeare knows nothing. What other option do we have? I am not staying here like a sitting duck waiting for this thing to descend upon us. We have to DO something; seek this devil! Maybe take it by surprise!"

Tiger looks to Lucy and Edgar thinks she gives her a slight nod.

"I cannot face it, not after dark," says Lucy. "Perhaps tomorrow I will be able. I am going to bed." She squeezes Edgar's leg, gets up and makes her way to her room.

"It is just you and me," says Tiger to Edgar, "like the old days. Let's go to Thomas Street this minute." Her face is lit up as if she were possessed.

"Uh . . . no, not now."

"Why?"

Edgar is wondering what it would be like to be alone with an armed Tiger Tilley if she wanted to harm you, if she were under the influence of Satan: alone in that dark room in Thomas Street.

"I . . . I think we should have Lucy with us."

"Lucy? We would be better off without her!" Tiger's voice is rising.

"I . . . I don't want to leave her alone."

"But—"

"I am going to bed too. We will be more rested in the morning and will be able to function better in that dim room with some daylight getting through its windows." He turns quickly and makes his way down the hall to his bedroom before she can respond. "Go alone, if you must," he says over his shoulder.

She doesn't, which worries Edgar even more.

His room is the middle one in the hallway, between the two girls. Edgar lies awake trying to sleep, worrying that enemies surround him, terrifed that Satan will attack at any second, wondering about the devil-man who visited Shakespeare, and frightened that the hag will come for him again, tonight. *The devil can take on her form,* he thinks, *walk around the streets of London!* He tosses and turns, with all his clothes on under the sheets, forcing himself to stay awake. Then he hears Tiger's door open: there is just a slight creak. It moves slowly, tentatively, as if whoever is pushing it does not want to be heard. Edgar leaps to his feet and rushes to his own door. In an instant, he is in the hallway and sees a dark form standing outside Lucy's room. It turns.

"What are you doing?" asks Edgar.

"Oh," whispers Tiger, "just checking on Lu. I won't be a minute."

But she is. Edgar goes back into his room, lies on his bed and listens. Tiger seems to stay in Lucy's room for a long time, making no noise. Finally, Edgar hears her sneaking back past his room and then creaking her door open again. Then there is silence. Edgar shakes his head. He is not sure if he has stayed awake for the last little while: he has no idea whether Tiger was in Lucy's room for ten seconds or ten minutes. Then he falls into a deep sleep. So many dreams come to him that he cannot keep track of them— shaven-headed, black-eyed devils fly about, and so do vampires, Frankenstein creatures, Mr. Hyde and other monsters—but none are in coherent stories. They merely rush through his mind in a kind of Walpurgis Night, vague and unrealized, like beasts seeking forms, born of his fears. The hag does not come. He wakes to dead silence.

He gets up, takes off his socks and pads out into the little kitchen at the back of the house. Tiger, never much for the culinary arts, is standing over a couple of burnt pieces of toast she is trying to butter. She looks up at him and smiles.

"Edgar. Are you ready for action now?" Both the rifle and the cannon are in the kitchen with her, within her arm's reach.

"Where is Lucy?"

"Not with the land of the living yet. Haven't heard a sound from her."

"That is strange." Lucy is always the first one to rise in the morning and usually makes breakfast for the others.

"Oh, I don't know. She is awfully frightened right now and perhaps cannot face this day."

"I will check on her."

"No," says Tiger.

Edgar pays no attention. He pivots and returns down the hall.

"Edgar, let her be!" cries Tiger, rushing after him.

Edgar stops before opening the door and turns so he can see Tiger clearly. She is standing there, unarmed, with a pleading look on her face. Edgar opens Lucy's door and goes in.

It is neat and tidy, extraordinarily so, filled with beautiful colors and things—two lovely little lamps on either side of her bed, a photograph of her grandfather on her white dresser, and a warm rug where her feet first touch the floor in the mornings. The lights are off and the drapes are drawn shut. Everything is as it should be, except . . . her bed is empty.

Lucy Lear is nowhere to be found.

Edgar stands there with his mouth open.

"She may have just gone out," says Tiger.

"And told no one?"

"Perhaps she was up very early."

"You said you hadn't heard a sound from her room."

"Well, I may have slept through her departure."

There is no sign of Lucy for hours.

"Something is wrong," says Edgar, breaking another long silence as he and Tiger sit on the settee again. She is cleaning the rifle, seemingly completely unconcerned about their friend's absence.

"You are jumping to conclusions. Don't worry about Lucy, for she can take care of herself. We have better things to do. You promised you would come with me to Thomas Street."

"I didn't promise." *Why would she say that?*

"When I have this gun cleaned, we are going, whether Lu is back or not. If someone has abducted her—"

"Or murdered her."

"Whatever has happened, then all the more reason to take a weapon to that room and search it from top to bottom."

Edgar wonders again why she has become so anxious to go there. He thinks for a moment. "All right," he finally says, "just give me a moment."

He gets up and heads to his room.

"Who knows why Lucy is gone," calls out Tiger, "maybe she has cracked and is helping whomever is opposing us, maybe her disappearance is all about survival."

Edgar wonders if Tiger really said that. He gets to his room, his jaw set and his hands sweaty on the doorknob. Once inside, he opens the window and wedges himself through the tiny opening into the two-foot-wide walkway between the Lears' house and the neighbor's. Then he scurries along it and out onto Progress Street and runs as fast as he can, far away from Tiger Tilley. A half hour later, he is in an alleyway in central London, bending over and out of breath. "I am running from my dearest friend!" he exclaims. "What is wrong with me?"

"Nothing," says a gasping voice near him, "and she isn't your dearest friend, not anymore."

He looks up to see Allen Brim standing near him, bending over too, with one hand on a knee, the other over his heart.

"Father!"

"You were moving very quickly, my son. What is going on back at the Lear house? You appeared to be running from it."

"Lucy has disappeared."

Allen straightens up, hands on his hips now.

"Things are coming to a boil, Edgar. You need to—"

"I am almost certain he is inside my head."

"Who?"

"The devil. Satan!"

"You look perfectly—"

"He may be turning me against Tiger. I cannot believe what I am thinking about her, imagining she is saying. He may have taken Lucy! He may have killed her!"

"Calm, Edgar, calm. You must trust yourself and your thoughts. Now, you spoke of two things you might do in order to oppose your enemy yesterday. The first was speaking to William Shakespeare and that got you nowhere; the second was going back to that room on Thomas Street, was it not?"

"I cannot. I am unarmed. Tiger may be heading there too, bearing the rifle!"

"Not to worry. You shall have me. You must explore that place more thoroughly, Edgar, it may be your only hope. We shall deal with Tiger if we encounter her."

Edgar believes that no one is a match for Tiger Tilley, and he is terrified about what he might find in that upper room on Thomas Street, so he makes his way to the East End with his father with great reluctance.

They enter through the big door with the black-horned handle and find no one to intercept them when they step inside. Edgar wonders if Tiger could have gotten here already and disposed of the big thug. They walk up the stairs to the fifth floor as quietly as possible, concerned by the creaks they are making on the steps, eyes upward for an attack coming down at them.

They reach the top floor in safety and are surprised to find the big door there unlocked. It is almost as if someone is inviting them back. Inside, everything is as it appeared before, waiting there in the dim light cast by the rows of candles and the few high windows, stained in red and black. They walk slowly forward past the frescoes of pyramids and staring eyes on the walls, up the center aisle between the carved wooden chairs and the jars filled with red liquid, all still arranged there as if waiting for an audience. They approach the stage with its black throne.

"It doesn't seem as if Tiger has been here," says Allen.

"But she said she was coming."

"Perhaps she was lying or perhaps she was only coming if she could draw you here. Did she seem to want to be alone with you in this place?"

"Yes."

"Let us examine everything in the room. There must be something in here that will give us a clue. Look at the colors, the carved snakes and horns, the eyes. It is a room for devil worship, there is no question; and remember, William Shakespeare came here. Tiger wanted to bring you to this place, the devil speaking inside her head. This is your enemy's lair!"

They search the whole room, examining the walls, looking for disguised doors, but they find nothing.

"What about this column?" asks Edgar.

He is standing next to the dark marble pole that goes from the floor nearly to the ceiling at the front of the room, topped with that oblong box, decorated with images similar to those on the throne and chairs.

"I wish we could climb up to that thing," says Allen.

They run their hands around the pole looking for anything that might help them ascend it, but it is smooth like marble, and they cannot find switches of any sort, or levers that might move the column up or down.

"How did they get it up there?" asks Edgar.

"I don't know, but if we could look inside it, maybe that would answer some questions."

Lately, when his father speaks, it is as if his voice were right inside Edgar's head, clearer than a human voice, as though Allen's mind was speaking directly to him.

They spend another half an hour searching the room, looking for trapdoors, false walls, anything. "There's nothing here," sighs Edgar, standing in the center of the room, gazing around, "nothing that tells us anything." He has not heard the sound of the hooved beast either. He still feels a presence though. He keeps thinking he is missing something.

"Hello?" he shouts. "Hello!" His voice echoes in the room.

They wait a long time for a response, certain one will come, but there is only silence.

"Well, we aren't coming away empty-handed," says Allen, picking up one of the jars of red liquid. "Take this," he says, giving it to Edgar. "Bring it to your Mr. Lawrence at the hospital and get him to have it examined so we know exactly what is inside it. His attitude about it may tell us something too."

Edgar looks at the jar.

"Blood."

"We don't know that for certain, though if it is blood, whose is it?"

An image of Lucy's smiling face flashes through Edgar's mind and then an image of someone hurting her. He closes his eyes to shut it out.

"Watch for Lawrence's reaction. You must be wary of him at all times."

"Why?"

"You know why. And the worst of my concerns may be his sending you to that alienist woman, the strange one with the dark ways."

"Dark? Why do you say that?"

"Do not trust her either."

They leave the building cautiously, descending the stairs slowly with as little noise as possible, Edgar keeping the open jar of red liquid under his black suit coat, moving gently so he does not spill it. They get out onto the street but then see someone coming along the pavement toward the door from their right, head turned in the other direction as if concerned about pursuers.

Tiger Tilley.

They slip into an alcove next door.

Tiger turns back to her destination. She still looks wary and has the rifle tucked under her arm, holding it vertical so it appears to be part of her coat. She moves in that stealthy, Tiger way, quick in her trousers and low hard-soled boots. She comes to the door, looks behind her again and enters.

"Let us remove ourselves," says Allen Brim. "I shall wait for you outside the hospital."

Edgar turns back to the door that Tiger has just entered. *She is alone in there.* Then he has another thought, perhaps worse. *Maybe she isn't.*

17

Alone

As Edgar enters the London, he wonders why he is having anything to do with Sir Andrew Lawrence, but despite his concerns, he reminds himself that the chairman offered to help them, and he has resources that might save them from destruction. It is a tantalizing offer he knows he should be considering. Edgar climbs the flights of stairs to Lawrence's office, the precarious jar of blood still in hand, though held under his coat, and when he reaches the top floor, sees the door wide open way down at the end of the hall. That is not surprising since the chairman likes literally to have an open-door policy. He is available to everyone in the hospital at any time, whether doctors, nurses or even patients. Edgar senses something different this time though. He can see right through the doorway and into the room. Lawrence's big gleaming wooden desk is straight ahead and behind it one of his nearly floor-to-ceiling windows. The midday sun shines in and lights up the office with a sort of heavenly glow. There is no one, however, in Lawrence's chair.

"He is always here at this time," says Edgar. "He must be some-where in the room." He moves quickly down the hall and enters, but there is not a soul in the office. Edgar wonders what to do with his jar. He does not want to give it to anyone other than Lawrence. What it is and what he wants done with it would be difficult to explain. He needs the chairman's clear authority—his request to his best doctors to have something tested without any questions asked.

Ignoring the doubts he has about this puzzling man, Edgar dips a pen in ink and writes him a message on the stationery he finds on the desk, placing the jar on top of it when he is done, but when he turns to leave, he hears someone coming down the hall-way behind him. His senses are acute and he picks up the soft gait and knows who it is. He slips the jar and the paper into a drawer and turns.

"Dr. Berenice."

"Edgar," she says with a lovely smile, her long black hair fram-ing that aging but exotic face. It occurs to Edgar that she is like a raven, a large, beautiful olive-skinned raven, striking, intelligent and dangerous. She glides into the room, moving like a ballerina or a ghost, shoulders back, chest out, chin up and focused on her prey. Hilda Berenice, navigator of the mind. "What are you doing here?" she asks.

"Well . . . I . . . I came to see Sir Andrew but it is obvious that he is out. Might you know where he is? Is it not rare for him to be away from his desk at this hour?"

"I suppose, yes. I believe he had an emergency."

"Then why are you up here?" He says it quickly, without think-ing. It takes her a while to respond.

"Yes, why indeed, I get so used to coming to see him that I forgot that I'd heard he had left the building."

"Do you know the nature of the emergency?"

"I try not to pry. Neither should you."

Edgar nods and slips past her, their shoulders almost touching as he tries to evade her. He gets nearly halfway down the hall before he hears her call out.

"Edgar?"

He stops and considers running, but turns back to her. *Do not trust her either*, he hears his father say. She seems to be floating toward him.

"How are you today?" she asks.

"Fine, just fine."

"No more devil in pursuit?"

"A temporary malaise."

"Back to that, are we?"

"I am working my way through my difficulties."

"Well," she coos, "stay at it."

It sounds like a command.

She does not follow him down the stairs and he imagines her returning to Lawrence's room, looking through his desk and finding the jar of blood. Then he remembers the word she used in reference to him. *Paranoid*. He knows what that is. Used by a mind doctor, it has a clinical meaning.

Edgar walks through every hallway as he makes his way down to the ground floor, but there is no sign of Sir Andrew Lawrence. He stops by the matron at her high imposing desk near the main entrance and asks after him. She glares at this impudent youth.

"It is not your business to know the whereabouts of the most esteemed man in this institution."

"I am his assistant."

She takes in a long breath. "I received a note saying that he had left for the day but—"

"Is that not unusual?"

". . . I did not see him leave the premises."

Allen Brim is dutifully waiting outside.

"What did he say? Was he acting suspicious?"

"He wasn't there."

"Oh dear."

"What do you mean by that?"

"Why would he not be in his office at this hour?"

"Why do you keep asking me the questions that are already in my head?"

A puzzled look comes over Allen Brim's face. "I do not know, son. Perhaps because I am your father, I love you, and we think alike."

"Well, I appreciate that, but I need more than your love right now."

Edgar is thinking about the fact that Dr. Berenice told him he must encounter his father and speak with him. Then, there was Allen Brim in flesh and blood, not long after the words had come out of her mouth.

"We will defeat this thing, together. I keep telling you that."

"I want to see Annabel Thorne, my mother."

"She is not your mother."

"She has been for a long while and she loves me, just like you."

"And yet she has been running about with this insolent Lawrence fellow, a scant month after her husband's death. She and your mother were best of friends but I can assure you that Virginia would do nothing of that kind. If I had passed from this life and Lawrence were attempting to seduce your mother, your real mother, and I could return to earth to deal with it, I would challenge him to a bloody duel. He and his fancy motorcar!"

"She is unusual, extraordinary. If she wants to enter into a romance with a wealthy, handsome man, then she has every right—"

"But you do not agree with it, do you, Edgar?"

He does not want to answer the question. They have been moving westbound along Whitechapel Road. He picks up the pace.

"I will not enter Thorne House with you, Edgar, but I will come along and wait somewhere down the street."

As he promised, when they reach the Thornes' street in Mayfair, Allen stops a good ten houses away and leans against a lamppost.

Edgar makes the familiar trip alone along the footpath feeling better with every stride. Yes, Thorne House is his home, his real home, and Annabel might as well be his real mother. Just the sound of her voice will make him feel safer.

The house looks dark and silent. He creaks open the black-iron gate and rushes up the steps to the front door, but it will not open. He pulls the cord and waits. No one comes. Then he notices the shutters pulled across the windows.

"Shuttered?"

It does not make any sense. In all the years he has lived at Thorne House, he has never once seen the windows boarded up.

Even Beasley is not about. Then Edgar wonders about the butler. "Is he part of all of this?" he says quietly into the door. "Is he part of a conspiracy to drive me insane? Did he make up the story of the hag walking down the stairs in Thorne House?" Edgar hammers on the door with his fists.

"Mother!" he cries. No one comes.

He feels a slight tap on his shoulder and whirls around.

"Son, you are shouting. There is no one here."

"But . . . but have they abandoned me? Has she abandoned me?"

"I am not sure that is the best way to state it . . . though it certainly has that appearance. It seems strange that she would unaccountably be away when you need her the most. Not in our interests to speculate though. We do not know exactly what has happened here, and we must not stay and be conspicuous on the street. That isn't a wise thing when you are being pursued by a powerful enemy, an all-seeing and all-knowing—"

"But what else can I do, Father? Where else can I go? William Shakespeare knows nothing that can help me, the devil-worship room told us nothing, and Andrew Lawrence seems to have vanished! I do not trust Tiger anymore, so I cannot go back to her." It is difficult for him to believe that he is saying this.

"Well, you could—"

"Lawrence! He has a home in Kensington! He might be there! I think I can find it!" Edgar has suddenly remembered Annabel gushing about Sir Andrew's fashionable address on one of the richest streets in London, Phillimore Gardens, in a wealthy neighborhood on the western side of Hyde Park. Lawrence had shown it off after walking out with her one evening.

Edgar races south to Piccadilly Street leaving his father far behind. When he turns on that busy street and heads west, he sees several hansom cabs pass and an omnibus rattles by, but he does not want to wait for them and keeps flying on foot until he gets to Hyde Park Corner. He slows a little to cross into the great park and then cuts through it, rushing along Rotten Row, the wide dirt path where fashionable Londoners still sometimes come to ride their horses or carriages and "be seen." Soon he is sprinting again, perspiring heavily in the still hot late afternoon, his father nowhere in sight behind him, a sinking feeling overtaking him as he thinks more of the disappearance of Lucy and Annabel, wondering if they are dead, anxious to get to Lawrence. He feels the blood pulsing through his body, his feet pounding on the ground, fear chasing him westward. It is as if he is trying to run to the end of the world and right out of it: away to an impossible place that is safe. He reaches the Albert Memorial, passes Kensington Palace and is finally in the posh streets where Sir Andrew Lawrence has his city residence. He turns north onto Phillimore Gardens and slows to a walk, nearly half an hour after he started out, his chest heaving. The houses here make the ones in Mayfair near Thorne House look ordinary. They are mostly white, in fact everything here is pristine and white—houses, doors, stone fences, even the footpaths—it is like walking into heaven. Only the gleaming wrought-iron low fences are black. Annabel had said it was the biggest house on the block and Edgar has no problem finding it, easily the most spectacular of many spectacular residences. He rushes up to it, leaps over the short fence, climbs the few outdoor steps on shaking legs and uses the knocker, black and iron in the shape of the letters A and *L*, pounding so hard on the door that he can hear the thuds echo in the house. He glances up and down the street and sees nothing suspicious behind him.

The entrance opens in seconds. A large footman stands there glowering at him, dressed in a spotless red-and-cream outfit that looks a century old. His breeches are velvet, his knee-high socks silk.

"Yes?" says the sour man, looking down his nose, barely able to observe the perspiring visitor.

"My name is Edgar Brim. I am a friend of Sir Andrew Lawrence's. I must see him!" He begins to push past the man but feels a heavy hand on his chest.

"Entrance has not been granted to you, sir."

"But I must see him."

"You cannot."

"But—"

"He is not in."

"Not in to me . . . or not in at all?"

"He is, actually . . . not in at all. He usually comes home for tea, but for some reason, he never appeared. He seems to have been delayed."

Edgar's heart pounds.

"Delayed?"

The door closes in his face.

Edgar walks up and down the street for hours and is careful to keep an eye on Lawrence's residence, but the chairman does not appear. At one point, the footman comes out onto the street and walks up and down it too, as if looking for someone. Finally, as the day begins to grow dark, Edgar gives up.

Where will I go? he asks himself. *Back to Tiger Tilley?* It seems like the only option. *I need to trust her.*

"Don't do it," says his father, who has been sitting on a wrought-iron fence a few homes south of Lawrence's for a while now, watching Edgar pace back and forth. "Stay with me, out on the streets. We will find a place to hide. The devil wants you to go back there. Miss Tilley will kill you, Edgar. You know how capable she is."

"That is insane," says Edgar under his breath. He starts to move toward Kentish Town, trying to find it in his heart to believe in his oldest friend. His father does not follow him. Edgar could find himself a ride, but he has to think, decide if he go can through with this, so he remains on foot again, walking all the way back along the southern edge of Hyde Park, past the great palace, the monuments, and elegant trees and into Mayfair, everything dreamlike in the dimly lit night. It is a dazed, two-hour nighttime stroll and he tries to make his mind up with every step. Should he spend the night on the streets out in the dark with his father and risk an open-air attack from the devil or keep making his way back to the Lear home on Progress Street and spend it with Tiger, who may mean him harm?

He moves north through Marylebone, up Baker Street, past Madame Tussaud's Wax Museum with its famous Chamber of Horrors advertised in red letters and farther north along the edge of shadowy Regent's Park and on and on to Kentish Town. He cannot bring himself to turn back. He approaches the Lears' home, but its appearance shocks him.

He had imagined a single light on, perhaps Tiger staring out a window with the rifle in hand, but it looks dim and empty as if only the ghosts of his dear friends were lingering inside. If the creature has murdered Tiger and is in this house, then it will have the rifle and the cannon at its command too.

Not that Satan would need a weapon.

Then again, perhaps Tiger is in there, lights off, ready to ambush him.

He opens the door quietly and steals into the nearly pitch-black interior. It seems to take him a minute to land each footstep though his head swivels quickly on his neck like a buoy in rough sea. He goes through the living room, the parlor, the little kitchen at the back, and then dares to turn on a light. No one. If Tiger were here, surely she would show herself by now, even if she meant him harm. He heads down the hallway. For some reason, he investigates his room first and then poor Lucy's. Finding both empty, he approaches Tiger's place. He puts his ear to the door. It seems deadly quiet. He opens her entrance ever so carefully.

Tiger's room is deserted, her bedsheets disheveled, her portmanteau open on the floor, her few clothes strewn about in it. *If she were going somewhere, why is it still here?* He remembers her untidy room at the College on the Moors. *Is this normal,* he asks himself, *or has she rushed out . . . or been taken? Or did she meet the devil in that room on Thomas Street?*

He cannot find the rifle anywhere and assumes that either Tiger has brought it with her or it too has been taken by their enemy. The cannon is gone as well. Again, he thinks that Satan would not need weapons. He wonders if he should leave, go back out onto the streets and find his father, or stay here where perhaps the beast will return to finish its dirty work. He is exhausted and cannot decide what might be best, so he simply remains. He goes to bed expecting to awake to the attack of a creature so horrible that he cannot even imagine its appearance. *What form will it take now?*

The empty Lear home at night is everything he thought it would be in this situation and he cannot bring himself to fall to sleep. Instead, he gets up and sits in the living room, still fully clothed, nodding off once or twice only to come violently awake, and each time reaching out for a nonexistent weapon. There are creaks and groans in the house and the distant sounds of voices and of people moving on the street outside. Several times, he thinks he sees a shadow at the door. There is absolutely nowhere for him to flee now, and no one to run to. He is alone. Even his father appears to have disappeared.

"They are all dead," he says in a monotone.

He begins to believe that he is asleep and dreaming all of this. After all, he is an expert at nightmares, this must simply be his worst, or a particular sort of insanity where dreams and reality mingle. It is not possible that all of his friends are suddenly dead or have vanished into the air; it is inconceivable that his dead father has been walking the streets with him. It is madness that the devil is after him. He convinces himself that he is awake but still cannot stop his mind's downward spiral. He sits next to the imaginary cannon, hallucinating. First, he thinks that the devil is actually in the room and that he cannot move a muscle and it is somehow sucking out his soul. Satan appears before him in black clothes with a hideous, shifting face, taking on different forms, eight feet tall, hag-like, then in red like Henry Irving on stage as Mephistopheles, cloven hooves banging on the wood floor.

Then he realizes that someone is actually knocking on the front door.

"You forgot something," says a voice behind him, and he turns to see Allen Brim standing in the entrance to the kitchen. He must have slipped in during the night.

The knock comes again. Edgar swings back around toward the front door with its little glass window, thick and translucent, and observes that it is raining outside, but cannot see anyone at the door; some spirit is knocking.

"You forgot something he said," continues Allen Brim.

"Who?"

"Our little friend."

"What did he say?"

The pounding grows louder.

"He said that his dark-minded visitor asked him to report to him. Now, how might he do that? How would the little man know where to go?"

"He would need the address."

"Indeed. Open the door."

For the first time in his life, Edgar fears his father, whose words sounded ominous, who stands there dry as a bone, fresh from a rain-soaked night, glowering in a dark coat. Is this really Allen Brim? There is no avenue of escape. Edgar must open the door to the invisible creature or face his menacing father.

He advances toward the entrance as it almost bursts inward with the incessant knocking. He peers out through the thick glass and sees nothing there but rain, hard pelting rain in the hot, humid night. He opens the door.

"Master Brim!"

Edgar looks down to see William Shakespeare, short like a child, his big head not even reaching the window. He is drenched and wearing the Zouave clothing. Edgar gasps and steps back. *Is this how Jon died?*

There is no old woman present, though, and the little man does not lay a finger on him. He is clutching something, something small, to his chest, and he slips past Edgar and into the living room, trailing a river of rain behind him until he reaches the settee and slumps down on it. Shakespeare's eyes look even wilder than usual, darting around in his head. Edgar approaches him cautiously and Shakespeare extends the small item in his hand toward him. Edgar takes it. It is a calling card, a black one with red lettering, its borders marked with snakes, pyramids, eyes and horns.

"What is this?"

"What . . . I should . . . have given you . . . when you graced me with your anxious presence some eighteen hours, forty-six minutes and twelve seconds ago. Take it, Sancho Panza! You lump of foul deformity!"

There is a name on the card and an address.

"I don't know this person," says Edgar.

"It is HIM! The devil-man! He gave me his card, you roast meat for worms!"

William Shakespeare's eyes look as though someone is shining a bright light through them from the inside of his head. Edgar expects his father to say something but he seems to have left the room, perhaps the house too. Edgar looks at the address on the card again: 13 Thomas Street.

"Is this the devil-worship room?"

"Next . . . next . . . next . . . door!"

Edgar looks at the name again.

"Alexander Morley."

18

Dead Man

"You cannot go there, Edgar Broom!" shrieks William Shakespeare. "It is HIM. He is not just a messenger! He is Satan. I KNOW it! HE SAID SO!"

"He did?"

"YES! I could not bring myself to tell you that! . . . Where are the others?"

"Gone."

"What do you mean, sir?"

"They have vanished."

"That is what he wants. You are ALONE! Do NOT go to him!"

"But you brought me his card."

"Yes."

"Why?"

"I do not know. I could not stop myself." He looks down at his bright apparel. "I do not know why I am wearing these clothes either! I have no memory of putting them on!"

"You have worn them before, haven't you?"

"Yes."

"Here."

"Yes."

"And Jonathan greeted you at the door!"

"Yes. No! Yes."

"You and the hag killed Jonathan and now you are sending me to see the devil!"

"The hag? . . . I did not KILL him!"

"Tell me what happened now or I will put a bullet through your brain with this rifle!" Edgar points the barrel of Alfred Thorne's extraordinary weapon at the little man's big head.

"But you have nothing in your hands."

Edgar looks down, realizes it is true, and it horrifies him. He remembers that Tiger must have the rifle . . . or someone else. He staggers toward the settee and falls onto it next to William Shakespeare.

"I do not remember how I got here that morning," says the little man in a voice so small that Edgar can barely hear him, "though I do know now, through some vague and hideous memory, that I was wearing these clothes. I knocked and Jonathan looked through the window and then opened the door to me. I could see a wild look in his eye when he first peered out, but then he saw it was me and his face relaxed, at least a little. He looked terrible, Edgar Broom, terrible! Oh my Lord sakes almighty! Then he looked out toward the street and his face changed again. That is what I remember. I could not have killed him. NOT ME!"

"You do not recall Jonathan lying at your feet, you little beast!"

"I remember scurrying away and I think I know who sent me."

"Who?"

"The devil."

"This Morley fellow."

"I believe so. I tried to resist coming, Edgar, I know I did."

"What about the hag?"

"Why do you keep saying that?"

"She was with you!"

"No one was with me . . . the hag is a figment of—"

Edgar seizes the little man and throws him across the room and his head smashes into the ridge on the top of the baseboard on a wall. Blood comes from a sickle-shaped wound on his forehead and tears from his eyes.

"When I fled," says Shakespeare, looking pitifully up at Edgar, "I mounted my noble steed, Rocinante, and galloped through the streets of London all the way home to the Crypto-Anthropology Society of the Queen's Empire, windmills at my back, my gallant friends Messrs. Sprinkle, Winker and Tightman awaiting me to soothe my fevered brow!"

Edgar walks to Shakespeare and stands over him. "When did you last see him?"

"Who?"

"Morley! You told me two days ago that he had been to see you a few days before that. Has he been in your presence since then?"

"He has been to see me three times this week . . . the last time was yesterday, and I had a note from him just hours ago, telling me that if I ever revealed his identity he would deliver me to hell. Something good inside me, Edgar, something deep down, made me come to you tonight. I have seen his handwriting. The note was in his hand! I believe he brought it himself! I burned it upon my fire!"

"Hours ago?" Edgar gulps. "He might be in the streets now? Near us?"

"The note said he could be found at home."

Edgar turns his back on Shakespeare. "Thirteen Thomas Street," he says quietly. "He's there."

"FLEE, Sir Edgar Broom, there is room on my horse!" Shakespeare struggles to his feet, the blood dripping down his big face.

"No."

"I beg your pardon?"

"I am going there."

"NO! NO, SIR!"

"And you are going with me."

The little man's big head looks as if it will explode.

"I would rather descend into hell."

"Perhaps you will be accommodated, and shortly. You know the truth, William Shakespeare, and it is that you cannot run from fear. You must face it. Now, come with me!" He grabs him by his collar and escorts him out the door, realizing as he goes that they are unarmed.

Edgar and his tiny companion move at a good pace south and east toward the East End in the now-dry early day through crowded streets. Shakespeare keeps pulling back and even trying to run away, but Edgar maintains a grip on him. The little man mutters at high speed, dabbing his forehead with a handkerchief.

"The devil has spells. He has black magic. He can make you do anything! He will kill us. He will kill us by simply looking at us! He said he could do it. He knows who you are, Edgar Brim, exactly who you are, and you fascinate him. You, the young knight of fear, the king of the hag phenomenon, you discombobulate him; you energize him! He is in your mind making you do what he wants! He wants to play with you more than anyone else! He wants you to come to him!"

"Then that is what he will get." Edgar is grinding his teeth.

"This is not simply a creature, lad: this is Satan himself, alive in London!"

Edgar Brim feels powerful. His brain is telling him that it is working better than ever before, his muscles are stronger, his quickness greater. He has ejected fear and the confidence that has replaced it is like a narcotic bursting inside him. At this moment, Edgar Brim is a genius and a superman.

"Morley is reading about the monsters!" shouts Shakespeare in desperation. "He is reading and re-reading *Dracula* and *Frankenstein* and *Jekyll and Hyde*! He has been studying them! Ever since I told him about our missions, about you and the others! He reads Poe from day until night! He reads *Inferno* and *Paradise Lost*! And he reads the Bible! It infatuates him! He says he is IN it! He recognizes himself! Do you hear what I am saying! He says we have proven to him who he is!"

Edgar keeps pulling Shakespeare forward, feeling more powerful with every word the little man shrieks.

By the time they reach Thomas Street, he is almost dragging his companion behind him, the diminutive fellow digging his boot-heels into the pavement. They march past the building with the devil-worship room and up to the entrance of the residence next door. Edgar pins his prisoner to the wall with one arm on the scrawny chest and hammers on the door with his other fist. Shakespeare's head wound has begun to clot.

"You were here in this street before, weren't you?"

"I think so," whimpers Shakespeare. "I may have come once . . . or twice. I do not know! Neither I nor you or anyone can resist his will!"

No one appears for a while, but then there are noises inside, someone approaching.

"Lord have mercy on our souls!" cries Shakespeare. "The saints in heaven preserve us now!"

The door opens and an old woman appears. For an instant, Edgar thinks it is the hag. He staggers back. She is, however, an ordinary woman, with a broom in her hand and a stained white apron over her dark-blue cotton dress. Edgar releases Shakespeare.

"May I 'elp you?"

Edgar turns away from her to his companion and whispers, "Have you ever seen this woman before?"

"No," says Shakespeare in a shaky voice.

"May I 'elp you?" asks the crone again.

"I . . . I am looking for Alexander Morley," says Edgar.

"Alex Morley?"

"Yes."

"Well, 'e isn't 'ere."

"Then, where is he?"

"That is up to the Lord our God."

"Pardon me?"

"You see, Mr. Morley is no longer with us. Atticus Cleaners 'as employed me to sort 'is residence. I will 'ave it ship-shape before the end of the day!"

"That is impossible," says Shakespeare.

"No it ain't!" replies the woman, losing her brief attempt at respectability. "I is among the best cleaners in the city of London, I is, and I will 'ave you know it can be done by the likes of me within the time allotted!"

"That is not what he means," says Edgar.

The woman's hands are on her hips and she is glaring at her interrogators.

"Then 'e 'ad best explain 'isself."

"He means that Mr. Morley cannot have passed from this life."

"Alex Morley is as dead as a doornail, for a week now, in fact."

"OH!" cries Shakespeare.

"Is there somethin' wrong with this little man, somethin' more than meets me eye?"

"He has had personal contact with Morley within the past day or two and a note from him this morning."

"Now that, sir, is impossible. 'E was carted out of 'ere and taken to the dead 'ouse a good seven days back, and I know so because I was told it 'appened and instructed to begin cleanin' 'is place before all the furniture was toted away and sold at auction."

"Oh!" cries Shakespeare again.

"Is 'e goin' to keep doin' that?"

"You are sure Mr. Morley is dead?"

"As sure as I'm standin' 'ere."

"How did he die?"

"Don't know for certain. There may have been some funny business. 'E was a strange one, Mr. Morley was, with 'is shaved 'ead and 'is black clothes and 'is 'orrible eyes. A weird one. Weird and smart as a whip. I've cleaned 'is hovel before, you know, a good dozen times or more. As I says, near everythin' 'as been taken away as of this mornin', but if you'd a seen it when 'e was livin' 'ere you'd a known what I mean by strange. The whole place was black, the walls and the ceilin', there was obscene little statues everywhere, knives all about the place, not a bed in sight. The police came 'ere to look around when I was doin' the first of this last cleanin'. It 'as been a long job. I heard them talkin'. There was no burial, someone claimed 'is corpse and took it away when the 'thorities was done with it."

"What do you mean by funny business?"

"I knows there was buckets of blood because there was still red all over the floors when I first came in and I knows blood stains and 'ow to remove 'em. No one did it to 'im, though, if you knows what I mean, not by the way those Bobbies was talkin'."

"Suicide?"

Shakespeare turns to the wall and lowers his head as if he is about to be sick to his stomach.

"I don't like that word."

"Do you think there was a doctor, a coroner?"

"Oh, 'parently they did it up right, took what he'd left of himself off to the hospital, before that someone came and claimed him."

"The London?"

"Course. These coppers said he knew someone there, an old friend, one of them mind doctors."

"Berenice," whispers Edgar, and a chill goes down his spine. "That's it, that's the name."

Edgar immediately turns and starts to walk briskly down Thomas Street toward the hospital.

19

The Devil's Friend

S hakespeare can barely keep up. He looks behind as he runs, his little legs moving as fast as he can make them go. He reaches out for Edgar several times, almost as if he wants to take him by the hand.

"Edgar! EDGAR BRIM!" he cries. "Alex Morley was sending me messages when he was dead! He butchered himself and THEN he came to see me! This proves who he is!"

"Nonsense!" shouts Edgar, not even looking back at him. "It proves precisely the opposite. The devil cannot die!"

"He looked perfectly well yesterday, Edgar, perfectly well! Quite striking, actually."

They cross wide Whitechapel Road and enter the hospital. It is approaching mid-morning and both the street and the London are hot and bustling. The wilting matron is fanning herself. She stares at them and even calls out, but Edgar ignores her, crosses the crowded, noisy reception room and begins to climb the first set of stairs, his little companion huffing and puffing as he tries to stay close. As they approach Berenice's door, Shakespeare throws himself at Edgar's legs and slows him down.

"Edgar Broom," he whispers, "before you open that door to this woman, this mind doctor who is connected to the evil that pursues us, I must tell you something! It may make you come to your senses and flee with me! It is about a particular visit that the devil Morley made to the Crypto-Anthropology Society of the Queen's Empire."

Edgar sighs. "What is it? And quickly."

"One day . . . one day . . . one day . . ."

"Out with it."

"He turned on an electric light."

"Why are you wasting my time?"

"And . . . and he moved an inkwell across the table."

"This is ridic—"

"He did not touch these items when he did these things."

"Shakespeare, you are a fool."

"He did not touch them, Edgar Broom. He turned on the light and moved the inkwell by simply looking at them. He used his powers. That was how he made me go to Master Jonathan, I am certain, and he somehow caused him to die. He many times told me that if I did not do the things he instructed me to do, tell him the things he wanted to know, he would take my soul with merely a look."

Edgar swallows and hopes it does not sound as loud to his little companion as it does to him. They are just a couple of steps from Berenice's door. He turns to it. The blind is pulled down on its window. He doesn't knock and enters without saying a word.

The alienist has her back to them, on her knees against the bed as if in prayer, but with her hands held out to either side of her shoulders, palms open and downward, as if receiving some sort of spirit from below. She is naked from the waist up: her tight brown dress pulled down to her wide hips, her back slim but taut, an extraordinary network of fine muscles evident, as if her torso belongs to an athletic woman in her twenties. Her feet are bare too.

"Dr. Berenice!" shouts Edgar. Shakespeare comes to a halt and gasps.

The mind doctor does not move even one of her well-defined muscles. She remains motionless for a moment, then, still turned away from them, reaches behind her waist, her shoulders popping out and back into place, pulls up the top of her dress to cover herself and does up all the buttons, right to the bottom of her neck, her arms, wrists and fingers remarkably supple. Then she gets to her feet, seemingly without effort, and turns to her visitors, swinging her long black hair around so it falls over her back. Her exotic face betrays her age, perhaps approaching seventy or maybe older.

"Oh, my Lord!" cries Shakespeare.

"Good day, Edgar. Who is this little man?"

"This is William Shakespeare."

"I see. Are you sure it isn't Charles Dickens?"

"It is what he calls himself."

"You . . . you look familiar, s-sound—" stutters Shakespeare.

"I doubt that."

"H-how . . ." stutters Shakespeare again, pointing at her, "how do you do that?"

"Do what?" asks Berenice.

"Reach behind yourself like that. Be so supple, so . . . so . . ."

"So young of body?" She stands towering over him, a perfect and strong hourglass shape. Something about her seems to terrify the little man.

"Yes."

"It is an ancient Indian art, where one stretches the body daily. It is that and other things that keep my body young, but the mind retains all the true power. Its power is limitless. A great man taught me that. He showed me how to keep my body the way he liked it to be. He and I were experimenters in life and love and magic. He believed that your mind might have the power to allow you to live forever."

"Alex Morley," says Edgar.

Berenice's eyes flare at the mention of the name. "Yes," she finally says. "How did you know that, Edgar?"

"I want to know more about him."

"Once you know a little, you will want to know a great deal."

"He is the devil incarnate!" says Shakespeare. "He is Satan in the flesh!"

"You are mad, little man," says Berenice.

"Then I am too," says Edgar.

The alienist turns away. "You will not defame a dead man. You will not defame a man who took his own life . . . in such a horrible way."

"How do you know that he is dead?"

"I saw his corpse, here at the hospital." She keeps her back to them.

"You claimed it and took it away too. Where is it?"

"I did not. I did not have the right to do that."

"Then who?"

"I don't know. Perhaps one of his insane followers." Her voice sounds bitter.

"I saw him alive, yesterday," shrieks Shakespeare.

Berenice whirls around. "That is impossible!"

"He sent me a note this morning too!"

"Do NOT say that!" cries Berenice.

"Because it is true?" asks Edgar.

"No, it is not true. He cannot defeat death. He was merely brilliant. Merely." She sniffs. "He truly understood the secret abilities of human beings. His brilliance was too much for even the Order." Shakespeare takes in his breath with a start. "He was under the impression that he could have taught me so much more."

"Perhaps his power comes from below," says Edgar. "Perhaps he entranced you because he had more than mortal power."

"I could believe that," says Berenice, gripping her arms with shaking hands and running them up and down as though to warm herself. "But I do not. You are not sane when you say these things, Edgar Brim. You need to send this little man to Bedlam and then lie on this sofa for me and tell me why you would believe that any man, or woman, is not mortal. You have said such things before."

Edgar steps back. "I will do nothing of the sort."

"I beg you to reconsider." There is aggression in her voice.

"Where is his body? I need to know that he is dead."

"I do not know."

Her mouth is a straight line, her face unreadable.

"Where is Lawrence? I need to speak with him."

"I told you before, he isn't here."

"But that was yesterday. He still hasn't returned?"

"He must have gone home."

"I went to his residence and there was not only no sign of him but his footman seemed perplexed as to his whereabouts."

Berenice turns her back on them again. "He has another home. In the country. A place he calls Lawrence Lodge. It is in Surrey, a few hours from London near the village of Hindhead on the road to Portsmouth, just past the Devil's Punch Bowl."

"What is that?" asks Shakespeare, barely able to say it.

"You will see."

"You speak of his estate and its location as if you have been there," says Edgar.

"I have not. He merely mentioned it during a session here. It is a place he is very fond of, a remarkable place, mysterious he called it, with a stunning view of the countryside." She keeps her back to them.

"Why did Lawrence need your help, Dr. Berenice?"

She turns on him. Her face is red. "I have told you! One cannot reveal such things!"

There is silence in the room for a moment.

"We are not going there, Edgar Broom. We cannot trust him. We cannot trust anyone anymore. We are fleeing!"

A whirlwind of thoughts invades Edgar's mind. *Where is Annabel? Is she with Lawrence? Is the countryside, safely away from things and with this rich man's resources and protection, the best place to be? Or is Lawrence in league with our enemy and drawing me out there to finish things in a remote location where no one will see what happens?* Edgar looks to Dr. Berenice and something makes him ask a strange question. It is as if he cannot resist saying it. "What would you do?" he asks her.

She seems to be holding back a smile. "I . . . I cannot tell you what to do." She takes several steps toward a window and looks out it. Edgar advances to her side and casts his gaze downward, in the direction she is looking. Sir Andrew Lawrence's motorcar sits there, pulled up close to the side of the building where the carriages are sometimes left. It gleams in the midday sun. Edgar wonders why Lawrence would not have taken it to his country estate, if indeed that is where he has gone. It occurs to him that the roads in the countryside might not be fit for such a conveyance . . . or that Lawrence may have had too many people with him to carry them in that slight machine. Does he have Lucy, Tiger *and* Annabel? Edgar knows that he cannot afford a hansom cab's fare that far out into the countryside. Something also tells him that he must get to Lawrence as fast as he possibly can.

Ten minutes later, when Edgar and Shakespeare arrive at the vehicle, the little man literally trying to dig his heels into the footpaths again to keep from being brought along, they notice that someone is sitting in the front passenger seat.

"Hello, my boy," says Allen Brim.

"Hello, Father."

"He is here?" asks Shakespeare. "In which seat? I should not sit upon him."

"Take the rear bench," says Edgar. "We have a long trip in front of us."

"Oh! I cannot actually ride in such an infernal machine! What is it, steam? Electric? Petrol powered?"

"It is electric and quite safe," Edgar lies.

"ELECTRIC! Oh my, oh my, oh my, oh my! Electric is evil, Edgar Broom. It has such power! Everyone knows that! It frightens me to my very soul!"

"Get in or I will frighten you far past that."

The little man, seeing he has no option, steps up into the carriage and squeezes himself into the back and onto the tiny rear bench. "She spoke of the Order," he says, barely above his breath.

"I meant to ask about that," says Edgar. "What did she mean?"

"The Hermetic Order of the Golden Dawn."

A memory, a difficult one, comes back to Edgar from many years ago, when he was being reprimanded by the headmaster of the College on the Moors, the Reverend Spartan Griswold, a six-and-a-half-foot praying-mantis of a man with wicked ways. The old tyrant had mentioned this very same group, an offhand reference that had sent chills down Edgar's spine. Edgar knew it was a secret society, that it had something to do with the occult and black magic and perhaps even evil. Its members had some sort of belief that invisible powers could, and perhaps did, run the world, the universe. Bram Stoker, creator of the blood-soaked *Dracula*, was a member. Now, it turned out, so was Alexander Morley. Edgar thinks of what Berenice had said about Morley's involvement. "He truly understood the secret abilities of human beings," she had said. "His brilliance was too much for even the Order."

Edgar does not want to think about that, not now. He must focus on the task at hand. He slides onto the front seat and gets behind the steering mechanism. "Now," he says, trying to sound calm, "how to operate this."

He thinks back to the day when he sailed through London with Lawrence and considers how this machine was piloted. He recalls Lawrence did very little to start it, simply turned a key, if he is correct, somewhere under the seat. He reaches down, finds it and turns the switch to start the battery. Nothing seems to happen. That makes sense though. This is not one of those petrol-powered cars with a starting crank that can break your arm and a noise that pierces the eardrums of anyone within a mile. It is much simpler and quieter. Edgar pulls the tiller bar toward himself, finds the two foot-brakes and settles his hand onto the lever that extends up toward him from the floor, just to the right of his right leg. There are goggles on the dashboard and he puts one pair on and hands the others to his passengers. He remembers how careful Lawrence was with this lever that accelerates the vehicle, pushing it forward in slow motion, as if it would allow the car to travel at a certain speed partway up and faster and faster as the lever was pushed forward.

He realizes that his heart is pounding and it surprises him to feel the sort of fear that has plagued him in very different circumstances throughout his life. This is not psychological . . . or is it?

"This is ridiculous," he says out loud. "This is a machine. It is new and different, and everyone fears things that are different, usually without reason. Be rational, calm down, pilot the carriage."

"Are you talking to your father?" asks a frightened little voice from behind.

"Just to myself," says Edgar, "trying to talk some sense."

He pushes the lever forward and the car moves out onto the street. He only allows the machine to advance very slowly at first, trying to get the hang of the tiller steering mechanism. He pulls up to the intersection with Whitechapel Road, decelerates and gently touches the brakes. The car lurches to a stop. He falls forward and Shakespeare comes crashing into him from behind, banging his big head on the back of the seat. He groans. Somehow, Allen Brim sits there as still as a statue.

"I beg your pardon," says Edgar, and then he looks out onto bustling Whitechapel Road. Fear envelops him again. The wide street is teeming with activity—horses and carriages, hansom cabs, rivers of pedestrians, shouting hawkers and even the odd motorized vehicle. It seems as though he sees all the colors of a rainbow out there and smells all the odors known to humanity. For an instant, he cannot move. It is as though the task of stepping from the womb into life confronts him.

"There is a solution to this," says his father, "and you know what it is."

Edgar steels himself, pushes the tiller forward, and turns left onto Whitechapel Road. "Oh, my Lord!" shouts Shakespeare from the back seat and covers his eyes as they enter the melee. Edgar wishes that he could conquer all his fears this way.

"It is possible, actually," says Allen Brim.

Edgar drives cautiously through the mob of traffic as he makes his way out of the East End, picks up the pace through the Old City and then hums along the Embankment beside the brown River Thames into Chelsea until he reaches the Battersea Bridge and crosses over that narrow, five-span passage into Brixton and the southern suburbs. He knows the way to the road to Portsmouth. It takes a while to emerge out of the heavily populated area, which worries Edgar, since he thinks they are easy targets there for anything that might be pursuing them, but once they reach Wimbledon, the population begins to decline. They are soon near the countryside, buzzing southwest into the sweltering county of Surrey where the roads are dirt or gravel, meant for horses and coaches, rough for the hummingbird motor vehicle. Mud flies up and splatters on their goggles as they whizz along at something that seems terribly in excess of thirteen miles an hour, trying to find the smoother parts of the bumpy road. As the natural world around them grows greener and more beautiful, Shakespeare sits on the back bench, looking terrified; Allen Brim in the passenger seat, a picture of intensity; and Edgar at the tiller, frightened that their enemy may be finding a way inside his very soul. He wonders if it has already done that to Lucy and Tiger. Perhaps it has taken them away to join the evil side, against him. "Perhaps they are all against me," he says to himself, "every single one of them. Perhaps that is what this is all about, what it has always been about." All the while, he is worrying about material problems: that they will break a wheel and, left alone in the country, become sitting prey. His mind swirls one way and then the next. "Is a dead man somehow in pursuit of me?" They pass through villages, past the great Epsom Downs horseracing park and onward, drawing stares from people everywhere they go. It takes them several hours to get to their destination.

Edgar begins to calm a little as they near the village of Hindhead where Lawrence's estate must sit on one of the hills overlooking the surrounding area—Berenice said it has a "stunning view of the countryside."

Then the car begins to slow. It does so on its own, as if possessed. No matter how far forward Edgar pushes the lever, the car keeps slowing down, and then it comes to a complete halt.

"Edgar Broom? What is going on?"

"We have come to the end of our ride," says Allen Brim. "This is an electric car powered by six batteries at the front and rear of the machine. They have limitations and thus the vehicle has a finite range. Thirty miles or so, I would say, and we have done it."

"We have to get out and walk," says Edgar, looking up at the sun, which has descended a good deal in the sky. He gets from the car. They are in a heavily wooded area. Something could emerge out of the trees and attack them without giving them much chance to respond, or run. "The vehicle is spent. We have, I'd say, another half hour to walk."

"But it will be pitch-black in an hour or two!"

"All the more reason to hop to it," says Allen.

Edgar pushes Lawrence's amazing horseless carriage a couple of feet into the trees. Then the two Brims begin to move along the wooded road and Shakespeare scrambles to keep up to them, moaning and whining as he comes. In ten or fifteen minutes, the scenery suddenly changes. In fact, the entire world appears to fall away to one side of the road. It seems that the trees, the rocks, the earth are instantly miles beneath them, and the vista is extraordinary. It is as though a giant or a god reached down and shoveled out the ground with one enormous hand for as far as one can see. It is remarkable to behold. They are moving along the road on the edge of this mammoth pit and one has the sense that if you took a couple steps toward it, you would vanish into its depths. Edgar stares at it.

"It's beautiful," he says. *Is it real?* he asks himself. *What delusion is this?*

"I don't like it," says Shakespeare. "It isn't right; it isn't natural!"

"Look," says Allen Brim, "there is a sign here."

Expecting to see a marker giving them the distance to Portsmouth or hopefully even an indication that Hindhead is just around the corner, the sign instead contains no numbers, just four words.

The Devil's Punch Bowl.

The three of them stand stock-still for a moment, listening to the breeze, to the crows cawing in the distance as they fly high above this aberration in the earth.

"It is just a coincidence," says Allen Brim.

"Yes," says Edgar.

"Yes? Yes?" cries Shakespeare. "What does that mean? There is no 'yes' about this. This is a 'No!' A NO ALL THE WAY! We must remove our posteriors from these premises and skedaddle at unheard of speed back to London!"

"I am going to Hindhead and you are coming with me!"

Edgar's mind, however, is swirling again. There are too many coincidences, too many delusions. He has to press himself to keep moving forward.

Two more signs, however, almost make him turn back. One marks the death of a sailor here long ago, killed by three highwaymen later hanged for their crime on a nearby hill, and the second is a remarkable stone Celtic cross sitting on the very edge of the abyss, described by the engraving as being erected there to ward off evil spirits. "The Devil Made This Place," someone has written across it in chalk.

"We are not in a story," says Edgar to himself. "This is not just inside my mind. This is real." By another force of will, he keeps himself and his companions moving farther, and in ten minutes, they pass a few homes and a public house, just past the sign for the village of Hindhead. They have no need to ask for directions to Lawrence Lodge. It appears above them before they have gone far, huge and looming on a hill that must command a magnificent view of the countryside. From the road, with the setting sun behind it, the big house, stretching along the horizon, has a dark, ominous look.

"I am not going up there, no indeed," says William Shakespeare, who turns and begins to walk back the way they came.

"Then we shall leave you to the wolves," says Edgar.

"Wolves?" asks Shakespeare, stopping on a dime. "Are they not extinct in England?"

Edgar gives him an evil smile.

A dirt road winds up the steep hill toward the residence. Edgar and his father begin to climb it. In a second, their little companion is following them.

"Berenice wanted you to come here," whispers Allen. "I think she has sent you here. It is a trap."

"What did you say?" asks Edgar, but his father does not respond.

The house does indeed look down upon its surroundings. Once they reach the grounds, a whole world opens up, as if separated from the rest of Hindhead. There is a small dark pond in front of the building and vehicles must travel across a short causeway to reach the front door. Lawrence Lodge is an elongated brick home, almost the full length of a ridge, with a sloping lawn laid between it and the water. It has three floors with gabled windows and a wide wooden entrance bearing Lawrence's trademark *A* and *L* doorknocker.

Edgar expects a liveried footman to step from the huge door to greet them, dressed in the family's red-and-cream-colored uniform and with a phalanx of other servants behind him.

The house, however, is silent.

They walk across the causeway and up to the entrance. The big doors do not open. It is as if the building is dead, while its backdrop of singing birds, wind in the trees, and the beautiful scenery descending below it, are alive with sound and sensation. The setting sun lights it all in an eerie way.

The stables are to the left of the main house, but they are dark too, giving no evidence of whether or not anyone has come here recently.

They stop and stare at the doors. None of them says anything for a while.

Then a light comes on in an upper room and then another dim one on the ground floor. A big black bird sits in the upper window.

"It is time for us to leave this place," says Shakespeare, and it is as though his tiny voice is broadcast across the county.

"No," says Edgar, "we are going indoors."

20

Lawrence Lodge

dgar leads the way. He walks up the six steps, presses the latch on one of the big wooden doors. It is hot like a furnace, baked by the boiling country air. In all his life, he cannot remember weather this searing. He pushes the door wide open and waits to see if anything comes at them. There is silence. He goes in. No one greets them in the vestibule. It is not entirely dark, one of the lights they saw from outside remains on in an adjoining room—the dining room, perhaps, or a sitting room—and it is dimly illuminating the vestibule too. Edgar leads them toward that light. There are animal heads nailed to the walls amongst clutters of paintings and dark paisley wallpaper in this hallway that leads inward. The eyes of these creatures seem to be staring at them. They reach a large sitting room and see that there are papers left on tables and knitting with the needles still in them on a love seat, as if the room's occupants have disappeared from the premises in a flash. Then Edgar sees something that chills his heart. It is a bonnet, but not any bonnet. It is black with peach lines in it, little threads that spell out the word *Love*. Annabel's!

He gasps and picks it up.

"What is that?" asks his father.

"It belongs to my mother!"

"That may not mean—"

"It means HE is here!" shouts Shakespeare and his voice echoes in the big room, bouncing off the paintings and the animal heads. "He has her here! Lawrence is in league with him!"

"Nonsense," says Edgar, but his voice is quavering. "There is no proof of that."

They remain silent for a moment, listening for sounds in the big house, but it seems deserted.

"Let us go upstairs to where the other light is," says Allen Brim.

Edgar starts moving toward the staircase.

"No!" cries Shakespeare, as loudly as he dares.

"All right then, you stay down here, alone."

"But we are not even armed!"

"We have our courage," says Edgar, as if trying to convince himself, "and our stealth." He notices a suit of armor standing against a wall near the foot of the stairs, the headless figure holding a long sword. "And we have this." He takes it into his hands, surprised at its weight. It reminds him of Professor Lear's big sword-like kukri knife. He wonders where that weapon is.

They ascend the stairs onto the first landing, then up the second set to the third, and tread carefully since there is almost no light here. Then they begin to hear muted voices.

"Lucy!" says Shakespeare, and Edgar has to put his hand over the little man's mouth. It isn't just her voice though; he can hear Lawrence's and Annabel's too.

Shakespeare seizes Edgar's hand and tries to pull it off, mumbling about their friends and loved ones being near.

"We cannot trust them," whispers Allen Brim.

"He is right," says Edgar. A part of him is thrilled that they are alive and another part terrified of them.

"What?" mumbles Shakespeare.

"We cannot trust them. None of them."

"What?" repeats the little fellow, this time a little louder.

"Lucy ran off on her own. She was acting suspiciously before that. Lawrence deceived me more than once and . . . and my mother, lately she has not been the person I knew as a child. She threw herself at that man just weeks after Alfred died!" There is anger in his voice.

"What?" says Shakespeare again. Then he mumbles something that sounds like, "You cannot be serious, Edgar Broom."

"They mean you harm, Edgar," says his father. "Dr. Berenice as much as said it. They are talking together as if they are in conspiracy with each other. And where is that strange girl, Tiger Tilley?"

Edgar does not want to think about it. It is bad enough that Lucy and Annabel are against him, perhaps plotting with the devil up here in this strange house, drawing him out to a lonely place in the countryside, but Tiger is another story entirely. Her capabilities are formidable to begin with, and if she were in league with Satan, her powers would be so much worse.

Edgar takes his hand from Shakespeare's mouth and puts a finger to his lips to make him keep silent. "We need to get closer to them, hear what they are saying."

The little man's eyes are wide. He looks at Edgar as if he terrifies him, but he nods his big head.

They move along a hallway in the direction of the voices, which grow louder and soon appear to be coming from inside a room at the end of the hall. The door is closed and a line of light is apparent under it.

"We cannot stay here forever," says Lucy.

"We have no choice but to wait." Lawrence sounds tense. "Who knows what is out there and what they are capable of."

"Are you referring to Edgar or the devil?" asks Annabel. She sounds unlike herself, like someone impersonating her.

Shakespeare draws in his breath and Edgar puts his hand on him. Then he tightens his grip on the sword.

"Either," says Lawrence. "I don't like saying it, but it is the truth."

"If Edgar is indeed mad," says Lucy, "if what you say about him is true, sir, then he could be capable of anything. I just hate to think of it."

"I will kill him if I have to, with one of these."

Annabel says nothing in protest and Edgar drops his head.

"Your guns won't be useful, sir," says Lucy, "if he has Alfred Thorne's rifle or the cannon. Common shotguns like these might as well be from the Middle Ages in a fight with those weapons."

"Why are we assuming he has them?" asks Annabel.

"How do we know he hasn't?"

"Maybe Tiger has them."

There is silence for a moment.

"I have no idea where her loyalty is in all of this," says Lucy. "I don't understand her at all, never have. Lord help us if she is against us."

Edgar thinks of Lawrence telling him that he would excavate the revenant's corpse from the basement of the Lyceum Theatre. He had promised, but it seems he had not done it. In fact, he had never mentioned the subject again. Had he ever intended to do it?

There is a sound in the building, a thud like something or someone falling to a floor. Quiet reigns for a minute, both inside and outside the upper room.

"I will kill anyone or anything that I have to," repeats Lawrence. "Dr. Berenice has taught me how important it is to know who my enemies are, and how to identify them."

"I can hear someone," whispers Allen Brim. "Someone is walking through the house."

Edgar listens carefully and thinks he hears footsteps too, far off in the building, perhaps one floor beneath them, perhaps lower, but he is not sure. He thinks of Poe's magnificent sensation story *The Fall of the House of Usher* and of the woman in it who had been given up for dead and put in a coffin in the basement of a building not unlike the one they are in right now . . . only to appear, very much alive, right before the eyes of the narrator. The footsteps are coming upward, just as hers had.

"One of us needs to venture out and search the building," says Lucy. "I'll do it, if necessary."

"No," says Lawrence, "I'll go, just give me a minute or two to brace myself."

Edgar motions to the other two to move back from the door and down the hallway. When they are far enough away, he gathers them together.

"If someone is moving about in the house, we have to find him or her. We have to do it before Lawrence sees us too. We have to do it now."

"That is an excellent idea, my son."

"No," says Shakespeare. "All the servants seem to be gone. They have somehow vanished! We know where the lovely Lucy, the wealthy Mr. Lawrence and your apparently dearest mother are at this moment, Edgar. So, that leaves only a couple of possibilities as to the identity of this intruder."

"Satan," says Allen Brim.

"Or Tiger," says Edgar.

"Yes, indeed," cries Shakespeare, "and neither she nor the devil are opponents we want to face, especially if the valiant Tilley has that blunderbuss weapon or that infernal cannon!"

"We could take whatever is lurking by surprise," says Edgar.

"YOU, you could take it by surprise. I will have nothing to do with this! For it will mean certain death!"

"You are as brave as a lion."

"I am a survivor!" says Shakespeare.

"You must kill whatever you find," says Allen. "Tiger Tilley is no friend of yours. Kill her and cut off her head with that sword. Bury her in a deep grave with her severed head between her feet, just like you did with the vampire creature."

Edgar wonders if he ever told his father what they did to the revenant's corpse. If he did not, then how could he know all that? He regards Allen Brim for an instant and wonders again if he too is his enemy. He glances at William Shakespeare. *I am alone in this. I always have been*, he thinks.

"You two stay here and I will search the house," says Edgar out loud. "If I do not come back in a short while, then flee. There is no use in all of us perishing."

His father takes him into his arms and hugs him but offers no resistance to the idea of his confronting their enemy alone. Shakespeare stands there watching with a puzzled expression on his face.

Edgar leaves them at that intersection in the hallway and heads out into the house with his sword held in front of him, stepping quietly and stealthily, every one of his acute senses alert. The moonlight filters dimly through a window or two. When he gets to the top of the staircase, he stops for a long time and listens. For a while, all he can hear is his own breathing. Then he hears that sound again, those quiet footsteps, a single floor down.

He descends the stairs.

21

The Electricity of Fear

When he reaches the bottom of the stairs, he stands still and again listens for a long while. There it is once more, but now he can distinguish some subtleties in the sound. It is indeed as if someone is walking and he or she is doing so carefully, so it is difficult to tell if the intruder is large or small, but there is another element to the sound, a steady little noise like what you might hear if someone were rolling something behind as he or she walked.

It cannot be Morley, says Edgar, inside his head, *for he is dead. But if Morley is Satan*, he reminds himself, *then how can Satan be dead?* He thinks again of *The Fall of the House of Usher* and the dead woman who came up from the basement. A terrible thought occurs to him. *Is that apparition moving about in this building?* He hears a caw, a deep guttural one, not from a crow, but a raven . . . then he remembers that big black bird they saw in the window as they approached this House of Usher. "Once upon a midnight dreary," he hears a voice inside his head say, "while I pondered, weak and weary" . . . the first lines of Poe's great poem, *The Raven*.

"I am living in reality," he says to himself in as steady a voice as he can muster, "and my friends are near, not my enemies. I am not in a poem or a story and I am not hearing Poe's 'ominous bird of yore' speak to me from a windowsill." Then the black bird offers another utterance, three quick caws like the syllables of a word . . . *Nevermore!*

"This is madness," Edgar whispers. "Shake your head and send all the fiction out!" *The Raven* spoke of death, its finality, its terror. *The Raven* spoke of fear! He hears Dr. Berenice telling him not to avoid the devil but accept him. He hears her telling him to be suspicious of his friends. "Did she really say that?" he asks himself. He can smell her perfume.

The footsteps begin again, and the rolling sound. They are getting closer!

Edgar moves behind the staircase, crouches down and waits.

A spectral figure emerges out of the darkness with a long weapon in hand and trailing a larger one behind.

It is Tiger Tilley.

She does not see him and walks past. Edgar rises. He can see the smooth white stretch of her slim but muscular neck, so vulnerable there with her face turned away. He will take off her head indeed! He will bury her on the grounds here, her skull resting between her feet. He raises the sword to strike.

22

Friends and Enemies

t the last minute, Edgar hesitates, and Tiger Tilley turns so quickly that he cannot react. She raises Alfred Thorne's incredible rifle, equipped with its remarkable expanding bullet, squeezes the trigger and hits a target a few inches from Edgar's hand, exploding the sword into a thousand pieces, the shards rocketing through this floor of the house like so many bits of a supernatural bomb. The sound is earsplitting.

Both Edgar and Tiger stand there speechless in the wake of the explosion. It slowly recedes. Then she smiles.

"You thought you might get the drop on me, Edgar Brim? Me? No one gets the drop on Tiger Tilley." Her grin makes her appear possessed.

"What are you going to do?" he asks.

"To you?"

"Yes. And after that."

"Well, what were you going to do to ME?"

"Are you in league with him?"

She raises the rifle and points it at his head. Edgar Brim has a strange sensation. His heart is pounding, but he isn't just frightened by his imminent death, it is who is going to be the cause of it. His dearest friend. This is not like any story he has ever read. It is the worst nightmare imaginable, to be slaughtered by the one you trusted, the one you loved, and whom you thought loved you. He imagines the bullet coming at him, entering his skull, exploding his brain. He wonders what it will feel like after that.

"Do what you will," he says.

At that instant, they hear someone descending the stairs directly above them. This clever person is already halfway down, no more than fifteen feet away. He or she has approached with great stealth.

"Move a muscle and I will shoot you, Miss Tilley," says a voice.

Tiger remains motionless, her rifle still pointed at Edgar who looks up and sees Andrew Lawrence approaching on the stairs in a crouch, his old-fashioned shotgun in hand, its barrel pointed directly at Tiger's head.

"I know you are quick, as quick as lightning, but my finger is on the trigger. Dare you test me? Like you, I have lived a difficult life and been on the streets, so make an intelligent decision about your situation. You of all people should know the correct response."

Tiger drops the rifle to the floor.

"Wise choice."

"Why are you doing this?" asks Edgar.

Lawrence swings the gun around to him. "She is not to be trusted. And neither are you." The handle of the sword is still in

Edgar's hand. "What were you doing here in the darkness?" asks Lawrence. "Were you trying to kill your friend? What sense does that make? You are mad, Edgar Brim."

"And you?" says Tiger. "What sense are you making? Are we your enemies? Are you in league with him?"

Edgar looks at her. "I just asked YOU that."

As the two former friends stare at each other, there is a dull thud and Lawrence tumbles down the stairs, as limp as a rag. Annabel Thorne comes into view directly behind Lawrence, with an iron candlestick in her hand.

"Silly fool," she says.

"Mother!" cries Edgar.

"Silly fool!" she shouts at him.

"Mrs. Thorne?" says Tiger.

"Another idiot," says Annabel, pointing at her. "I assume you are the famous Tiger Tilley, though not so admirable right now!" She descends the stairs and turns at the bottom to confront Edgar. She looks down at the sword handle in his hand. "What were you doing? Considering killing your friend?"

"Considering?" snaps Tiger. "That is an understatement."

Annabel strides over to her and slaps her in the face. "Hold your tongue! I know perfectly well what YOU intended with that horrible rifle Alfred invented!"

"Nice to meet you too," says Tiger.

Edgar smirks.

Annabel turns, takes a few steps back and slaps him across the face too.

"What the devil is going on here!" she shouts.

"I—," begins Edgar.

"Oh, be quiet, Edgar! I was not really asking you. You have nothing to say at this moment."

"I—," says Tiger.

"And neither do you!" She looks down at Andrew Lawrence. "Or you!" He groans, still unconscious. She keeps looking down at him. "Did you actually think I would consider a relationship with you so soon after Alfred's death?"

"Mother—"

"Hold your tongue, Edgar, or I shall cut it off!" Her face is red and Edgar clams up. "I took the liberty of insinuating myself into your life, my boy, after you returned from Scotland with that look of desperation in your eyes again. All the anxiety that you had as a child, which I thought I had helped you, in my own little way, shake off somewhat, appeared to have returned. I knew something was going on, something that has been a part of your life for some time now, which you have kept from me. I knew you would never tell me, since you are so good at keeping things inside. I befriended this fellow lying at my feet here, suspicious as I was of him and his intentions, and got closer to you and your troubles through him. As your mother, as one who knows your very soul, I could tell he was the sort of fellow in whom you would confide. I could see he was working on you, right off the bat. He has told me a great deal about what he now knows of your life and situation, things I knew I could get out of him if I arranged the right set of circumstances and approached him cleverly."

"But he told me he kept my secrets from you!"

"That tongue is still in danger of being removed, young man! I am speaking!" She glances down at Lawrence again. "He is a man who is not without troubles himself. He had a very difficult time as a child, even more difficult and desperate than I think he has told me. In reaction to that, he has spent his whole life being manly and careful, paying little attention to his feelings and concentrating on his own wealth. He is good fellow inside, I think, but he was susceptible to the charms of Dr. Berenice, who seems to have influenced him somehow and perhaps you as well, my son. What in the world did she tell you? You know that I know something of these alienists, these mind navigators, and the power they might have over someone if they wanted. That is why I have been reading that young Professor Freud fellow. Do you know that uncontrolled fear induces paranoia? I understand that you told Dr. Berenice that you were being pursued by the devil?"

"He is," says little William Shakespeare, who has come to the top of the stairs. "We all are!" Allen Brim appears behind him.

"I trust that this is the strange little man who takes the great bard's name, who keeps telling you that monsters are in pursuit of you? Mr. Lawrence has filled me in on that too."

"The monsters *are* pursuing us!" cries Shakespeare, "and each one is worse!"

Lucy now appears at the top of the stairs. "I heard a horrible bang!" she exclaims. She stares down at the scene below her.

"There is a good deal of truth to what the little man is saying, Mrs. Thorne," says Tiger. "There are indeed aberrations about on the earth, monsters if you want to call them that, some glimpsed in distant versions of themselves in story books. Circumstances have drawn us into battle with a few of them. That is true."

"Even if that WERE the case, it does not mean the devil himself is after you now!" cries Annabel.

"We cannot say that for certain," says Edgar. "Ask my father."

"Pardon me?" asks Annabel. "Do not speak of Alfred Thorne in the present tense. That is cruel, Edgar. He is gone."

"No, Mother, my real father. Ask him yourself!"

"Ask him?"

"He is right here. He will tell you how it all began."

"Where?"

"Where . . . what?"

"Where is your father?" asks Annabel, her voice sounding shaky.

"Why, he is at the top of the stairs, glaring at you."

Annabel looks up the stairs, then back at her adopted son. "Edgar . . . if you ever again so much as mention the fact that your father is alive and talking to you, I will get a switch and give you a thrashing, even if you are thirty years older than you are now! DO YOU HEAR ME?"

"Yes . . . Mother."

Allen Brim slowly fades from the top of the stairs, and Edgar feels as though he is awakening from a long sleep. When he looks at his mother, her face seems clearer, sharper to his senses.

"This Freud fellow talks about something he calls *delusions* and he also discusses a phenomenon he terms *suggestion* and, of course, *hypnosis*. Someone is playing with your mind. It may be Dr. Berenice or Mr. Lawrence or . . ."

"The devil!" shouts Shakespeare.

Annabel takes a step toward him and he scurries up the stairs to the top and gets behind Lucy.

"Mother!" cries Edgar, stopping her in her tracks. "You may be correct about many things. It does seem that I may have allowed myself to spiral inward . . . somewhat . . . perhaps to be taken in by delusions . . . of a sort." He wonders about Dr. Berenice's perfume, its strange odor, how it lingered on his clothes. He thinks of her holding her warm hand tightly to the side of his head, her talk of the black magic skills that Morley had taught her, her suggestion that he encounter his dead father and consort with the devil in his head. "Perhaps I have been guided by expert hands that mean me and others harm, people who have discovered things about us and found the right circumstances to manipulate us, and thus may have pitted us against each other, but there is something in all of this, someone, who is not playing at tricks and who is no delusion."

"What do you mean?"

Lawrence rouses and gets to a seating position. He rubs his temple. "Oh, my head," he moans.

"There is a man named—"

"MORLEY!" cries Shakespeare.

"And he is real."

"He is DEAD and he is LIVING!" adds the little man.

"Explain yourself, my boy."

"Alex Morley. He believes he is Satan."

"HE IS!"

"That is preposterous!" Annabel cries.

"We did not believe there could be a revenant on earth, a vampire, or a Grendel, or a human being made by the hand of man."

Annabel's eyes widen. "Is . . . is that what the last one was?"

"Yes," says Lucy quietly at the top of the stairs. "It is certain."

"Morley turned on a light with his mind," whispers Shakespeare, "and moved an inkwell across my table!"

"He put our friend Jonathan to death by taking the form of the hag from my nightmares and then using her to enter his brain or his heart or his bloodstream, employing some strange power, a sort of electricity of fear," says Edgar. "He turned off the light inside our dear friend!" Beside him, Tiger cannot stop herself from gasping. "Only one force could inject that sort of terror into someone."

"And now he is dead . . . but he is still here!" sobs Shakespeare. "He is the devil, I tell you, HE IS SATAN HIMSELF! He is in all the great stories, all the great books! He is the greatest villain of all time, the greatest monster! Morley recognized himself! I told him about the aberrations and he recognized himself! It lit up a realization inside him! He is Satan, I tell you, and now he knows it!"

"Nonsense," says Annabel, but she says it so softly they can barely hear her.

"He killed himself in a bloody mess . . . several days ago," says Edgar. "We know that for a fact. We also know that he has spoken to people in person, written to them, since he died."

"Someone is here," says Lucy suddenly.

"What do you mean?" asks Tiger, picking up the rifle again.

Lucy Lear has hearing like no one else in the group. Tiger knows that if she senses something, it is no delusion.

"Downstairs."

Lawrence staggers to his feet. "I feel as though apologies are in order. First, to this lovely lady, Mrs. Thorne. I fear I have been a cad. I know not why. I thought I was long past that. Please accept my sincere regrets. I have also harbored ill feelings toward others in this company and—"

"Oh, close your mouth!" says Annabel.

"Yes, my lady," he says, glowing at her. She looks back at him and Edgar thinks he detects a slight smile on her face. Then they all hear the sound and her smile instantly vanishes.

"Downstairs, indeed," says Tiger, and she turns toward the stairs with the rifle in hand, trailing the cannon, moving quietly but on the double.

"Why does she always get to have all the weapons?" asks Lucy.

"You try to get one from her," says Edgar.

At the stairs, however, Tiger lets Edgar and Lucy help her, giving up the cannon for them to carry, so she can hold the gun at the ready.

They all descend, Tiger out front.

It takes them a long time to go down this single set of wide stairs. It is a good thing that the steps are covered in rugs and that the beautiful polished wooden balustrade is thick and easy to grip with trembling hands.

They reach the ground floor with Tiger still in the lead and her rifle pointed this way and that in the darkness, the half-moon in the windows casting shadows everywhere here too. They head toward the big living room. Edgar and William Shakespeare know that there was a dim light of some sort here, but when they reach the room, it is dark and they can barely make out the sofas, the love seat with the knitting or the animal heads on the walls.

"Someone has turned off the light," says Edgar. "It was on when we were here just a short time ago."

"Did you actually see a lamp that was lighted?" asks Lucy.

"Perhaps your father turned it off," says Tiger.

Edgar wishes she could see the intensity of the glare he gives her.

"Quiet," says Annabel. They all listen. She squints into the dimness in front of them. "It seems deserted here now."

Their path lit only by the moonlight, they carefully make their way farther into the room, look around as much as they can, and still finding no one, gather on the seats, Lawrence groaning as he lowers himself near Annabel, Lucy sitting next to Edgar, and Tiger on a love seat alone, pointing the rifle into the darkness. Shakespeare remains standing in the middle of the room, as if ready for escape at a second's notice.

There is silence for a while. If there was an intruder down here, then he, she, or it, truly seems to be gone.

"Perhaps we can try to make sense of things now," says Annabel.

"Well," says Lucy quietly, "I need to explain my actions. We all do." She takes a deep breath. "You see, I was only trying to help. I thought if I left home without you two . . ." She looks at Edgar and Tiger. "Maybe it would help somehow. Maybe that was not rational. After Jon's death, I was terrified, though I eventually tried to pretend I was all right, but I could not get away from the terror and it made me so anxious I just had to flee. It was an awful feeling. I had to run . . . somewhere, I did not know where . . . and I had to do it secretly. It was almost as if I felt it wasn't just the devil who was after me, but you two as well. I was ill with it. Once I got out onto the streets though, late that night, the air against my skin seemed to make me come to my senses, at least a little. I could not go back, admit what I had done, I thought that would just cause more problems, create more suspicion among us, so I went to the hospital to see Mr. Lawrence. He had seemed so kind and his offer of help had stuck with me. It was almost as if he was calling to me. He was there even though it was the middle of the night, and Mrs. Thorne was with him—"

"He had asked me to come away with him," says Annabel.

"I am sorry," says Lawrence. "I am not sure what I was thinking. I needed this knock on the head!"

"And I was fine with that," says Annabel. "I can look after myself, Edgar, and the more suspicious Sir Andrew's actions were, the better, since to my way of thinking that meant that he was doing something that might shed some light on your situation. He was telling me more and more as time went on."

"Dr. Berenice has been counseling me," says Lawrence, still holding his head in his hands. "I have some difficulties still, about my childhood, all that I saw, the poverty, other things, the people I stepped on to get ahead and now have such regrets about. I often try to forget all of that, not admit that any of it ever happened. I . . ." He looks around at his friends and drops his head. "I am a bit of a sham . . . I was a thug in my youth, my hard-bitten youth, in Ireland. I was a criminal, to tell the truth. I made the beginnings of my fortune that way, by threatening people, hurting people . . . even killing. That is long past me now. Once I came to England, I began a long road to being a better person. I try with the very fiber of my being to be a good man, at least most of the time. I changed my name, I invested in the hospital, the world's greatest, and I help it with everything I have, my finances, my soul. I want to heal people, like I learned to heal myself." He pauses. "Berenice found out about me. She asked me many personal questions in casual conversation when we first knew each other, rooted out some of the details of my past and then told me she could help me learn to live with the difficult parts. It was magical, how she did it. She found out more when she had me on her psychiatrist's sofa. I . . . I realize now as we speak of our situation . . . that she may have been using me. I believe she made suggestions to me. She suggested I draw in Edgar Brim, I know that, his mother, his circle. As I say, I am not sure exactly how she did it, though I recall she often focused on my guilt, which haunts my life. She must have discovered that and gone right to it, right into that pain to use me. It would be terrible if any of this information about my past ever got out." He takes the monocle, tosses it on the floor and grinds it to dust. "I was somehow compelled to do some things that were not right, especially in squiring about and compromising Mrs. Thorne . . . whom I adore, who is a fine and beautiful lady."

Annabel blushes.

"As I was saying, there they were," says Lucy, "in the middle of the night in Mr. Lawrence's office. They told me they were going out to his country estate, that it would be safer there. They said I should come with them. When I suggested to Mr. Lawrence that perhaps I shouldn't leave Tiger and Edgar behind, he said that he felt Tiger was acting strangely and I could not trust her, and that Edgar could fend for himself, that his stories about the devil and the eight-foot man were worrisome anyway. He said Edgar was dangerously unhinged. I argued with him but he said the doctor, a specialist in the hospital, had confirmed it all. I was still feeling terrorized too. He said I should escape with them and save myself."

"I am sorry for—"

"I thought that a little strange," says Annabel, "to say the least, but it thickened the plot of your situation, Edgar. I even made it appear to them, to Sir Andrew especially, that I too was deeply worried about your sanity, and suggested that maybe you could not entirely be trusted. I told Sir Andrew that my son had begun to frighten me. It seemed to embolden him."

"I couldn't believe she said that," says Lucy, "but I was in an awful state and beginning to accept almost anything. You will do that when the devil is after you . . . or in you."

"He isn't," says Annabel.

"Yes he is!" says Shakespeare.

"You were talking to your father, Edgar, your dead father!" says Tiger suddenly. "He was walking around the streets with you! I heard you speaking to him at the Lears' door, even though you pretended to me that you were just talking to yourself. When I went into Lucy's room that night and she was gone, when I realized she had run from us and that I was alone with you, mad as you were, spouting outrageous things, I knew I had to deceive you, say she was still in her room. I had no idea what I should do next. I have always been able to summon courage, but a sort of terror was growing in me as well and it was making me think awful things. It was a horrible feeling, unlike anything I had ever experienced. You must know I was traumatized by Jon's death!" Her eyes fill with tears. "I wanted to take you to that devil-worship room on Thomas Street, Edgar, and do something . . . perhaps to you, eliminate you . . . I don't know."

"I felt that, deep down."

"The day we were in that room, I heard the footsteps too, the hoofbeats!"

He nods at her, but does not say anything. Then they smile at each other. Edgar wants to embrace her and she looks like she wants the same.

"When we got here," says Lawrence, "the place was empty! I have a dozen servants in this estate. They were all gone! It was as if something had not just harmed or scared them off but made them vanish, destroyed them!"

"It is a trap," says Shakespeare. "We have been drawn here for a purpose!"

"The three of us went upstairs and secluded ourselves in a room there," says Lucy, "and we talked, everyone suspicious of everyone else, though not saying it, and terrified of anyone who might be coming here. It was as if our talk was getting darker as the hours passed. You, Edgar, and you, Tiger, because you were not with us, started to seem more like our greatest enemies, in league with whatever was after us. It is amazing now to think of it, of what possessed us! We wondered about the weapons, who had them. I was glad I had this." She pulls her grandfather's big kukri knife, nearly as long as a sword, curved and as sharp as a guillotine, up from her side. She had been carrying it all along, holding it close to her leg. She drops her head. "I was ready to use this on anyone!"

Suddenly, the lights come on in the room. There was no click from an electric light switch, no hiss from gas. Everything, however, instantly illuminates in an intensely bright glow. It hurts their eyes and they all look down and shield themselves from it with their hands.

When they try to look up, they begin to realize that rows of people surround them, gathered there in dead silence. There are black-robed men with shaved heads on chairs at one end of the room, an eight-foot man with his gigantic legs propped nearly up to his chin sitting at their center, a big thug with a big black beard and squashed nose beside him. There are rows of women against the other three walls, all with long luxurious hair, dressed in plain brown dresses that reach the floor, fitting them tightly to emphasize their shapes. Sitting in the center of them at the end of the room opposite from the men is Dr. Berenice. She holds a portrait of Alexander Morley in her hands.

23

Revelations

Edgar stares at Berenice, but she seems incapable of looking back at him. She avoids his eyes and gazes down at the portrait. Lucy and Lawrence gape at the sight in disbelief, Annabel gasps, and little Shakespeare drops to the floor holding his hands over his big head. "Thou art boils, plague sores!" he cries, but there is no force to his words.

Tiger leaps to her feet and tries to train the rifle on everyone at once, pivoting around, locking onto one head and then the other until she settles on the eight-foot man, who is now rising way up to his feet. Tiger raises the rifle as he looms above her. His red face seems small on his gigantic body, but his features are remarkably sharp—thick, black eyebrows on a face caked with makeup, his shaved head somehow glistening in the dim light. There are markings on his black robe, red symbols representing eyes and crosses and pyramids, the number 666 evident right over his heart. He twirls a huge black cane in his hand and pulls back his robe to reveal his long black trouser legs.

Edgar turns toward him. "Mephistopheles," he gasps, "the servant of Satan!"

"Fire at will," says the tall man to Tiger Tilley in a deep voice. She hesitates. "You may kill me, that is true, but the holy beast is immortal. You cannot kill him as you murdered the others. He is alive though he is dead. He is in the air and in your brains."

Tiger fires. The expanding bullet strikes the eight-foot man below the left knee and explodes his leg. He instantly collapses, falling face forward onto the floor, hitting it with the crack of bone on hardwood.

"Change your mind?" asks Tiger.

There is no blood, however, no shards of bone or splatters of ligament or muscle against the wall, at least not from the tall man's leg. The bullet, which has made a crater in the wall as a small meteor might, has simply blown off a short wooden extension, a stilt covered by the bottom part of one huge trouser leg. The tall man groans and lifts his head. There is blood dripping from his face and his nose is smashed against his cheek, but he smiles and sits back in his chair, the other extension still on his right leg. He is a tall man indeed, but not eight feet. He smiles and licks the blood that is dripping from his nostrils toward his mouth.

"Shoot again, abominable young lady who takes the form of a male; shoot a hundred times, a thousand times, a billion. You will kill us, but you will never slay what torments you and your friends! We brought you here. We have you!"

Tiger trains the gun on his head, and then turns it on the other men, all those shaved heads, all those black-robed bodies dressed similarly to Mephistopheles. Then Tiger turns the weapon on the women, all looking passive, no expressions on their faces, their backs arched and strong against their chairs, their chests thrust out. She focuses on the woman who appears to be their leader, clutching the portrait of Morley.

"No!" says Lawrence, "that is Dr. Berenice!"

"Then," says Tiger, "she needs to speak, explain herself and all of this, or I will take her to hell, which is where it seems she belongs. We may not be able to defeat the demon that haunts us, but at least I will have the satisfaction of destroying his wife!"

"I am NOT his wife!" shouts Berenice.

"Then, what?" asks Edgar, getting to his feet and taking a few steps toward her.

"I believed in him," says Berenice. "I still believe in him."

"What . . . do you believe? Who is he?"

"SATAN!" cries Shakespeare.

There is a murmur of approval from the others but Berenice says nothing at first.

"It seems it may be true," she says eventually.

"Seems?" asks Edgar.

"I do not know if I want it to be true, but I know he is dead, and I know he is somehow here. I told you that he came to understand the power of the mind. We human beings, most of us, have no idea what rests within our brains and in our souls. He knew. Why did he know, why did he understand when no one else did? That is an important question. He may be the chosen one. There was a time when I thought he loved me and that intoxicated me. But as you see, there are many more who love him." She glances at the other women and does not look pleased. "He taught me things and then he abandoned me, but he said it was because he had higher goals . . . it seems he may have been correct. Neurology was just child's play for him, then the occult and black magic were much the same. He joined the Order and then ascended past it so quickly that he believed he had powers. Kinetic strength, astral projection and an understanding of the universe . . . of evil . . . and perhaps now . . . much more."

"It is reality," says Mephistopheles.

"Reality," say all the women and men in unison.

"He slaughtered himself," says Mephistopheles, "in order to prove who he is. He told us he would return. He said he would live in our minds, in other minds, as alive as he has always been since before the beginning of human life. We saw him perform miracles many times. He is not dead. He is Satan. He is immortal. Seek and you will find him."

Edgar notices a man sitting two seats from Mephistopheles. The man stares straight ahead, his head shaved, looking long and lean with a skeletal appearance. He seems familiar and Edgar struggles to place him. Then, it comes to him. He could easily pass for Mr. Sprinkle, at least as that apparition appeared in William Shakespeare's apartment not long ago.

"He used me," says Berenice softly.

"What did you say?" asks Edgar.

"He used me to mold you and your friends," she says, staring at them. "He discovered who you were, Edgar, and your susceptibilities, your knowledge of monsters. He found you through little William Shakespeare. He sent me to the hospital to convince them they needed someone like me, where I could do what was required.

He knew he and I could influence you there, Edgar. I used Andrew Lawrence and his low Irish birth and his secrets, and he delivered you to me and attached himself to your mother. Alex used the power of his unparalleled mind, the electricity of fear, the use of tinges of mescaline and other potions in my perfume and drinks, and the psychological techniques I could bring to bear to influence all of you, to make you think yourselves insane, to make you distrust each other, hate each other . . . want to kill one another."

"That is nonsense . . . the last part," says Lucy.

"Did you not do all of that? Did he not locate the evil inside you all? Did he not locate the truth?"

Edgar wants to object, but he knows she is correct.

"You were brought here to destroy each other," says Berenice.

"But we are all still here!" exclaims Tiger.

"Yet he made you do—" begins Mephistopheles.

"We are all here!" shouts Tiger again. "We did not, in the end, turn on each other. We are all alive and united, and we will kill him. We will destroy Alexander Morley, just as we did Grendel and the revenant vampire and the Frankenstein creature."

"How?" asks Mephistopheles.

"Yes . . ." says Berenice, her hand on Morley's face in the portrait. "He is still inside you, not finished with you. How will you kill him?"

"Will you shoot him?" shouts another man.

"Will you hunt him down?" cries a woman.

"He cannot be found!" they all shout. "And yet he is here!"

"He is somewhere," says Edgar quietly.

"He made a covenant with us," says Mephistopheles. "He told us what he would do, how he would destroy his earthly body, how he would experiment with you all and prove who he is, and then return in his darkest glory."

"Return!" shout all of the others in unison.

"It was all just tricks!" shouts Annabel at the women. "Can you not see that?"

"He used you!" says Lucy, glaring at Berenice. "You said it yourself! He used you as a woman the way a twisted MORTAL man would!" Berenice cannot look at her and instead stares at Morley's portrait, gripping the frame with shaking hands. It seems as though she wants to smash it.

"She is right!" cries Edgar. "All the things he did to all of us were just tricks, HUMAN tricks, not Satan's. Yet you believe in him." He finds himself staring at Berenice, who will not look back. He turns on Mephistopheles. "You are NOT an eight-foot man!" he cries. "You and he are shams!"

Mephistopheles grips his chair, pushes himself up onto his one remaining stilt and balances there, towering over them. Lucy steps forward and with one mighty swing of her grandfather's kukri blade—the same one Edgar drove into the chest of the revenant vampire and of the same sort that killed Count Dracula—cuts Mephistopheles down, slicing off the extension of his other leg below the knee. He falls again though this time he gets his hands out to protect himself. He glares up at them.

"You had best not test him!" he screams.

"Best not!" shout the others. Hilda Berenice says nothing.

"That devil-worship room is just a show," says Tiger, "the red liquid in the jars simply dyed water, the huge black feathers manufactured and those footsteps just one of you acting a part to frighten us. The posthumous letter to Shakespeare was written long before Morley died, wasn't it? And his appearance at the Crypto-Anthropology Society rooms after his supposed death either the work of a man dressed up to look like him or—"

"No," whispers Shakespeare, "it was him!"

"—or he is, in fact, not dead! His death faked!"

"He is dead," says Mephistopheles. "He butchered himself in a ritual esoteric act. An ancient Far Eastern rite. You may question other things, but he is dead. I saw the result." He shivers and stares at Berenice and then into the distance. "He has survived, risen." Mephistopheles looks at Shakespeare. "But I did not know that he may have gone to visit this little human being . . . after that. When did you see him?" he asks.

"Two days ago," says Shakespeare.

Mephistopheles appears to turn pale even under his red makeup. There is a shriek from the group, then shouts of glee and applause.

Berenice just smiles.

"The snakes!" shouts Edgar in the din. "Which one of you arranged that?"

"Snakes?" asks Mephistopheles, his voice shaking now. "Snakes? When?"

"Which one of you," repeats Edgar, turning around in a mad swivel and surveying all of his enemies, "put those snakes in our beds? A week ago today!"

There is silence.

"He DIED the day before!" cries Mephistopheles. "Praise the holy beast! He is real! The covenant is fulfilled!"

It is the second time he has used that word, but this time it has meaning for Edgar Brim.

"*Covenant!*" he says to himself. He looks at Lucy and takes her hand, then turns to Tiger and takes hers too. "I know where he is!" he says.

24

To Thomas Street

Edgar rushes out of the room toward the front door with Tiger and Lucy, and Annabel and Lawrence follow, the chairman rolling Alfred Thorne's remarkable cannon behind him. Shakespeare pauses for an instant and then scurries in pursuit.

"You know nothing!" shouts Mephistopheles behind them. "The prophecy will come to pass. You will all destroy each other! The electricity of fear that HE has his finger on will do it. HIS powers will do it from the afterlife. He will prove who he is, a monster, a holy beast beyond compare. We shall live under his guidance. We shall live in lust, greed and material gain. We shall please ourselves under Satan's coming reign. We shall do what we will! We shall put fear in all who do not follow! His influence will grow everywhere. Seek him, Edgar Brim, and he will annihilate you! He is itching to test his powers!"

Edgar leads his friends out onto the lawn in the dim light of the half-moon.

"We need to get to Thomas Street, London, immediately. Morley is there, and I think I know exactly where." He glances back and sees Mephistopheles, Berenice and the others coming to the big front doors of Lawrence Lodge. They are talking animatedly.

"No!" cries Shakespeare. "Morley will destroy us if we seek him! That is what he wants!"

"I wonder what they did with all the servants?" asks Lucy.

"We need to go fast?" asks Annabel. "In the night? Through the countryside?"

"If we only had my horseless carriage," says Lawrence. "It won't tire like horses and I know how to make it travel extremely fast."

"We have it," says Shakespeare.

"Pardon me?"

"We brought your motorcar here," says Edgar, "but the batteries died near the Devil's Punch Bowl."

"Not to worry," says Lawrence. "Come with me!"

He leads them to his stables where he gets Edgar and Tiger to help him lift six fully charged batteries into a dogcart. Lawrence then lets out all the horses in the stable but one and smacks them on their hindquarters, sending them off into the forest. Then they hitch the remaining horse to the cart, lift Shakespeare onto it with the batteries and head back onto the lawn, and then over the water and across the causeway in the darkness. Morley's followers are still at the front of the house, gesturing toward them. Then Mephistopheles rushes to the stables.

Edgar and his friends move faster, jogging along beside the dogcart and horse.

"It will take them a while to realize that we have sent the horses away, but then they will be after us!" says Lawrence. They pick up their pace.

Once they are over the causeway, Edgar gazes back at Lawrence Lodge in the moonlight. Glancing down into the dark pond in front of it, he sees the building's twin in the water. The image shimmers, and for an instant, it looks as though there is a crack in the center of the house, and as the wind blows across the water, the building seems to crumble and implode as it appears to crash to the ground.

When they are out of Hindhead, the six of them barely glance at the Devil's Punch Bowl beneath them to their left. Instead, they rush forward, seeking the location of the horseless carriage. Annabel runs with them, lifting her skirts, as quick as the rest, in fact, competing with Tiger for the front of the pack.

They find the vehicle in the trees, pull out the dead batteries and replace them with the fully charged ones. The chairman of the London Hospital produces some matches and lights the two lamps at the front of the car and the one in back, then they leap in and Lawrence, the expert driver, takes the tiller bar. Annabel is beside him on the front seat and the others are jammed into the rear bench, Edgar in the middle with Shakespeare on his knee.

Lawrence has a way of building the speed of the machine by slowly moving the floor lever forward as it gains momentum and somehow gets it to go at a devilish rate, forcing the lever so far toward the front of the carriage that it seems almost pushed through the metal. They absolutely fly along the road, bumping and banging on the rough surface, humming away, almost bouncing out of their seats, hanging on for dear life. Edgar imagines the speed they must be going. *Nearly twenty miles an hour!* He tries to suppress the fear that this is creating within him. He notices that the others, even Tiger, are tight faced and anxious.

It seems to take barely an hour to get to the London suburbs, and soon after that, they are across the Battersea Bridge and the River Thames. Crowds increase as they advance, as do the numbers of horses and carriages, and the sounds and smells. Lawrence seems to pay all of it no mind, expertly swerving in and out of traffic, doing even better than his and Edgar's previous trip, moving along the river, and then cutting up through the busy parts of the city on a straight line toward the East End. Surely Morley's people cannot follow them at this pace. It is getting late now and play and concertgoers, men in black-and-white evening suits and women in colorful long dresses, many pursued by drunks and mongers, are still about. Lawrence eludes them all. They reach Whitechapel Road and the car dies, so they leave it pulled off to the side and race through the dangerous arteries to Thomas Street. The door with the black horns is unlocked again. They climb the stairs quickly, Tiger with the rifle, Edgar and Lawrence carrying the cannon, but when they come to the doors at the top floor, none of them reaches out for the handle. They pause. Shakespeare is hanging back.

"I . . . Don Quixote . . . cannot go in there!" he whispers. "If that terrible man is inside, he will glare at me and I will be taken straight to hell!"

"He is just a man," says Annabel, "and they were all tricks."

"Then, you open the door," says Shakespeare.

She cannot make herself do it.

"There have been strange things happening, some that cannot be explained, we must admit," says Edgar. "Even Morley's followers were surprised by some of the things we told them. So . . . we must be honest, fooling ourselves will not help us here . . . we are about to face another monster."

"The worst one," says Shakespeare.

Annabel puts her hand over her mouth.

"If the Bible is right," says Edgar, "it could be a dark angel, an unearthly lion, a dragon or a beast—"

"That's what his followers called him! The holy beast!" cries Shakespeare. "What if he has transformed in death?"

"Whatever form this demon takes," says Edgar, "we must face it."

"We have this," says Tiger, pointing the rifle at the door.

"And this," says Lawrence, nodding at the cannon.

"We have never unleashed it on a creature," says Lucy. "It is incredibly powerful. Maybe this weapon can blow our monster apart!"

Edgar Brim's mind is temporarily far away, at war with itself. He fears that he knows what their greatest enemy really is—not an angel with black wings, a lion or a three-headed beast, not a gigantic red demon with cloven hooves. He remembers the passage in the Bible where Satan, invisible and undescribed, confronted the Lord and seemed to enter his brain. Perhaps it is truly inside their minds. The devil was there for a while, there is no doubt. That means it can return. Edgar knows where to look for Satan.

"I will open the door," says Lucy.

"And I will go in first," says Tiger. "Take off the head! That is what Professor Lear always said! We have triumphed before and we will do so again. Mr. Lawrence, we will open both doors wide, so ready the cannon behind me, fire it if you must, even if you have to blast through my body. Should nothing come, roll it in slowly and be prepared for anything!"

Lucy reaches for the doors and begins to open them wide, but before she can pull them completely back, Edgar steps through, directly in the path of Tiger's rifle and Lawrence's cannon.

He looks up at the box on top of the pillar at the front of the room.

25

The Thing in the Box

"Edgar!" cries Tiger and darts after him and pulls him back. The others rush in, dispersing to either side, giving Lawrence a clean shot with the cannon from behind them. He points it into the space. Tiger veers to the left and puts her back against the wall as she moves toward the front of the room, her rifle cocked and aimed here and there.

The dim room is as cold as before, and silent, as if waiting for the creature to explode onto the scene, the interior lit in the same way as before, with candles everywhere. The jars of red liquid are still on the floor, lining the center aisle of a dozen rows of large and elegant wooden chairs. Images of pyramids and inner eyes remain on the walls. That big black throne still sits on the stage.

"There is no one here," says Lucy.

"No one human," whispers Shakespeare.

"If Morley's followers have been at Lawrence Lodge since yesterday," says Annabel, ". . . then who lit these candles?"

Andrew Lawrence wheels the cannon up the aisle, his eyes wide and alert.

Tiger is listening for sounds between the walls, the footsteps of a cloven beast, but there is nothing.

Edgar gathers himself and ventures to the center of the room, stepping in front of the cannon again, much to his friends' dismay. He is not surveying his surroundings like the others. He is still staring up at the ornately decorated oblong box at the top of the dark pillar near the stage. It is almost touching the ceiling, and its appearance is as he remembers it: a sort of Ark of the Covenant.

"Covenant," says Edgar quietly.

"What?" asks Lucy.

"That was the word that Mephistopheles used. He said that Morley made a covenant with them." He examines the box. "No one knows where his body is? I do."

They all look up to the top of the pillar.

"In the Bible, it is said that God left the Ten Commandments in that sort of box. In other words, he left his instructions to humanity there. Morley is Satan. His body, its miracle of defeating death, IS his instruction to humanity, his covenant. His very existence beyond death puts the fear into others that he requires, shows them his power, his immortality. We must destroy him!" Edgar points up. "He is in there."

Tiger snaps the rifle upward and aims it at the box.

"In what form?" asks Lucy.

In the silence that ensues, they all imagine a black-winged angel or some other unimaginable beast rising from the box and descending upon them.

"We all must leave," says a voice from the shadows at the front of the room. It is a woman and she sounds terrified. Hilda Berenice emerges into the light.

"How . . . long have you been here?" Annabel asks.

"I arrived before you did."

"That is not possible," says Tiger, who has now trained the rifle on Berenice.

"It is impossible. You are correct." The mind doctor looks as white as a ghost and she is trembling. "When you raced away from Lawrence Lodge, I prayed that I could get here before you. I prayed to Alex . . . to Satan . . . and here I am. I do not know how. He spoke often of astral projection, in other words of traveling through space with the power of your mind. We must all leave!"

The others are not able to say anything. Edgar smells her perfume. He looks at her aging face, down at her fit young body in that tight plain dress and knows that this woman is incredibly powerful. Edgar Brim is sensitive to a fault and he can feel something indescribable emanating from her. *She would pray to no one. She has come here under her own power!* He notices that she is holding her hands in front of herself, like an actor who wants to display how they tremble.

Suddenly, Tiger runs down the aisle toward Lawrence, knocking some of the blood-filled jars over as she rushes. The liquid spills across the hardwood floor. She flings the rifle into Lucy's hands, shoves Lawrence aside and trains the cannon on the base of the pillar. "OUT OF THE WAY!" she cries. The others scatter. "Let us see what this big gun can do." She pulls the cord on the cannon, the chemicals mix and the mighty weapon fires, finally fires at an enemy target. The concussion inside the room is otherworldly, a deafening roar. Edgar imagines Alfred Thorne standing there watching his killing machine finally put into action, his pale face and dark mustache evident in the dim glow. Edgar wonders if his adoptive father would smile or frown. Annabel looks on with the same expression, as if she too is imagining her husband seeing his infernal idea unleashed.

The big cannonball rockets out of the mouth of the weapon and strikes the thick stone pillar just a few feet above the base. It slices through stone like a sword through soft skin, strikes the wall on the other side and makes a hole the size of a door. The column seems to shiver for a moment and then it begins to collapse. The covenant box at the top hovers for a second and then descends, dropping toward the floor like a bomb. It does not, however, crash through the floor, but instead sticks a perfect landing like a powerful gymnast touching down unharmed on a mat from an ethereal apparatus.

They wait for the sound to subside. Even when that has happened, no one dares to move toward the coffin. Then it rattles.

Shakespeare runs to the far end of the room and buries his head into the floor, covering himself with his hands. They can hear him praying, shouting at God to save him.

Tiger steps toward the oblong box.

"No," says Edgar, "I will do it."

He looks back at Berenice, who for an instant almost seems to be smiling. He turns and moves forthrightly toward his target. The top of the box beneath him has a lid, not fastened in any way, just set into the coffin. He reaches out and touches it. It is surprisingly warm. He waits for a reaction from it, but it sits there, an inanimate marble box. Then, Edgar starts to slide the lid away. It grinds like fingernails on a chalkboard. Edgar's heart is pounding and he dares not look in. In fact, against all sense of self-defense, he keeps his eyes shut. The others stand back, weapons ready, faces tight. The lid slides all the way across as Edgar pushes it, but when he is almost done, it seems to move on its own. Edgar opens his eyes and glances back at Berenice again. She has her hands over her mouth now, her eyes apparently filling with tears. He lets go of the lid. It balances perilously on the edge, then falls to the floor and breaks in two.

Everyone holds their breath as the sound reverberates in the room. And for a long moment, nothing happens.

Then something rises up. It lifts into the air, a mass of black eyes and teeth and horns trying to take shape, as if in search of its body. Wings try to materialize and three skulls attempt to emerge from one set of massive milk-white shoulders. It howls and reaches out its black-and-red arms, with claws for hands, to seize Edgar Brim. It struggles to do so, its body forming and fading. It shrieks again, in a scream that rattles the walls, and then it collapses back into the coffin. There is silence. Edgar wonders if the others have seen what he has. He takes a deep breath and peers into the box.

The sight is stomach turning. Alex Morley lies there dressed in black from head to foot, his hands across his chest with two long-nailed thumbs upright like knives, and a smile on his face. He is motionless. His shaved head is skeletal and his body has begun to decompose; the smell, which Edgar in his terror had not registered at first, is horrible.

"Morley is dead," says Edgar.

"No!" cries Berenice and she rushes toward the coffin and reaches in, weeping as she touches the corpse. Edgar smells that perfume again.

"He cannot be!" shouts Shakespeare, rushing up to see him too. "He visited me, wearing these very clothes! He conjured up snakes in your beds! He transported Dr. Berenice here through an act of black magic! HOW CAN YOU SAY THAT HE IS DEAD! This is simply his body! He is inside us! He is the greatest monster ever!"

"Then we must resist him!" cries Lawrence.

"If he is alive in here," says Lucy, pointing a shaking finger to her head, "then . . . we should kill ourselves."

It is quiet for almost a minute. There is only the sound of the alienist's gentle crying.

"Get that woman out of the way, Edgar," says Tiger, "and prop him up! I will put a cannonball through him. Let us see what powers he has when there is not a single piece of him left!"

"NO!" cries Berenice. She glares at Tiger, as if she wants to eat her.

As the sound of her shriek fades, there is a pounding on the stairs, like something galloping upward, and this time it is evident that everyone hears it.

Edgar and Tiger stare at each other. Neither says what they are thinking.

Hooves!

There is a rustling too, like the beat of gigantic wings. The sounds are multiplying.

"He has summoned his army!" shouts Shakespeare.

"Or it is simply him, freed from his body!" cries Berenice, and there is another smile on her lips. "I am here, Alex," she whispers, but loud enough so everyone can hear. "I am here, Satan." She drops to her knees and turns her young body and old face to the ceiling.

"PROP HIM UP!" shouts Tiger. "We must disintegrate him!" She seizes the cannon and points it at the covenant box. Her face is devil red. "This will explode his very soul!"

Edgar, however, does not make a move to lift the corpse into position or push the mind doctor aside. A realization has come over him. He looks at Berenice acting like a schoolgirl waiting for her dangerous lover.

"You!" he says to her.

Lucy stares at him in disbelief. "Edgar! Do as Tiger says and get out of the way! We must wipe him from the face of the earth! His spirit may live in his corpse! He may gain his powers from it!" She rushes toward the coffin.

The door opens with a crash behind them and they all turn to it.

The man who calls himself Mephistopheles is standing there. Slowly Morley's other followers materialize behind him, flowing into the room in robes and long dresses, staring at the covenant box on the floor, Lucy reaching out for the putrefied corpse as Edgar holds her back, and Tiger at the cannon no more than ten feet away, her weapon trained directly at the coffin.

"What are you doing?" shouts Mephistopheles.

"We are about to destroy your devil forever," snaps Tiger. "You can watch!"

Mephistopheles smiles. "Go ahead, attempt it."

"Attempt it," say Morley's followers in unison.

Tiger turns back to Edgar. "Lift him up and get yourself and them out of the way or I will blow you all to hell with him!" She reaches for the cannon's cord.

"Move," says Annabel quietly.

"No, Tiger," says Edgar, "there is no need for that."

Berenice rises up from beside the coffin, towering over Lucy and looking straight into Edgar's eyes. She places her left hand on the side of his head at his temple, its soft, warm surface feeling as though it is touching his brain inside his skull again. She runs it down his cheek to his chin and smiles, then turns and regards the others in the room, without releasing Edgar.

There is the sound of something moving on the other side of the wall. It is like a two-footed creature walking on hooves. There is no doubt. Morley's followers drop to their knees. Standing in front of them, Mephistopheles stares at the wall, transfixed.

"Come, oh holy beast . . . come Lord!"

"Get out of the way!" screams Tiger again. "I will blast him to the underworld and then I will turn this weapon on the wall if that doesn't end things. This is for Jonathan!"

"ATTEMPT!" shout the followers.

The footsteps grow louder and move closer.

"COME SATAN!" shrieks the crowd.

Edgar reaches a shaking hand up to Berenice's. Her hot flesh feels as if it will burn him. He pulls the hand off his face and steps back from her.

The footsteps stop.

"I . . ." says Edgar, his voice shaking, trying not to look into Berenice's eyes, "I know who you are."

"Of course," says Tiger, "she's—"

"And I know what that is," he adds, pointing at the coffin. "It is merely the rotting corpse of a man named Alexander Morley, a misguided human being with an ego the size of this room, who actually believed that he was Satan in the flesh." He points at Berenice. "There is your devil!"

"Nonsense," she says, but not with much feeling.

"You want me to believe that Morley is the devil, don't you, Dr. Berenice? You want all of us, even these pitiful people at the door, to believe it. You want us to blow him sky-high and believe we are done with him. That way, we will not know that it is you. You have been behind all of this. If we believe that this man is the culprit then you can go on doing what you do, in anonymity, like the monster you are."

"You are not a fool, Edgar Brim," says Berenice with a smile. She reaches a hand out for him but he slaps it away.

"You learned about William Shakespeare and his hag phenomenon pamphlets through Alex Morley. You learned about us. It was you who began to believe that *you* were like the creatures we hunted, more than human. Morley's claims were always nonsense to you."

"Not necessarily. He may indeed be what he thinks he is . . . but I am more."

There is a gasp from the crowd behind Mephistopheles, who stares at Berenice, his mouth wide open.

"You were in Scotland," says Edgar to the alienist.

"At your door, whispering that the hag on your chest was the devil," she says quietly.

"It was a woman's voice. You may even have been in Spitsbergen, howling in the arctic air." Berenice merely smiles. "You got yourself into the London Hospital, into Andrew Lawrence's life and heart, and into mine, and my friends'. You entered our unconscious. It is you who really understands the power of the human mind."

"And the gateway to its control . . . fear. The electricity of fear!"

"It was you, really you, on my chest in my bedroom at Thorne House, with your long dark hair flowing down, your breath like strange perfume. Beasley saw you. You brought the snakes too."

Edgar can see and hear it now as if it were happening at this instant. He hears someone gently waking him, his door open and close, her distinctive floating footsteps descending the stairs, and he sees the lurid green skin of the snake writhing in his bed.

"AH!" he cries out.

"I am inside you," says Berenice.

Edgar shakes his head. "Not if I know about it, about you. That is how I will defeat you."

"We shall see."

"It was you who wrote the note to William Shakespeare in Morley's hand after he died . . . and it was you who appeared in Drury Lane the next day."

"No!" cries Shakespeare, "I saw him."

"I made you see him," says Berenice, glaring at him. "I was him right before your eyes." The little man shrinks back. "I can do it again!"

"You did not pray to Alex Morley to come here from Hindhead in an instant, you did it yourself!"

"Or perhaps I was never there . . . in Lawrence Lodge."

Mephistopheles takes in his breath.

"And it was you who murdered my friend," says Edgar.

Tiger begins to turn the cannon toward Berenice. Lucy pulls out the kukri blade.

"It was a WOMAN!" cries Shakespeare. "I remember now! I heard a voice in the night in my bed! It told me to get up, put on the Zouave clothing and meet her in Kentish Town! It was a woman's voice! But I have no memory of her being with me!"

Berenice smiles again.

Now Edgar can see it. William Shakespeare knocking on the door like a zombie. Jonathan, bursting with fear and anxiety but hiding it, coming to the door and opening it to his strange little friend in relief. Then Berenice stepping in front of him . . . doing . . . what?

"There are many ways for me to kill," she says, "if I have my victim primed correctly. I saw the beautiful Jonathan Lear in the hospital searching for you the day before. I knew what I could exploit. I do not need physical strength! I have greater power. Men are such fools."

Shaking with anger, Tiger points the cannon's barrel directly at Berenice's head, but Edgar steps between it and her intended victim.

"No, Tiger," he says, "that is not the way."

"No," says Lucy, stepping forward with the big blade out, "this is!" She rushes forward and swings at Berenice, who deftly dodges her, missing her swipe. Edgar seizes Lucy by the hand.

"That is not the way either," says Edgar. "Let me finish with her first."

Lucy steps back.

"If we kill her, then that means we are afraid of her," says Edgar. "We are afraid of the power that resides within her. It will live on then, inside us."

"It is inside all of you anyway," says Berenice. "I made you hate each other, want to kill each other. It was easy. I have my finger on your fears!"

"Why?" asks Annabel. "Why?"

"I am Lamia, I am Lilith and I am Hecate. I am in *other* stories not so easily found, not so popular, the ones you do not know. I am Adam's wife, who showed him what life really was since God would not; I am the spirit in the woman who seduced Zeus and had my children killed by his jealous wife; I am the goddess of the underworld and witchcraft. I am the child eater. I am the witch beyond all witches. I have the power of evil inside me. I understand the human mind, how to control it. I can navigate inside your unconscious. I can enter it on the pathway of fear. Edgar Brim was perfect for my experiments. I set out to control him, to control his very reality, to control those around him." She looks at Edgar. "Would you like to see your father?"

"Hello," says Allen Brim, pushing his way through the crowd at the door and emerging into the room. "Edgar!"

"LEAVE ME!" shouts Edgar at him, and Allen Brim disappears.

"Ah," says Berenice, "but he will return. He is your fears, your conscience. He told you to suspect your friends."

"What about Morley?" Edgar is anxious to change the subject.

"He is my inferior. I knew that when he betrayed me! I had no idea of my powers when I met him. I did not know who I was. He was my teacher. He taught me so much. We were lovers. Then he began to take others for his pleasure." She glares over at the women at the door. "That told me that he was mostly just a man. They are weak: guided and controlled by their maleness."

"That isn't true," says Lucy. "You are weak!"

Tiger stares at Berenice in fascination.

The mind doctor ignores them. "We had a child."

"A child?" asks Annabel.

"A boy. It is gone now, was not needed."

"By what means is it . . . gone?" asks Lucy.

"Never mind," says Berenice. "I took my place as just one of Morley's women, but I began to control him, help him believe that he was Satan, whether he was or not. I took the position at the hospital and told him I would use his techniques to control the minds of Lawrence and all of you, but I did more than that. I learned of Lawrence's childhood errors, of the crimes, the murder he committed." Lawrence drops his head. "One day, I will have more than his body, I will have his fortune. I will blackmail him and he cannot stop me. I will use my body, my young body that I nourish, to enjoy myself, and have his fortune too. Then I will move on to others. This world is a fearful place."

"No, you will not have my—" begins Lawrence.

"Yes," replies Berenice. "You cannot resist me. You will not."

"How did Morley die?" asks Edgar, shaking.

"Ah!" cries Berenice. She looks toward the people at the door. "I convinced him to kill himself. It was easy to do. I entered him and made him try the experiment of living on after life to prove he was Satan or had similar powers, controlling others from beyond the grave . . . instead of becoming the rotting corpse I knew he would be, and that you all see now."

"How did he die?" repeats Edgar.

"He and I went to his rooms. We had an intimate moment. Then I took out his big kitchen blade and put it into his hand. He grew frightened. He would not do it. Weakling. So . . ."

"You need not go on," says Annabel.

"There was a great deal of blood," says Berenice with a smile.

"Be quiet," says Tiger.

"Satan was an angel," proclaims Berenice, ignoring her. "He revolted against God. I revolted against Alex Morley. I butchered him. I was more powerful." She smiles. "The secret to it all is fear. It is God's little secret. Without fear, He rules the world. With it . . . my spirit rules."

"I do not know exactly how you have done all of this," says Edgar, "how you flew from Lawrence Lodge to here, how you made all the servants disappear, exactly how you caused life to slip from the soul of my friend, but I do know that you cannot do it unless we let you. We are giving you your power, and you will count on others to do the same."

Berenice turns around. She unbuttons her dress, her back to them. She lets it fall to her waist. From behind, she looks to be in her twenties, those many taut muscles in her back like a beautiful road map. She raises her powerful arms to her sides.

"Butcher ME," she says. "We will see what happens."

Lucy steps forward. Edgar has never seen such an expression on her face: potent and resolute. Her eyes focus on her foe, on her neck. She raises the blade.

"Do not be tempted," says Edgar. "She will elude you, somehow, even if her head falls from her shoulders . . . and leave you fearful."

Lucy swings the blade down hard at Berenice's neck. It cuts through the air like a bow whip. Somehow, however, in a feat of strength well beyond her size and muscle, she arrests it inches from Berenice's thick jugular vein, standing out like a river on her neck. "You are right," Lucy says and drops the sword with a rattle to the floor. She smiles at Edgar.

"We are not afraid of you," says Edgar to the back of Berenice's head. "We want you to live as you are, for the years or few decades you have left on earth, no matter how much you care for your body, and then you will die a natural death. For our part, we will not be suspicious of each other, hear hooved devils in walls, see our dead father or give all our wealth to you. We will take away your electricity, your power. We will contain your spirit, at least inside this body you now inhabit. We will do it by leaving you alone." He turns to Lawrence. "Where can we put her? Alive and impotent?"

"I have enough friends on the police force," replies the chairman, "and we have enough witnesses here to her tale of at least the assistance in the murder of Alex Morley, to quietly put her away, alone, in a cell." They all look toward the people at the door. Mephistopheles is trying to appear brave but several others are weeping. "I can arrange to have her held in solitary confinement in Bedlam, in the section of the Bethlem Royal Hospital for the criminally insane. There, she will wither and then expire, no one near her, to ever look at her or receive as much as a glance, no one to

271

speak to her or hear her, no one on whom she can practice her deadly arts. No one to fear her."

Berenice keeps her back to them and covers herself up. She seems smaller and older.

26

Fear

They take Berenice down Thomas Street and across White-chapel Road to the hospital, where they summon the police.

An hour later, Edgar Brim walks along the streets of the East End, arms around his friends but with a pounding heart. He did not think this was possible. He has banished evil and yet he is still afraid.

There is one last thing he must do. If he fails, all will be lost.

27

The Hag

Annabel invites everyone to Thorne House the next day, even Andrew Lawrence. In fact, she spends a good deal of time with him. Beasley and the other servants have returned after the two-day holiday Annabel secretly gave them while she explored her adopted son's situation at Lawrence Lodge. Everything in Thorne House shines: the chandeliers, the cutlery, the plates and even the people. Their meal is sumptuous—pork and beef and lamb, blood pudding and wine. There is a good deal of laughter.

Annabel leads it all, her laugh ringing off the ceiling as she throws her head back, her smile nearly splitting her face as she glows at the wealthy and handsome Andrew Lawrence, finally getting her wish that everyone around her stop thinking and worrying and being sad.

Even little William Shakespeare is happy. He sounds more lucid than he has in years.

"I had no real fear of the devil," he cries, "that was merely a pose, I tell you. Had he actually risen up from his sarcophagus, I would have seized that blade from you, dear Miss Lear, and smote him through the chest and head like a knight of old! But I knew it was the mind doctor all along!"

The laughter, at this, is nearly as loud as the cannon's blast.

"What?" the little man cries. "You doubt me? You infections that the sun sucks up! O gulls, o dolts, as ignorant as dirt!"

Edgar Brim's joy is forced. He sits between Tiger and Lucy wearing a new suit Annabel has purchased for him, his wild red hair somewhat tamed, pretending to be happy, but his greatest fear still inside him. It is not Alexander Morley or Hilda Berenice. The devil remains banished from his mind and he refuses to allow her or him back. It is something else. *Someone* else. Nighttime is approaching. Bedtime.

He says good night to Tiger at the door, while Lucy talks to Annabel. The dear friends embrace each other. Tiger feels so lithe and strong, and he admires her so much. It is difficult for him to believe that he ever doubted her.

"Now that it is all over," she says softly into his ear, "come with me."

"Where?"

She pushes him gently back and looks at him. He loves her dark eyes.

"To America," she says.

"America?"

"Yes, that is the only place for the likes of me. It is the land of opportunity! I can do what I want there. I can be whatever I choose to be. We could go together. I would look out for you."

275

It is such a tempting offer. His anxiety subsides a little as she gazes at him. He feels like a child in her arms. Then his heart begins to speed up again.

"No," he says. "America is the place for you, not me. You must go alone."

She appears shocked for a moment and he thinks he detects a slight reddening in her eyes.

"You do not need me," adds Edgar. "I need you. I must stop that . . . going away with you is not what I should do."

She takes in a breath. "You are right," she says, stepping away from him and turning her face so he cannot see it. "I do NOT need you. I do not need anyone." Then she turns back, her expression softens and she kisses him on the cheek. Then her lips tighten again and she goes out the door without another look.

"Edgar?" says a voice behind him. Lucy. She walks up to him, shy, looking down, her face reddening a little. He takes her hands in his.

"What will you do?" she says.

"That's what Tiger was just asking."

"Well, now I am."

"I'm not certain." He glances upstairs, thinking he hears something moving around in the dark hallway outside his bedroom. "Mr. Lawrence has made it known that he would have me. He would groom me to run the London, a chance to help heal others, a life at the helm of a great science. I am uncertain, though, what I am capable of, what my fate will be."

"You spoke of writing more than once."

"Yes."

"I know those stories your father read are still alive for you. I know you think about them all the time. All sorts of other tales too. Books are your strength, Edgar, perhaps your fate. No one has an imagination like you."

"I . . . I don't know," he says, glancing upstairs again.

"You would write frightening stories, wouldn't you?"

"Yes," he says in a small voice, and gulps.

"Meaningful ones." She pulls him close to her and hugs him tightly. "Come and see me. Read them to me. I'll listen," she says into his ear.

They slowly pull back from each other.

"What do you want, Lucy, in your life?"

She simply smiles at him. When she goes out, she glances back with a look. Edgar watches the door for a while after it closes, then sighs and turns toward the stairs. For a wonderful moment, he had forgotten what he must face. His greatest challenge is before him now. He starts up the steps and realizes that his legs are trembling. In fact, they are shaking so much that he stops halfway to the first floor. He hears a noise downstairs behind him, laughter, and turns to see Annabel and Andrew Lawrence heading toward the front door. When they get there, the chairman of the London Hospital takes her hand and kisses it, but she seizes him and plants a long smooch on his mouth. Lawrence almost staggers, but then goes out the door singing. His pitch seems to have improved.

"I know you are standing there, Edgar," says Annabel, turning to look up at him. Her smile is resplendent. "Mr. Lawrence is truly a charmer, my son. He is a gentleman and devilishly attractive, and that is how that adjective should be employed! It was truly not his way to try to push me in any direction—that woman put thoughts into his brain just as she put them into yours. Perhaps now though, I shall do the pushing. I really do not care a fig for anyone's reaction to that. Not even yours! I shall not be a slave to my late husband, as much as I deeply loved him, or to any role society asks of me. I shall live for today! In the moment! It is good advice. You, Edgar Brim, should heed it."

She walks past him up the stairs to her bedroom, so enamored that she does not notice the terror in his eyes.

He comes to his door.

The hag.

She was there before Berenice and the others and she will be there again. *Tonight.* He is sure of it. This is his final battle. If he loses it, he loses everything. He will be back at the beginning or worse. Berenice may rise from her cell. All the monsters had proved to be real, in their way, and that was good because he and his friends could fight them. He did fight them. He faced them and won, just as his father, his real father, told him to do. This, however, is different.

Edgar starts removing his suit and putting on his nightclothes and discovers that his whole body is quivering. He stands over his bed, looking at it, not wanting to get in, and remembering his days at Raven House, the sensation stories that came down through the heat pipe, the panic they put into his mind.

"Father?" he asks, but Allen Brim is not in the room, nor anywhere else. He is indeed dead, fully and completely. Edgar must do this on his own.

He thinks of the College on the Moors, of the bullies, of Fardle, of Spartan Griswold and the frightening teachers. He thinks of

Professor Lear, of killing the vampire creature, of destroying the Frankenstein beast with the harpoon gun. He thinks of Alex Morley and Hilda Berenice, trying to exert power from here and beyond the grave.

Then Edgar thinks of the hag. She has been with him for so long. She is as real as all the other monsters. He thinks of how easily Berenice controlled him, how quickly he slipped into a fantasy world of eight-foot men and friends who intended to kill him. The hag is the very oxygen behind all of that. The hag allowed it all to come alive.

"I need to live in reality," he whispers, and a tear rolls down his cheek. "If I cannot do that, then nothing else will matter. I will die."

He lays his head on the pillow and tries to stay awake. He knows he cannot sleep again, ever.

He drifts off.

She comes at him unlike before. He can see her, hear her and smell her. She descends from the ceiling, her weight upon him before she even lands on him. This is not Berenice. It is not the devil. This is much worse. Her stringy hair hangs down like white, dying vines and touches him first. Then her bony knees, then her wizened chest, then her toothless, wrinkled face.

"Be afraid!" she cries. "Let fear be in you and control you!"

He tries to twist and turn under her, sick to his stomach from the putrid smell of her breath.

"Look at me!" she shrieks. "Look at me!"

He wants to fight her and flee from her at the same time. His mind is on fire. He cannot move though. His arms and legs, everything, is paralyzed again. She clutches at his throat.

"The time has come to kill you," she says softly.

In seconds, he cannot breathe. The force on his chest is like the weight of a whale. He becomes very still. It is the moment, finally, to give up.

His father is somehow near again, though not alive, and Edgar cannot see him. For an instant, he struggles with that. "Where are you? I need you!" he hears a voice say, and realizes it is his own. Allen Brim is invisible.

"Do not be afraid," says someone. Edgar cannot pinpoint who is speaking. It is not his father and not his own voice. It seems, however, to be bearing the truth, telling him what matters in life.

"Do not be afraid!"

He moves his head and looks the hag in the eyes. He stares at her, boring a hole into her face. Slowly, the weight on his chest gets lighter. The old woman lifts from him. Her body begins to dissolve and her face registers the pain. She cries out as she disappears, sucked upward in a spiral, taken from his world for good.

Edgar Brim falls asleep.

When he wakes in the morning, he is refreshed and alone. He smiles, gets up, pulls back the drapes and lets the brilliant sunshine pour into the room. It illuminates everything. He looks around and sees rays of light glowing on his desk. Several novels rest on a shelf above it. The characters inside start calling out to him. They whisper, cry and scream. An inkwell and pen sit on the desk's surface next to a stack of blank paper, rustling in the breeze, as if alive.

He sits at the desk and picks up the pen, fearless.

Acknowledgments

Interviewers sometimes assume that I wrote *The Dark Missions of Edgar Brim* trilogy because horror stories intrigue me. Though there are certainly books in the genre that I find interesting, my motivation was different. I wanted to write about fear. It sometimes seems to me that it dominates our modern world, gets politicians elected, informs our moral decisions and has begun to enter the hearts and minds of so many of our young people (and the rest of us) in the form of anxiety. I did not want to write conventional novels that contained obvious discussions of this problem, but instead chose to create stories set in another time, before any real awareness of anxiety existed, or interest in the power of fear was prevalent, and follow a boy who is struggling with these issues, trying to kill his terrors. These fears, of course, take the form of famous monsters in *The Dark Missions of Edgar Brim*. Telling these stories also gave me the opportunity to explore literary art, and certain literary achievements and present my conviction that great art is, in a sense, alive. *Demon*, this third book in the trilogy, brings everything to a conclusion, exploring the role that our own minds have in giving us our fears, and the power they may have to eliminate or at least control them.

There have been a number of people involved in helping me bring this unusual tale to the page, right from the beginning. Tara Walker from Tundra Books and Penguin Random House Canada was there at the start, helping me develop the idea. Lara Hinchberger then did a great deal of the heavy work, editing these books with her unending grace and insight. Copyeditor Shana Hayes made sure it all made sense in the end, and Peter Phillips read and re-read each text, adding his invaluable input. I would also like to thank Rachel Cooper and Jennifer Lum for their wonderful cover designs.

The books would not have existed without the work of the legendary Edgar Allan Poe, who unknowingly (or not?) lent some of his style and vision, and his two first names to my stories. *The Fall of the House of Usher* and *The Raven* play specific roles in this installment. Other literary giants and their works appeared in the books, and this time, in *Demon*, in order to explore evil and the devil in literature, I reached all the way back to Dante Alghieri and John Milton, and leaned on their art. Re-reading *The Divine Comedy* and *Paradise Lost* was a great pleasure.

I want to thank, once again and most importantly, my family—Sophie, Johanna, Hadley and Sam—all of whom understand the horrors involved in making a life and a living out of the arts.

The Dark Missions of Edgar Brim was at times a difficult world to inhabit, but it has certainly been worthwhile for me, a fascinating journey into the world of fear and its powers. The arts, I think, should explore everything, even those things that daunt us.

THE DARK MISSIONS OF EDGAR BRIM

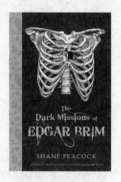

Edgar Brim has suffered from nightly terrors since he was in his cradle, exposed to tales of horror by his novelist father. After the sudden death of his only parent, Brim is sent by his stern new guardian to a grim school in Scotland. There, his nightmares intensify and he is ridiculed for his fears. But years later, when sixteen-year-old Edgar finds his father's journal, he becomes determined to confront his demons and his bullies. And soon the horrific death of a schoolmate triggers Brim's involvement with an eccentric society that believes monsters from famous works of literature are *real*.

With the aid of an unusual crew of friends, Brim sets about on a dark mission—one that begins in a cemetery on the bleak Scottish moors and ends in a spine-chilling climax on the stage of the Royal Lyceum Theatre in London.

THE DARK MISSIONS OF EDGAR BRIM: MONSTER

After vanquishing the terrible creature that stalked the aisles of the Royal Lyceum Theatre, Edgar Brim and his unusual crew of friends return to their mentor only to discover that he has been brutally murdered by an unknown assailant. The group go into hiding, Edgar desperate to protect his friends and family from what may be a second horrific creature torn from the pages of literature. Meanwhile, Edgar's guardian, Alfred Thorne, forces him to pursue a trade, and so Edgar begins working with his uncle, Doctor Vincent Brim, and a renowned vivisectionist, the brilliant yet mysterious Doctor Godwin.

The more time Edgar spends in the company of Godwin, the more he begins to wonder about the doctor's motives. And time is running out for Edgar and his friends. A monstrous creature is chasing them, a beast seemingly impervious to Thorne's weaponry. Can Edgar Brim once again defy the horrors that pursue him and protect those dearest to his heart?

Accolades and praise for Shane Peacock's
Boy Sherlock Holmes series:

Finalist, Governor General's Literary Award (*Becoming Holmes*)
Winner, Arthur Ellis Award's Best Juvenile / YA Crime Book
(*Eye of the Crow, Becoming Holmes*)
Winner, Geoffrey Bilson Award for Historical Fiction
for Young People (*Vanishing Girl*)
Finalist, TD Canadian Children's Literature Prize (*Eye of the Crow,
Death in the Air, The Dragon Turn*)
Winner, IODE Violet Downey Award (*Eye of the Crow, Vanishing Girl*)
Honour Book, Canadian Library Association's Book of the Year
(*Eye of the Crow, Vanishing Girl, The Secret Fiend*)
Shortlisted, Canadian Library Association's Book of the Year
(*Death in the Air, The Dragon Turn, Becoming Holmes*)
Shortlisted, OLA Silver Birch Award (*Eye of the Crow, Death in the Air*)
Junior Library Guild Selection (*entire series*)

"Creative references to Doyle's characters abound . . . and Sherlock himself is cleverly interpreted. . . . [made] both fascinating and complex. . . . plenty of readers will like the smart, young detective they find here, and find themselves irresistibly drawn into his thrilling adventures."
—Starred Review, Top Ten Crime Fiction
for Youth, *Booklist* (*Eye of the Crow*)

"The details of the plot are plausible, the pacing well timed, and the historical setting vividly depicted. . . . On balance, the characters enrich the book and help give Holmes's storied abilities credence."
—Starred Review, *School Library Journal* (*Eye of the Crow*)

"Shane Peacock has created . . . a thrilling, impeccably paced murder mystery. Peacock reveals the budding detective's very real fears and insecurities, providing just enough detail about the young Sherlock's methods to make him an entirely believable teenage precursor to the master detective. Peacock also neatly creates a sense of the bustle of Victorian London, making the squalid grunginess of the East End almost waft off the pages."
—Starred Review, Books of the Year 2007,
Quill & Quire (*Eye of the Crow*)

EYE OF THE CROW

I t is the spring of 1867, and a yellow fog hangs over London. In the dead of night, a woman is brutally stabbed and left to die in a pool of blood. No one sees the terrible crime. Or so it seems.

Nearby, a brilliant, bitter boy dreams of a better life. He is the son of a Jewish intellectual and a highborn lady—social outcasts—impoverishment the price of their mixed marriage. The boy's name is Sherlock Holmes.

Strangely compelled to visit the scene, Sherlock comes face to face with the young Arab wrongly accused of the crime. By degrees, he is drawn to the center of the mystery, until he, too, is a suspect.

Danger runs high in this desperate quest for justice. As the clues mount, Sherlock sees the murder through the eye of its only witness. But a fatal mistake and its shocking consequence change everything and put him squarely on a path to becoming a complex man with a dark past—and the world's greatest detective.

DEATH IN THE AIR

till reeling from his mother's death, brought about by his involvement in solving London's brutal East End murder, young Sherlock Holmes commits himself to fighting crime . . . and is soon immersed in another case. While visiting his father at work, Sherlock stops to watch a dangerous high-trapeze performance, framed by the magnificent glass ceiling of the legendary Crystal Palace. But without warning, the aerialist drops, screaming and flailing to the floor. He lands with a sickening thud, just feet away and rolls almost onto the boy's boots. He is bleeding profusely and his body is grotesquely twisted. Leaning over, Sherlock brings his ear up close. "Silence me . . ." the man gasps and then lies still. In the mayhem that follows, the boy notices something amiss that no one else sees—and he knows that foul play is afoot. What he doesn't know is that his discovery will set him on a trail that leads to an entire gang of notorious and utterly ruthless criminals.

VANISHING GIRL

When a wealthy young socialite mysteriously vanishes in Hyde Park, young Sherlock Holmes is compelled to prove himself once more. There is much at stake: the kidnap victim, an innocent child's survival, the fragile relationship between himself and the beautiful Irene Doyle. Sherlock must act quickly if he is to avoid the growing menace of his enemy, Malefactor, and further humiliation at the hands of Scotland Yard.

As twisted and dangerous as the backstreets of Victorian London, this third case in The Boy Sherlock Holmes series takes the youth on a heart-stopping race against time to the countryside, the coast, and into the haunted lair of exotic—and deadly—night creatures.

Despite the cold, the loneliness, the danger, and the memories of his shattered family, one thought keeps Sherlock going; soon, very soon, the world will come to know him as the master detective of all time.

THE SECRET FIEND

In 1868, Benjamin Disraeli becomes England's first Jewish-born prime minister. Sherlock Holmes welcomes the event —but others fear it. The upper classes worry that the black-haired Hebrew cannot be good for the empire. The wealthy hear rumblings as the poor hunger for sweeping improvements to their lot in life. The winds of change are blowing.

Late one night, Sherlock's admirer and former schoolmate, Beatrice, arrives at his door, terrified. She claims a maniacal, bat-like man has leapt upon her and her friend on Westminster Bridge. The fiend she describes is the Spring Heeled Jack, a fictional character from the old Penny Dreadful thrillers. Moreover, Beatrice declares the Jack has made off with her friend. She begs Holmes to help, but he finds the story incredible. Reluctant to return to detective work, he pays little heed—until the attacks increase, and Spring Heeled Jacks seem to be everywhere. Now, all of London has more to worry about than politics. Before he knows it, the unwilling boy detective is thrust, once more, into the heart of a deadly mystery, in which everyone, even his closest friend and mentor, is suspect.

THE DRAGON TURN

Sherlock Holmes and Irene Doyle are as riveted as the rest of the audience. They are celebrating Irene's sixteenth birthday at The Egyptian Hall as Alistair Hemsworth produces a real and very deadly dragon before their eyes. This single, fantastic illusion elevates the previously unheralded magician to star status, making him the talk of London. He even outshines the Wizard of Nottingham, his rival on and off the stage.

Sherlock and Irene rush backstage after the show to meet the great man, only to witness Inspector Lestrade and his son arrest the performer. It seems one-upmanship has not been as satisfying to Hemsworth as the notion of murder. The Wizard is missing; his spectacles and chunks of flesh have been discovered in pools of blood in Hemsworth's secret workshop. That, plus the fact that Nottingham has stolen Hemsworth's wife away, speak of foul play *and* motive. There is no body, but there has certainly been a grisly death.

In this spine-tingling case, lust for fame and thirst for blood draw Sherlock Holmes one giant step closer to his destiny—master detective of all time.